CHOSEN

Other books by Denise Grover Swank:

Rose Gardner Mysteries
(Humorous southern mysteries)

TWENTY-EIGHT AND A HALF WISHES

Chosen Series
(Paranormal thriller/Urban fantasy)

CHOSEN
HUNTED (November 2011)
SACRIFICE (Winter 2012)

CHOSEN

DENISE GROVER SWANK

Kelley:
We never know
when we will be
"Chosen"
Denise G. Sw

This book is a work of fiction. References to real people, events, establishments, organizations, or locations are intended only to provide a sense of authenticity, and are used factiously. All other characters, and all incidents and dialogue, are drawn from the author's imagination and are not to be construed as real.

IN memory of my husband Darrell—who always believed
I could do anything.

AND to Cody—this book wouldn't have been born
without your idea

CHAPTER ONE

EMMA bolted out the door of the rundown diner, pulling her five-year-old son behind her. She broke into a cold sweat that had nothing to do with the humid July heat.

Her boss, a balding man in a white uniform followed behind. He stood in the open door gnawing on a toothpick. "Where do you think you're goin', Missy? Your shift ain't done yet!" He waved a greasy spatula toward her.

She ignored him and opened the back door to her beat-up Honda Accord, strapping Jake into the back seat.

"They're coming, Mommy," Jake's quivering voice whispered in her ear.

His deep blue eyes filled with tears and she gently kissed his cheek. "We'll be okay." She tried to convince herself as much as she tried to convince him.

"I'm tellin' ya, don't think you can come back like nothin' happened," the man shouted as she opened her door.

She gave him a quick look and climbed in. It didn't matter. She wouldn't be back.

The Bad Men, as Jake called them, had found them more quickly. They used to be able to live in a place for months, but this time had only been three weeks. She tried to take comfort in the daylight, even if it was fading. The

Bad Men usually came at night, but she sensed their desperation was making them bolder. She drove home as fast as possible without the risk of getting pulled over by the police. She knew from experience they couldn't be trusted.

Home was an aged, pay-by-the-week, roach-infested motel. Their possessions were few and fit in a couple of boxes. She always took her sheets with them, although they might not make the cut this time. She turned into the motel parking lot and drove past the dated front office with its blinking neon vacancy sign. She glanced toward the desk clerk, a teenager who spent more time reading a book than paying attention to the comings and goings of the motel.

Their unit sat at the end, making it easy to observe the parking lot yet also made them easily trapped. But the benefits outweighed the risks.

She backed into the space in front of their unit, torn between bringing Jake in and leaving him in the car for a quicker getaway. The key was already in her hand as she unbuckled him. She pulled him past the rotted wood door. If someone tried to force their way in, the door wouldn't withstand much battering.

The chill of the air conditioner blasted her as they entered the room. As she waited for her eyes to adjust to the darkness, she pushed away the nauseating smell of mold and fear and tried to focus on what to grab. Jake cowered in the corner, eyes wide in terror. His fear spooked her. She rarely saw him this frightened. It made her hurry, tossing clothes in the battered suitcase she threw on the bed.

"They're here," Jake whispered in the monotone he used when he saw things only he could see.

Emma grabbed their few toiletries off the stained Formica counter, tossed them in the suitcase, and zipped it closed. Lifting the pee-stained mattress, she pulled out the gun she'd stuffed underneath and made sure it was loaded. "Let's go."

Emma pushed her weariness aside. She was tired of running, tired of dragging Jake all over the country. But she willed away the tears that threatened to spill. There was no time for self-pity; she had to protect her son. Jake stood in the corner, gripping his stuffed dog to his chest. Emma lowered herself close to the floor, and scrambled to the window to peer through the grimy vinyl blinds. A black SUV was parked at the entrance to the motel parking lot, next to the office about hundred feet away, facing their direction. "Shit."

Emma turned toward Jake, frozen in his nightmare. "Jake!" She knew there was no use trying to reach him. He would be like this, near catatonic, until the danger passed. She hoisted Jake on her hip, grabbed the suitcase with her left hand, and slid the door open with the gun in her right. Crouching as much as she could, she opened the back door to the car. His eyes glazed over as she set him in the center seat and tossed the small suitcase on the floor in front of him. As she buckled Jake in, she looked up and saw a man walk out the door of the unit next to hers.

"Hey, can you tell me where the ice machine is?" He carried an ice bucket in one arm and his room key in the other hand. She cast him a brief glance. He looked like he was in his early thirties, wearing jeans and a light blue button-down shirt with long sleeves rolled up below his elbows. His wavy dark hair could have used a trim. He didn't fit the Bad Men's usual look of jeans and black shirts, so she dismissed him as a threat.

"Uh, sorry… I can't help you…" She stood and shut the back door, looking over her shoulder at the SUV as she opened the driver door. She hid the gun behind her back and tucked it into the side pocket on the door as she climbed into the car, barely giving him a second glance.

The man leaned in the open window on the passenger side with an air of nonchalance. "You seem to be in a hurry." He turned to the black Navigator behind him. "Friends of yours?"

He raised his eyebrows a fraction of an inch. She noticed the muscles of his forearm tense.

"No," she reached for the gearshift, but he opened the door and climbed in the passenger seat. "What the …?"

"We need him," she heard Jake's voice in the back seat.

Emma jerked her head around to check on Jake. He seemed calmer now and stared at the man sitting next to her, a strange expression on his face. The man looked just as surprised as Emma.

"What are you saying?" Emma demanded. "We don't have time for this!"

The Navigator started moving toward them.

"Go!" the man next to her ordered.

She had two choices: Try to kick him out and give the SUV time to block her in or drive. She slammed her foot on the gas pedal. Loose gravel shot out behind the car and hit the building.

"You're going to have to get around them," the man said as he fastened his seat belt and braced his left hand on the dashboard. "It's the only way out."

She knew this already and cast him a quick glance of surprise. She considered protesting, but didn't want to waste the time. She hurtled down the narrow parking lot toward the SUV. With only twenty feet between the two cars, the SUV swerved toward them.

She swung left, avoiding the SUV and narrowly missing a parked car. She heard tires squealing behind them as her car barreled toward the parking lot entrance.

"Turn right," he ordered.

Emma turned, barely slowing at the corner. She raced down the four-lane divided highway heading out of town, knowing the SUV would soon be behind her. A quick glance in the rearview mirror confirmed it.

"I don't suppose this piece of crap goes very fast?"

She glared at him as she raced to get through a yellow light. The SUV pushed through the red light. Car horns blared and tires shrieked behind her.

"We can't out run them, so we'll have to outwit them and we'd better do it soon. They're catching up," the man said.

Emma saw the SUV in the side mirror, approaching from behind. A car in the left lane separated her and her pursuer, but the SUV rode its tail and the car moved to the right lane.

"Don't let them get on the side of us," he grunted as he turned around to see their progress.

The highway ahead was clear for the next two hundred feet so Emma straddled the center broken white line. The SUV was soon behind them and gave their bumper a tap, jerking the car forward.

"That was just a warning. Next time won't be so gentle." He braced himself as he looked back.

"No shit."

His eyebrows raised. "Done this before?"

She didn't answer, but instead weaved around the cars in front of her. An intersection with a stoplight appeared ahead. Blessed with a green light, Emma stayed in the right lane, keeping the SUV behind her and trapped by cars in the left lane. As she entered the intersection, she floored the gas pedal and made a hard left, cutting in front of the car in the lane next to her. The other car skidded to a halt, barely missing the Honda's back bumper. Cars coming from the opposite direction hadn't entered the intersection, avoiding a collision.

"Nice move."

"Thanks," she mumbled looking in her rear view mirror. The SUV was trapped by the cars in the left lane, but swerved and hit several as it fought to follow her. She knew she didn't have much time before it caught up.

She sped down the four-lane highway, whizzing past battered fast food restaurants and strip malls. This was the older part of town, the seedy section. The area she was used to.

The windows were open and a few strands of hair had worked loose of her ponytail, whipping her face. She glanced toward the man next to her while he looked out the back window.

"I don't see them." He turned to study her.

"They'll be back." Of this, she was sure.

"Turn left up here."

She knew this road and the one up ahead. She'd staked it out weeks ago. She went straight.

"I told you to turn left," he growled as she sped past the turn.

She didn't respond, but kept driving, the SUV approaching from behind.

"What the hell are you doing?"

"Saving our asses." She made a hard right onto a two-lane country road.

"More like getting us killed!" he shouted, the veins on his neck bulging. "There's hardly anyone on this road. We're sitting ducks. Turn around."

She ignored him and drove, wind rushing through the windows. Adrenaline surged in a familiar swell as they raced down the unpopulated road. Empty fields enveloped the road on both sides, with an occasional tree thrown in. They were alone in the middle of nowhere with the exception of the SUV. She saw it in the rear view mirror, gaining on her. She slowed down.

"What are you doing?" he yelled.

"Letting them catch up."

He reached over and grabbed the steering wheel in a firm grip. "Are you crazy?"

"Are you? Get your hands off the wheel!" She threw a sharp elbow to his left arm and he withdrew his hands with a grunt.

As she turned to look over her shoulder, she saw indecision on his face. She felt bad he was in the middle of this, but she didn't ask him to jump in the car and play Johnny Hero. "Look, I have a plan. Trust me. We're almost there." She suddenly jammed her foot on the gas pedal and his head jerked back. "Brace yourself."

His hand reached for the dash.

"Hold on, baby," she yelled over her shoulder.

The SUV reached the driver's side of the Honda, driving neck and neck on the two-lane road. The windows were blacked out, hiding the occupants. Thankfully, no one came from the other direction, but a sharp tree-lined curve lay ahead.

"I hope you know what you're doing…"

The SUV nudged the Honda toward the ditch on the side of the road. Emma held the steering wheel firm and nudged them back, easing off the gas as she recovered.

"We're almost there…" She floored the gas pedal again. The SUV pulled to the front of the car as the curve approached.

"You're going to kill us!"

With the curve only fifty feet away, the SUV drove into her lane, trying to force her off the road.

She reached down and jerked the emergency brake. The car whipped into a spin. The SUV hit the brakes and skidded forward, tires squealing. She fought for control of the steering wheel as the Honda spun off the side of the road, its own tires screeching in protest, but faced the opposite direction when it came to rest. The smell of burnt rubber hung heavy in the air. Emma hit the gas and plunged down the road. The sound of crunching metal and cracking wood echoed behind them. She looked in the mirror and saw the SUV had crashed into the trees lining the curve.

The man next to her let out a sigh of relief. "Where did you learn to drive?"

"On a race track."

"Really?"

She turned to face him and smiled. "No."

****

When she smiled, Will almost lost his composure. Her face completely changed, catching him off guard. After watching her for twenty-four hours, this was the first time he had seen her smile. She was attractive enough, lean but with curves in the right places, and long brown hair she pulled back in a ponytail. Looking at her now, he lost himself in her deep, dark brown eyes. But when she smiled, the tension in her face fell away, leaving an ethereal beauty he didn't expect.

"Who were those guys?" he asked, trying to refocus.

Her smile disappeared. "No one you want to know."

"What do they want?"

If possible, her face became even harder. "We need to get you back to the motel."

"Don't you want to call the police?" He had no intention of calling the police, but it sounded like the right thing to say.

"No."

Getting information out of her was trickier than he hoped. "What are you going to do now?"

She turned to look at him, the loose strands of long brown hair dancing in the breeze around her face. She looked wild and ruthless. "Look, we can take care of ourselves."

This turn of events had completely changed his plans. Of course, nothing about this job was what he expected. They never told him she had a kid and he'd complained bitterly when he found out. He didn't do kids. He was explicit about that. But the group who hired him said they didn't care about the kid. They wanted her and raised their offer. It was hard to refuse. Somewhere along the path of their self-destructive course he thought of a Plan B, which was much better than his original plan. Maybe things were turning his way. "Let me help you."

She pulled up to a stop sign at the four-lane highway. "No, thanks, we're good."

"We can trust him," a small voice in the back said.

She looked up sharply and spun around to look at the kid in the back.

Will turned, too. The boy looked like a cherub out of one of those Renaissance paintings he had studied back in his college art appreciation class. Short blond curls framed his face of pale skin with rosy cheeks. Big blue eyes with long dark eyelashes. Will thought the kid's beauty was wasted on his gender.

"We can trust him," the boy repeated.

She turned to look out the windshield and hung both of her arms over the steering wheel. "Are you sure?" she asked, staring straight ahead.

"Yes."

She rested her chin on her hands and closed her eyes. He decided she must be trying to figure out how to deal with this change of events. Personally, Will thought it was going too far on the permissive parenting scale letting a preschooler make a decision like that, but hey, it worked in his favor. He sure wasn't going to protest.

"Okay," she finally said, sitting up. "I need to leave town. They know we're here so we've got to leave as soon as we can."

"Who exactly are *they*?" Will asked. As far as he knew, he was the only one on this job. He'd be pissed if they hired someone else as backup.

"You don't need to know that," she said, turning at the corner. "How do you plan on helping us?"

"I can help you leave town."

"Why would you do that?" Her eyes narrowed as she looked behind for signs of the SUV.

Will had seen the damage. The SUV wasn't going anywhere. Where the hell had she learned a move like that?

He gave her his rugged, bad boy smirk and shrugged. "What can I say? I'm a sucker for a damsel in distress."

"Do better than that," she snorted.

He liked that she wasn't easily snowed, even if it made his job more difficult.

"Let's just say I'm hoping to get lucky, and maybe if I'm nice enough, I will." He gave her a slow, lazy smile as he leaned against the door, crossing his arms.

She rolled her eyes. "Don't count on it."

"Don't crush a man's hopes. Just wait and see. I might grow on you."

Raising her eyebrows, she twisted her lips into a wry smile. "That's what I'm afraid of."

He laughed. God, this might actually be fun. "I'm Will, by the way."

She hesitated.

"She's Emma and I'm Jake," the boy in the back said.

Emma scowled in the rear view mirror at Jake's reflection.

"We should go back to the motel get our stuff and figure out where to go from there," Will suggested, still formulating a plan.

"You know, your involvement isn't necessary. It's better for you if you just go your own way."

"So what's *your* plan?"

"Drop you off close to the motel and head out of town."

"What about your stuff?"

She pointed to the suitcase in the back. "That's it."

"Where are you headed?"

"Tell him," Jake said.

This kid was really starting to freak him out.

Her face contorted with outrage and she whipped the car into a deserted strip mall parking lot. She jerked to a stop and turned to Will. "Excuse me, could you step out for a minute?" she choked out. "I need to talk to my son. Alone."

He put his hand on the door handle. "You're not going to leave me stranded here, are you?" Will was afraid to get out of the car. He knew she didn't want him with her and if she ran off, it would be hard to track her down again. Not to mention all the money he'd lose. He still hadn't even convinced her to let him go with her.

She flashed him a tight smile. "No, of course not. Scout's honor." She held her hand up with three fingers pointed up in pledge.

"Somehow I doubt you were ever a Girl Scout," he mumbled as he got out of the car.

"I heard that."

Will leaned down and stuck his head in the window. "I would appreciate it if you didn't leave me stranded out here in the middle of Nowhere, Texas. What would I do if those bad guys came back and found me defenseless?" His words oozed the seductive voice he used to get what he wanted.

She looked at him for several seconds. "You expect me to fall for that bullshit? I promised I wouldn't leave and I don't break my promises. Now get the fuck away from the car."

He couldn't help but chuckle as he walked to the front of the car and leaned against the hood. There was no way in hell he'd let her out of his sight. The pocketknife he dropped on the ground and kicked into the front passenger tire was going to make sure of it.

****

As soon as Will walked out of earshot, Emma whipped around and glared at Jake. "What are you doing? We can't trust this guy!"

Jake watched her with his vast blue eyes. "You have to."

"Why? Why do we have to?"

His head leaned against the side window, watching the cars passing by. He sighed, sounding weary and despondent. "You need him. Our lives depend on him."

"What aren't you telling me, Jake?" The hairs on the back of her neck stood on end.

His eyes pierced hers. "You know what you need to know." He looked away again, his shoulders slumping.

Emma started to panic. He never withheld information from her. Her voice raised an octave. "What aren't you telling me, Jake?"

"Is everything all right in there?" Will called over his shoulder.

Jake sat up, now looking like a scared five-year-old. "Mommy, you need to trust him. You need him. Please." A tear rolled down his cheek. "*Please.*"

Her eyes filled with tears as her throat constricted in fear. "What aren't you telling me, Jake? You have to tell me."

Will's head popped in the window and looked from Emma to Jake. "What's going on in here? A touching family moment?"

Jake closed his eyes and Emma knew he wouldn't tell her anything else. She wiped her cheeks with the back of her hand. The last thing she needed was to let this asshole see any sign of weakness. "None of your business. Get in the car."

Will hopped in and buckled up. "Let's get back to the motel and get my stuff. Where are we headed?"

She cast a glance at Jake in the back seat. He nodded his head. "We were originally on our way to Austin when the Honda broke down. We got stuck here."

"Austin, huh? That's a good distance from here. Plenty of space for your friends to find you out in the open highway. What about Dallas? It's closer and bigger. I presume you're hoping to get lost in a big city."

Emma hesitated and tried to stuff down the irritation creeping in. "We came from Dallas. It's not a good idea to go back there."

"I disagree. They might not think you'd go back there. You know, I might be of more help if I knew who these guys were and why they were after you."

She appraised him. He was tall, his long legs stuffed under the dashboard of the Honda. He looked strong, which should have scared her, but she could take care of herself. "What makes you qualified to help us?"

"I used to be in the Marines, Special Forces. I have some skill sets that might come in handy." He winked and she suppressed a snort.

"What do you do now?" she asked skeptically.

"Oh you know, this and that. I'm a consultant. I'm currently between jobs." He flashed his cocky grin.

"That smile work for you much?" Living among the dregs of society made her well acquainted with guys like him. Lesson number one: Stay away from his type. "You still haven't answered why you're helping us." She saw Jake's disapproval in the mirror. "I deserve to know that much, Jake."

Will looked at her like she had lost her mind, but quickly recovered. "I told you, you know, the whole damsel in distress thing."

"You really expect me to believe that?"

Will cleared his throat and suppressed a laugh. "Okay, let's just say my duty to 'serve and protect' is deeply ingrained."

"I thought that was police officer's motto. Isn't the Marines' motto Semper Fi?"

His eyes widened in surprise. "Yeah, but it seems more appropriate than Always Faithful."

"How can I believe you were in the Marines? You could easily make that up."

"I can tell you a few stories no one wants to hear before bedtime. I've seen a shitload of bad things brought about by a lot of ugly people. Want me to tell you a few?"

She had enough of her own nightmares. "No."

They were almost to the motel when the car began to pull to the right. "Crap."

"What?"

"I think we've got a flat tire." Emma turned into another deserted parking lot. Will got out of the car and walked to the front tire. It made her nervous to get out without her gun, but she didn't want Will to see it. Emma pulled it out of the side panel and stuffed it in her purse. She got out with a sigh and walked to the front of the car where she was greeted by a flat passenger tire.

"Got a spare?" Will asked, his hands stuffed in the back pockets of his jeans.

"No." Her heart sank.

"It probably happened when you did your cool street-car move. That's pretty hard on tires, you know."

She threw him a look that would make lesser men run in fear then kicked the tire. "Son of a bitch! I don't have the time or money for this."

"Good thing I've got a truck we can use."

His casualness irked her. "What about my car? What am I supposed to do? Just leave it here?" She paced the length of the Honda. Could this evening get any worse?

"No one's going to be open at this hour to fix your flat. We could stay the night somewhere and get it fixed in the morning or we can leave tonight in my truck."

She'd rather take the bus.

"We need to leave tonight."

Emma and Will turned, startled by Jake's voice.

He stood by the open back door. "They're coming."

CHAPTER TWO

DAMN, this kid is freaky. "Who's coming?"

Emma was already pushing Jake back in the car. "How close are they?"

"Who's coming?" Will asked again, but Emma and Jake didn't answer.

"They're close. We don't have much time." Jake's eyes were wide with fear as he clutched his stuffed dog.

She buckled him and shut the back door. Will still stood in the parking lot, trying to figure out what was going on.

"Are you coming or not?" She leaned against the back door looking at him.

He knew she hoped he'd say no. He wasn't going to give her the satisfaction.

"What is he talking about? How does he know they're coming?" Will opened the car door and Emma walked around to her side and got in. "Are you planning on driving on the rim?"

"Have you got a better idea?" She turned the key.

They were only a few blocks away and they were ditching the car anyway. It seemed like a good plan. "Who's coming?"

"Who the hell do you think? Are you always this dense?" She scanned the road, probably looking for signs of new pursuers.

This whole situation seemed ridiculous. "How does he know they're coming?"

"He just does, okay? I don't have time to explain this to you. Do you want to help us or not? Because if you changed your mind, I've got to figure out what we're going to do."

It took more than this to shake him up. "No, I'm still at your disposal, Princess."

Her mouth pursed in a grimace. "We don't have much time and I sure don't have time for your shit. How long will it take you to be ready to go?"

Will didn't see a problem, but he could tell she was spooked. He knew there was no way those guys in the SUV were going anywhere, but there could be others, especially since he didn't know who they were. "A few minutes. I don't have much to pack."

"Okay, we'll park in the parking lot of the bar next to the motel and wait for you."

"No, I don't think it's a good idea for us to split up. Just park outside my room."

"I'm a big girl. I can take care of myself. Just get your stuff and come meet us." She pulled into the bar's parking lot and drove around to the back.

The low setting sun hid behind the dilapidated motel units next door. Will reached for the door handle. He glanced back at Emma, who wrung her hands on the steering wheel, her lips pinched together. "You're not going to leave me, are you?" It wouldn't surprise him if she drove off and left him, flat tire and all.

Tilting her head, her mouth broke into a slow smile that didn't quiet reach her eyes. "I wouldn't dream of leaving you." Her voice was sugarcoated and punctuated with a fake Texas drawl.

That was all the answer he needed. He reached over and pulled the keys out of the ignition before she realized what he was doing. Emma grabbed at his hand as he pulled the keys away, trying to pry his fingers open.

"Give those back." Her eyes were wild and desperate and her nails dug into his palm.

He grasped both of her squirming hands in his. He was careful not to crush her with the keys as he held them in a tight grip. "Calm down, Emma. You can't go anywhere anyway. We're taking my truck, remember? This is just a little insurance to make sure you don't go and do something stupid." Will turned to Jake in the backseat. He watched the scene with only mild interest. "Jake, will you tell your mother she needs to wait for me and not run off?"

Emma pulled frantically, still trapped. "Don't talk to my son," she seethed. "Don't you bring him into this."

"It seems to me we're running because of him, which means he's already in this."

She stopped tugging and gave him a blank stare. "What are you talking about?"

Will thought she looked like she'd been caught in something, but damned if he knew what it was. "Isn't he the one who said, 'They're coming?' And you freaking believe him and start running around like they're hot on your ass." Will waved his arm outside the window. "Guess what? There's no one here. But fine, we'll leave ASAP because Jake says we need to, but...," Will narrowed his eyes and lowered his voice, "don't tell me he's not part of this, Princess, because he most certainly is."

Will let go of her hands and she slowly pulled them back as the anger returned, the shocked expression quickly replaced by rage. "Don't ever touch me again." She spit the words out through gritted teeth.

A smile lifted the corners of his mouth. "You touched me first." He got out of the car and pocketed her car keys. "I'll be back in a minute. Don't miss me too much."

He jogged across the short parking lot. The motel had four units to a building with a gap between them. He turned back to look at the car before he slipped between them. She wasn't looking at him, but he could see the boy's passive face watching. What was up with that kid? And what had caused Emma to freak out?

Before going around the front of the building, he paused and looked for signs of anyone watching, but saw nothing unusual. The same tired, worn-out cars littered the parking lot from the day before. His new black Ford pickup truck stuck out in this dejected junkyard. He pulled his room key out of his pocket and edged his way to the door, checking the parking lot again before letting himself into the room. As he started to pack his belongings, he pulled out his cell phone and called his contact. Someone answered on the second ring.

"Who else is working this job?"

"I have no idea what you're talking about."

"Someone tried to grab my mark tonight. What do you know about that?" His suitcase already lay open on the other bed. He threw in the items scattered around the room without paying attention to how they landed.

"You're the only person working this case." But Will noticed the moment of hesitation before his contact answered.

"So what aren't you telling me?"

"There is another party interested."

Will paused with his hand in midair. "Go on."

"Another group is involved and has been known to make attempts to capture her in the past."

"And you didn't think this was something I needed to know? I almost lost her tonight because they showed up and she took off."

"If you had grabbed her the first day you found her this wouldn't be an issue at all."

"Are you a fucking idiot? You want me to drag a woman almost a thousand miles across the country against her will? Like no one's going to notice the screaming woman in the back of my truck? I told you it would take a couple of days and I could get her to go willingly and I was right. She's waiting for me right now."

He couldn't tell if it was a sound of relief or satisfaction. "She must be here within three days, sooner if you can. Our board would be most appreciative."

The other end went silent and he stuffed the phone in his pocket. He had second thoughts about this whole job. He couldn't figure out why anyone would want her, let alone two different groups. At first, he suspected an unpaid loan, but they wouldn't have him drag her a thousand miles for that. They'd have someone here take care of it. And that someone wouldn't be him. He delivered people; he didn't beat them up. He sure didn't beat up women. He might be a lowlife, but even he had his boundaries.

Sitting on the edge of the bed, he inhaled deeply as he rubbed his forehead with his hand. Something about all of this reeked and his instincts told him to run like hell. But the money called him back. It was a lot of money, another warning sign. Why would someone pay that much money for a woman who seemed like she was nobody? Just a mother with a kid. He'd grabbed a few women before, but they were criminals. Then again, Emma could be a criminal. But his instincts told him different, and Will's instincts were usually right. They had saved his ass time and time again in Iraq. He let out a string of curses. It pissed him off he'd thought of Iraq twice within the last hour. That shit was better left in the past.

Will heaved off the bed. He pushed aside the cheap sliding closet door and pulled a heavy metal case. The box dropped on the bed with a thud and the bed shook from the weight. He opened the combination lock and popped the lid open to reveal a small arsenal of weapons. Will liked to prepare for the unforeseen and this situation screamed for it. If Emma's friends came back, he was going to be ready. He scanned the contents of the case, grabbed a handgun, a rifle and some ammunition then stuffed them into a duffle bag. His pistol was still strapped to his ankle. He was grateful he didn't need to pull it out earlier. He had no doubt she'd never agree to go with him if she knew he had a gun. Let alone more than one.

Will slung the duffle bag over his shoulder and picked up the two cases. Cracking the door, he looked outside and found a black SUV idling at the back of the parking lot across from Emma's unit. *Holy shit.* He hadn't expected that. He shut the door and peered out the side of the cheap blinds. The setting sun cast deep shadows across the parking lot fringed with spotty streetlights. Most were burnt out and the remaining few pooled light on the entrance, casting the SUV in the shadows. He saw two figures in the front seat.

With his back against the wall, he weighed his options. Chances were they didn't even know he was involved. He could walk out to his truck and they might be none the wiser, although it was going to look suspicious leaving this late with his luggage. But the chances were that they did know. The other guys must have seen him get in her car and come out of this unit. *Shit.* This job was becoming a huge pain in the ass. He bent down and pulled the rifle from the duffle bag, along with a bulletproof vest. Stripping his shirt off, he put on the vest and then his shirt back. *Better to be prepared.* Will thrived on being prepared. He wasn't worried about getting away, but he worried Emma might change her mind if he drove up while playing Gunfight at the OK Corral. But he might not have a choice in the matter.

He pulled the keys out of his pocket, cocked the rifle, and hid it behind his back. The SUV was parked on the driver's side of his truck. Will's plan was go to the passenger side, load his gear, assess the SUV occupants and then determine his next move. Best-case scenario, he got lucky and they didn't notice him. Worst-case scenario, he wasn't and they started shooting. Will wasn't feeling very lucky.

Opening the door slowly, he glanced at the SUV as he walked casually to the passenger side, the rifle hidden behind his leg. The SUV's engine idled as he opened the passenger door and tossed the bags in the back seat. Will laid the rifle on the front seat, then saw the passenger window of the SUV slide down. He reached for the rifle again, pondering his next step. The idea of walking around to the driver's side and getting shot didn't appeal to him, but getting in on the passenger side looked pretty suspicious. Then again, looking suspicious was a whole lot better than getting shot.

Will ducked down and climbed up into the truck while watching the SUV. He laid the rifle in his lap and started the engine. Jerking the truck into reverse, he lowered the window just as he heard a gunshot. *God, sometimes I hate it when I'm right.* He grabbed the rifle and stuck it out the window. The truck was parallel to the SUV, and slightly forward of it. He aimed the rifle low and shot several rounds, hoping to hit a tire. More gunshots filled the humid night air, and he shifted into drive and floored it. The back window shattered as he turned left onto the highway and passed the bar parking lot. He sure as hell wasn't leading them directly to Emma. He only hoped she didn't run off.

****

Emma rested her head on the seat back while she watched Will walk away. She had never trusted anyone to help her escape before and now she was bound to this leech. She was furious. Her fingernails dug into her palms as she clenched her fists, fighting the urge to vent her frustration on Jake. What the hell was he thinking? She looked in the rearview mirror. The exhaustion on his face tempered her rage. The visions always made him tired, especially when they were intense. His head turned and he studied her in the mirror.

"You don't like him?" he asked.

"'No' doesn't even begin to cover it."

He stared with unblinking eyes. "You don't need to like him. You just need to let him help us."

Emma's anger erupted anew. She spun around and thrust her head between the front seats. "Why do we need him? We've done just fine on our own. We've never needed anyone before."

"Things have changed." His face implied wisdom older than his years. Every time Emma saw the fear and torment in his eyes after a vision, a piece of her heart withered in despair. Jake saw things no child should see. As his mother, her job was to protect him. But she was powerless to stop his visions.

"How have they changed? What aren't you telling me, Jake?"

"You only need to know we need him and you can trust him."

His unyielding gaze infuriated her. "Jake, I demand you tell me what you know right now." He wasn't usually a defiant child and his behavior unnerved her. What did he know that he wouldn't tell her?

He scrutinized her with ice blue eyes. The only response was the country music drifting from the propped-open back door of the bar and cicadas singing in the trees. Somehow, she knew he wouldn't answer. She flopped back in the seat, resting her head on the headrest.

The sky had darkened. The poorly lit parking lot behind the bar made her jumpy. She felt vulnerable and trapped, like a noose tightened slowly around her neck. Emma reminded herself she was the one who picked this place to hide. As she wondered if she should have parked in the motel parking lot, she heard a gunshot and jolted upright. She scrambled to grab the gun in her purse.

"We need to get out of here." She realized she didn't have the keys, and then remembered the flat tire. They were trapped. More gunshots echoed, coming from the direction of the motel.

"We're waiting for Will," Jake said.

"The hell we are! We're not sitting here waiting for them to show up." Her throat constricted, choking her last words. They had never come this close to being caught before. Will's piss-poor plan didn't help her anxiousness.

"We're not leaving. We wait for Will."

Emma expected his usual terror, but he was calm, unfazed by the gunfire.

She climbed out of the car with her purse and opened the back car door. She leaned in and reached in for Jake. "We're not waiting outside like targets. We have to hide in case they find our car."

He opened his mouth as if to say something, then smiled. "We can hide inside the bar. It's better than hiding in the trees."

Emma knew she should be irritated by his attitude, but at this moment, she didn't care why he came with her, as long as he came with her willingly.

Tall, barren trees lined the area behind the parking lot. They would fail miserably at hiding someone. She pulled Jake out of the car and she realized how backward everything was. She never thought she'd be raising a mini-tyrant, but experience trained her to trust him. This was only the second time she questioned his revelations. The first had been when he was two years old, when it all began.

She hid the suitcase behind a bush along the building, after removing a shirt. With a firm grip on Jake's small hand, she walked to the back door. She patted the gun in her purse for reassurance then opened the door to get her bearings. It opened to a storeroom with two other doors on the same wall. Her experience working in bars told her that one most likely opened to the bar area and the other to a hallway. If she were alone it wouldn't be a big deal, but bringing a five-year-old into a bar presented a host of challenges, not the least of which was it made them conspicuous. She pulled Jake into the building and heard the distant wail of sirens.

Emma decided the door to the left most likely led to the hallway, and it didn't disappoint. The storeroom door was at the end of the hall, with the bathroom doors on the wall to the right. The bar was at the opposite end of the hallway. They slipped down the hall and Emma dragged

Jake into the women's bathroom before anyone spotted him. Relieved to see it had two stalls, she locked the door behind them. She stood in front of the mirror and took her ponytail holder out of her hair, fluffing it with her fingers.

"I want you to hide in one of the stalls while I go out to the bar and wait for Will." She hoped Will was smart enough to look for them here. If he was still alive. He could have been caught in the gunfire.

"Okay, Mommy," Jake answered, to Emma's relief.

She put on lipstick, powdered her face and dug out a small bottle of perfume, hoping to mask any BO. Not that she needed to worry; it was already obvious the building was poorly air-conditioned. Her goal was to fit in without drawing too much unwarranted attention and a quick glance in the mirror confirmed it. The only thing left was her shirt. She stripped off the one she wore and replaced it with the one in her purse.

Emma ushered Jake into a stall and lowered the toilet lid. "Lock the door behind me, then sit on the toilet seat with your feet up so no one can see you. Okay?"

Jake nodded.

She leaned down and kissed his cheek. "Don't be afraid. I'll come get you as soon as Will gets here."

"I'm not afraid. Will is coming."

"Shut the door behind me." Jake obeyed and she heard the lock sliding into place as someone pounded on the bathroom door.

"Hey, open the door! I gotta pee." A woman's slurred voice was muffled by the heavy wooden door. "What did ya lock the door for?"

Steeling herself, she turned the lock.

A middle-aged woman with too much makeup and reeking of alcohol shoved her way in. "There's two stalls! You don't need to lock the damn door."

"Sorry, I had to go to the bathroom." Emma swayed to the side as if she lost her balance and giggled.

"Damn drunk," The woman mumbled, heading for the empty stall. Emma cast a glance toward Jake's hiding spot and walked out the door.

Emma assessed the room as she entered. An unoccupied table next to the hallway caught her attention. From there she could see when someone came and went to the bathroom. She could also see the front door. It provided the perfect vantage point.

She walked up to the counter and a bartender sauntered over. "What can I getcha, darlin'?" he asked with a wink. A cowboy hat hung low over his wrinkled brow and the buttons on his shirt strained over his extended gut.

"I'll take a glass of water and a scotch on the rocks."

He grabbed a couple of glasses and started making the drinks. "Ain't seen you here before."

"Just dropping in tonight." She handed him money as he gave her the glasses.

"You just let me know if you need anything." He tipped the edge of his hat.

She took the glasses to the table and sat down. The bar was busier than she expected on a weekday night. Wooden tables that looked like they had seen their prime in the 1970s cluttered the room, occupied by patrons who appeared to have seen better days themselves. A couple of beat-up pool tables filled the opposite corner; draped over them were men in cowboy hats carrying pool cues and beer bottles. A ragtag country band played on a makeshift stage, and the lead singer crooned slightly off key. Some patrons danced in a small area in front of the stage. Others were deep in conversation.

Emma picked up the glass of water and sipped it, scanning the room for signs of anything suspicious. She hoped Will wouldn't take too long getting there, and hoped he hadn't gotten shot. Her breath caught at the thought. If something happened to him, she and Jake were in big trouble. But Jake said he would come. She released her breath in relief. She just had to wait for him. That is, if the idiot thought to search for them in here.

As Emma turned to check the hallway, she saw a man approaching. *Here we go.*

"Can I get you a drink?" He looked young, probably younger than her. Instead of the usual leer, he appeared genuine in his request.

"No thanks." She raised her glass to him.

He sat down in the empty seat next to her. "Hi, I'm Eric. I haven't seen you here before."

Great, I picked a place full of regulars. But then again, it wasn't surprising. Small town, honky-tonk bar. "Just passing through."

"Lucky you. Everyone who lives here wishes they were passing through." He leaned his elbows on the table and smiled.

She sucked in her breath. Longing seeped through the crack of the door that she shut on her dreams years ago. He was cute and had a freshness about him, an earnestness that tugged at Emma's heart, making it heavy with regret. She sighed. If things were different, she could have had a life with someone like Eric. She had forced herself to accept her fate and never look back. She wasn't about to start now.

"Actually, Eric, I'm waiting for someone." Emma pointed to the scotch. "He just hasn't shown up yet."

Eric's grin fell and he stared at the glass in his hand. "Sorry, I didn't mean to bother you." He got up to leave and Emma had to resist an urge to tell him to sit down.

"That's okay. No harm done." She smiled, ignoring the ache that gnawed at her resolve. As he turned and walked away she wondered how long it would take for the next fool to show up. She didn't have to wait long. Two men dressed in jeans and black t-shirts walked through the front door, and it was obvious they didn't belong there.

CHAPTER THREE

EMMA really regretted sending Eric away.

The two men stood in the doorway, gazing around the room. A few patrons turned to check out the newcomers, who looked like they belonged on the cover of GQ magazine, not a small country bar. They sat at an empty table close to the door.

Emma shifted her gaze toward the stage, resting her chin in her hand. She fanned her fingers across her cheek to hide her profile.

Crap. She worried Jake might be upset with the Bad Men this close, but she didn't dare go check. She couldn't risk leading them to him. Instead, she sipped her water, pretending to be fascinated with the band, and hoped they didn't recognize her. A few moments later, another man approached her. A cigarette hung from his mouth and he held a glass in his hand. Cockiness oozed from his lanky frame as he slid into the chair next to her. "Hey there, sweetheart. How're you doin'?"

Resisting the urge to cringe, she plastered on a coy grin. "Just waitin' for you, sugar." Her voice dripped with her best Texas drawl.

A lecherous smile spread across his face in response and he leaned his shoulder into hers. "Well, then it's your lucky day."

Smoke from his cigarette blew into her face. She would have loved nothing more than to shove the cigarette up his ass. Her gaze shifted to the men at the table. They were watching.

Emma ran her fingers down the man's arm and glanced up at him through her eyelashes. "What's your name, handsome?"

"Carl." Carl looked like he was about to shit his pants with glee. She doubted his approach had a high success rate.

"Hi, Carl. I'm Lisa." Her fingers trailed down his arm to his hand. The men still watched but appeared less alert. Now, if she could just keep Carl here without having him jump her until she figured out what to do. "Tell me about yourself, Carl."

Carl's wrinkled eyes lit up as he began to give her what she was sure was the exaggerated version of his life. The men began scanning the room again. Emma nodded and fawned in the appropriate places, stifling a yawn. A woman went into the women's restroom and came out a short while later. Emma wondered when the men would leave.

The front door opened again. A man in a low-slung cowboy hat and a denim jacket walked in and sat at a table in the far corner by the pool table. He seemed relaxed but alert. Emma realized it was Will. Maybe he wasn't a total idiot after all.

****

Will got away from the parking lot without being followed and it worried him. The men were still close to Emma. Who was stuck with no keys to her car. *Shit*.

He drove around a few blocks to make sure he wasn't being followed before heading back to the building. Emma was close enough to hear the gunshots. She probably looked for somewhere to hide. The bar seemed a logical place.

He pulled into the bar lot, parking in the corner close to the street, and walked around to the back of the building to check out Emma's car. As he suspected, it was empty. Flashing lights of police cars swept between the gaps of the motel units. He walked toward the front of the bar and stood between two motel units, hoping to get a better look. The SUV sat in its original spot. Police milled around, but it didn't appear like they had apprehended anyone, which meant there were men with guns still on the loose.

While surveying the bar parking lot, he formulated a plan. A man and woman emerged from the entrance, headed toward their car. The man fumbled with his keys as Will approached him. "How much for your hat?"

The man looked up surprised. "What?"

"I need a hat. How much for yours?"

The man blinked as he digested the question. "I dunno. It's a nice hat. A hundred bucks."

The hat had seen better days. Will knew it wasn't worth that much but didn't have time to haggle. He saw a denim jacket lying on the back seat and pointed to it. "I'll give you a hundred and fifty if you throw in the jacket."

"It's hotter than a coon dog chasing a bitch in heat. Whatdaya want a jacket for?"

"I'm cold-blooded." Will pulled out his wallet and dug out his money. The man handed over a wadded-up jacket that reeked of horse. Will handed him the money, took the hat off the man's head, and put it on his own. "Pleasure doing business with you."

Will shrugged into the jacket as he walked to the entrance. It was a tight fit but it would work if he could overlook the stench. He pulled the gun out from under his shirt and tucked it into the waistband of his jeans. The jacket would hide the gun and it was easier to reach now. He only hoped he wouldn't need to use it with the police right next door.

His eyes adjusted to the dim light of the bar when he entered, and he spotted an empty table between the front door and the pool table. Surveying the hazy smoke-filled room, it took almost a minute before he realized the woman at the back of the room was Emma. Her hair was down and she had changed shirts. The fact that she was sitting with some slime bag had thrown him off, too, which he was sure was her intention. He was impressed. He noticed the men in the black shirts, but so far, they hadn't noticed him. They weren't paying much attention to Emma either so she must have fooled them too. Will suddenly realized that he didn't see Jake. His gaze returned to Emma and they locked eyes for a brief moment of recognition before she turned back to the man next her.

A waitress approached him. "What can I get you?"

"A beer."

"Any particular kind?" She put her hand on her hip, appraising him.

Cocking his head, he winked. "Surprise me."

The waitress walked to the counter. Will guessed there were close to thirty people in the room. He had to get Emma out without attracting interest from the men looking for her. The waitress came back with his beer. He placed his money on the table. "What do you know about that guy?" He pointed to the man sitting with Emma.

"Who? Carl? He's a dirty ole coot. I can't believe that woman is talking to him." She shook her head in disgust. "She looks way too high-class for him."

Will took a swig from his beer bottle. "Got a pen I can borrow?"

"Sure." She looked hopeful as she took a pen out of her back pocket and handed it to him.

He glanced up at her as he began writing. "Will you do me a favor?"

"Sure." Her eyes lit up. Will was used to women doing what he asked.

"I want you to take this over to the woman with Carl." She seemed disappointed. He finished writing, folded over the napkin, and held it out. Will leaned his head toward her and lowered his voice. "That's my sister over there. Take this to her and I'll owe you. Just name your price." He winked and knew she'd do it.

She took the napkin while Will still held on. "Don't tell her I sent it or she might not read it, okay?"

"When do I get to name my price?" She leaned over so he could see down her shirt.

"After you give her the note, we'll discuss it." She stood up and whirled around, looking over her shoulder at him as she walked away. Will only wished he had time to settle up on his debt.

****

Between Carl's constant smokestack and the tension that gripped her shoulders, the pounding in Emma's head became intolerable. Will made eye contact with her so she knew he recognized her. But instead of doing something, he was busy flirting with the waitress. Just another guy thinking with his dick.

"What?" She realized Carl had asked her a question and turned back to him, feigning interest again. *Seriously, when are those guys going to leave?*

"What about you, darlin'?"

Emma hadn't paid attention so she smiled. "What about me?" She batted her eyelashes and couldn't believe it actually worked. Talk about a guy thinking with his dick.

"What do you do?"

Will's waitress walked up to the table. "Can I get you guys anything?"

"Give me another beer. Let me buy you a drink, Lisa." Carl took Emma's hand and stroked the back of it. Emma swallowed the urge to vomit.

"A glass of white wine."

The waitress left and walked over to the bar. Emma turned back to Carl. "Oh, you know, I do a little bit of this and that. Mostly waitressing."

"Where do you work? I wanna have you wait on me."

Gag.

When the waitress returned and handed Emma her wine, she slid a folded napkin with it and winked. Carl dug out his wallet as Emma opened the napkin.

I'm going to create a diversion. Go out the back door. My truck's in the back of the parking lot. I'll meet you there.

So maybe he was useful after all. She still couldn't figure why he wanted to help them. It didn't make sense and the whole situation didn't feel right. Instinct told her to ditch him, drag Jake to the bus station, and catch the next bus out of town. But Jake insisted they needed him and if she learned nothing else, it was that she should listen to Jake. Emma folded the napkin in half and put it in her purse as she glanced at Will again. The waitress had gone back to his table and he gave her his undivided attention. Will represented everything Emma avoided these last six years. He was a player. A good-looking player, but a player nevertheless.

Carl returned to talking about himself and hadn't noticed Emma's distraction. Will didn't seem in a hurry to create his diversion. Which meant Emma got to spend more quality time with Carl.

In a moment, she was sorry she lamented her boring time with Carl. One of the men in the black shirts got up and walked in her direction. Her chest tightened and she fought the instinct to gasp for air. She reached under the table and into her purse. Her fingers wrapped around the cold metal handle of the gun, reminding her she wasn't helpless. In reality, it did her little good. She couldn't use it in here. The man continued toward her and Emma cast a quick glance to Will, hoping he wasn't too busy with his new friend. Will's eyes locked with Emma's, the tension evident in his face. The man walked past her and his leg brushed against her elbow. She resisted the inclination to flinch, especially as he continued past her and down the hall. She wondered if Will saw the alarm in her eyes; he had no way of knowing Jake was in the bathroom. Her heart stopped as the man stopped in front of the bathroom doors and then went into the men's restroom.

"Hey, are you okay?" Carl asked, staring at her with a puzzled gaze.

Emma forced a smile. "Yeah, sorry, I just got a sudden headache."

The disappointment was evident in Carl's eyes—*nothing like the classic headache excuse*, she could see him thinking— but Emma wasn't ready to let him go just yet. He might be slimy but he was excellent cover.

"It's okay. It's just one of those sudden muscle spasms." She smiled at him and rubbed his arm. "See? It's all better now."

He appeared wary but accepted her answer.

Emma resisted every motherly instinct to race down the hall to the women's bathroom to check on Jake. If she drew attention to herself, they might realize who she was. So far, it seemed that she evaded recognition. She looked over at Will. If he had a plan, she hoped he would put it into motion soon.

****

Will saw Emma's look of terror as the man walked past her. He knew it had something to do with Jake. He had to be close and Will guessed Jake was in the back somewhere,

where the man in the black shirt went. Emma seemed pretty calculating so her fear concerned him. It was time to do something, but first he had to ditch the waitress.

"I get off at midnight. Can you stick around and wait for me?" She leaned over again and Will had to admit the view was nice. It really was too bad he didn't have time.

Will stood up and grabbed his beer. "Wouldn't dream of leaving." He rewarded her with his grin. "But I don't want to keep you from your job, sweetheart. You run along and I'll shoot a game of pool."

She pouted and walked away as he moved to the pool table. Will watched the players, deciding his best course of action. A guy shaped like an old tree trunk had been hanging out with a girl since Will walked in. When it wasn't his turn, he draped his arm across her shoulders. The other player was leaner and looked intent on his game. He leaned over the table, taking a shot. Will thought it was the perfect setup.

He watched them play for a few minutes. The lean guy missed his shot.

"Your turn, Wilson."

They were both drunk, making the situation even better. He cast a quick glance toward Emma. She stared down the hall, biting her lower lip. Momentarily torn between going to investigate the back or moving forward with his plan, Wilson's girlfriend walked over to the bar, and that made his choice easy. Wilson made his first shot and missed his second.

"Go easy on me, Morgan." Wilson stumbled over to Will's area.

Will angled his hat low on his forehead and leaned on a table close to him. He held his beer bottle against his chest, pointing to the man looking for Emma, still sitting at the table. "Not sure if you realize it, but that guy's been hitting on your girl."

Wilson whipped his head to stare at Will and teetered from the sudden movement. "He's been doing *what?*"

"He's been winking and checking her out. I heard him telling his buddy he couldn't wait to 'hit that up'. I wouldn't want some guy hitting on my girl, so I thought I'd do the friendly thing and let you know."

Turning a deep shade of red, Wilson's mouth twisted into a snarl. He stumbled over to the man sitting at the table. Will quickly hid his smile with his beer bottle. *God, that was too easy. On to phase two.*

Morgan looked up from his game. "Where'd he go?"

Will shrugged. "Who knows, but I'm curious why you've taken his slop all night."

Morgan stood upright. He put the cue end on the floor and leaned against the handle. "What did you just say?" From the tone of his voice, Will guessed that Morgan was a guy you didn't want to mess with.

Moving closer, Will leaned his hip against the table. "Look, how you play pool is up to you. But I thought you should know," Will lowered his voice and leaned his head toward Morgan. "I saw him cheating a couple of times. Thought I'd do the friendly thing and let you know, in case you've got money riding on it."

"Son of a bitch!" Morgan whacked his pool cue on the table and stormed off in Wilson's direction. Will met

Emma's eyes. He held her gaze for a moment before the sound of breaking glass filled the room. Phase two, complete.

The other man emerged from the hallway in time to see his buddy being hauled out of his chair by Wilson. He rushed to help his friend as chaos over took the room.

Will turned in Emma's direction to tell her to move, but she was already gone.

****

"Hey, where you goin'?" Carl shouted behind her.

She ignored him as she rushed down the hall and pushed the bathroom door open. "Jake!"

The stall door opened and he stood before her, unmoved by the excitement in the other room.

"Time to go." Emma reached her hand toward his. She pulled him down the hall and out the back door. When outside, she pulled out the gun, unafraid to use it here. She found her suitcase behind the bush and headed for the front of the building. They hugged the wall as Emma pulled Jake behind her, making their way along the side. The sounds of the fight echoed in the parking lot once they reached the front. A quick glance around told Emma it was safe to leave the cover of the building.

Will said to go to his truck out front, but this was a country bar in Texas. The parking lot was packed with pickup trucks. She wondered how she'd know which one was his.

"Took you long enough."

Her head jerked up to see Will, minus the hat and jacket, standing next to a black pickup truck on the back row.

"Yeah, well, I had to visit the ladies' room."

Will gave her an odd look and opened his door. "Get in."

Emma opened the passenger door and Jake scrambled up into the front seat. She tossed their small suitcase in the back as she climbed in and noticed the back window missing. Glass covered the backseat. "Nice touch."

Will scowled as he started the truck. He stopped at the exit of the parking lot, checking over his shoulder at the bar and then over at her. The look he gave her, a combination of curiosity and irritation, confused her. But it left as quickly as it appeared, and he pulled onto the highway.

CHAPTER FOUR

THEY drove in silence for about thirty minutes while the headlights of Will's truck lit the empty highway. Jake fell asleep against Emma's arm. She leaned her elbow on the window ledge and rested her chin in her palm, looking dejected.

"You okay?" Not that Will cared, but he wanted her to think he did. He needed her to trust him.

"No. But that's all right. I'll figure it out."

He wasn't sure how to answer. "Want to tell me who those guys were?"

Her silence was his answer.

"What's your plan when we get to Dallas?"

She sighed and paused. "I don't know yet."

Her honesty surprised him. He expected her to bluff. "Why Dallas?"

The dashboard lights lit up her face, making it easy for him to see her roll her eyes. "I never said I was going to Dallas. You're the one who decided on Dallas."

He held his hand up in mock defense. "Whoa, down girl. You said Austin, but I never took it that you had any actual plans there. Where do you want to end up?"

She leaned her head back on the seat. "I have no car, no money. Everything I own is in a fucking suitcase. Where do I want to end up?" Sitting up, she shook her head. A derisive laugh escaped. "There's no where I can go and be safe. They always find us. Always." Her voice trailed off as she looked out the window again.

"Who finds you? Tell me who they are and maybe I can help you."

When she didn't answer, he knew it was useless to keep asking.

They rode in silence before he spoke again. "We'll be in Dallas soon. I suggest we find a motel, get a good night's sleep and figure this out in the morning."

She raised an eyebrow. "Get a motel room? I'm not staying anywhere with you."

He cast her an appraising glance. "Hate to break it to you sweetheart, but you're not my type. I prefer my women unencumbered." He motioned his head toward Jake.

"Somehow I doubt that would stop you," she mumbled. "It doesn't matter. We'll be going our own way once we hit Dallas."

"You're going to end up in Dallas around midnight with no transportation and no money and you're going to just dump your son out on the street? Do you really think that's a good idea?"

He could tell that pissed her off. *Good.* That meant he got to her. "Look, Emma. I promise it's purely innocent—"

"Hah! You? Innocent?"

Will laughed. "Okay, how about platonic? We'll get a room with two beds and I promise, cross my heart and hope to die." He made the motions as he spoke the words. "I'll stay in one bed and you can stay in the other."

She scowled. The idea seemed repulsive to her, but he had hit a mother's nerve.

They drove toward the downtown area and Will split off onto I-30.

"Where are you going?"

"I don't know yet, but figured I shouldn't make it so easy to find us."

"You mean Jake and me."

"Like it or not, I'm part of this now too." He pointed to the back window. "They know my truck so it won't take them long to figure out who I am. All the more reason to stick together." That wasn't entirely true. His truck was registered under an alias.

"No! I never asked for you to help us," Emma groaned.

"Too late now."

Although Emma was quiet, Will could tell an undercurrent of anger threatened to break loose. It amazed him how easy it was to get her to follow his lead, but he had a feeling she didn't usually cooperate this well. The fact she felt guilty dragging him in her trouble proved she had some sort of conscience. He planned to use that to his advantage.

About fifteen minutes outside of downtown Dallas, Will turned off an exit and pulled into a motel parking lot.

"You stay here with Jake and I'll check us in." He got out of the truck and locked the doors with his handheld remote and walked into the lobby.

****

Emma was exhausted. The evening had turned into an utter nightmare. She hadn't even stopped to consider that the men who chased them now knew about Will—and now he was in danger too. She groaned and Jake stirred against her arm. It was getting more and more difficult to keep Jake safe. How could she take care of someone else?

Will is perfectly capable of taking care of himself. Talk about an understatement. There was no way she was going to be saddled with him indefinitely. In the morning she would just have Jake confirm that Will's help was no longer needed and then they could go on their way. Wherever that turned out to be.

What were they going to do? Their circumstances had never been this dire. They had nothing. She glanced down at Jake and brushed the curls from his cheek. He looked so peaceful when he slept. He didn't deserve the life she gave him.

Tears burned her eyes and her anger returned. There was no time for tears, no time for self-pity. Tears were useless. She learned that hard lesson years ago. She had no idea why the men wanted Jake, but she would do anything to keep him safe. Looking up, she saw Will emerge from the motel lobby. *Even if it means sticking with him.*

He unlocked the door and climbed into the truck. "I got a room on the other side of the building so no one driving by can see the truck."

Emma nodded. She had to admit that while he didn't seem trustworthy, he was turning out to be useful.

Will drove to the back of the motel and parked in front of a row of doors. He got out to unlock the door as Emma unbuckled Jake and carried him to the door. Pushing the door open, he flashed a smile. "Ladies and children first."

She scrunched her face in disgust. "Save the charm for your waitress friends."

Will laughed as she went through the door and looked around. It wasn't a five-star hotel, but it was several stars above their last one. "Why don't you take the bed by the bathroom and I'll take the one by the door," he suggested. "Just in case."

Just in case was a heavy burden on her shoulders. Emma pulled back the thin polyester bedspread and laid Jake down. She wanted nothing more than to curl up into a ball next to him, but her suitcase was still in the truck. She turned to go to the door as Will entered with her suitcase and his own. He placed hers on the dresser. "You can use the bathroom first. I want to go out and check some gear on my truck."

"Thank you."

Will nodded and went outside.

Emma was so tired she didn't even bother brushing her teeth. She quickly took off her jeans and replaced them with a pair of loose shorts. Her purse lay on the floor next to the bed. She pulled out the gun and held it in her palm. Although she had been well-trained in its use, she'd never had to shoot at anyone. But she had a feeling the day she had to use it was coming, and soon. Could she do it? One glance at Jake's sleeping face and she knew the answer.

Tucking the gun under her pillow, she curled up next to Jake. She knew she should stay alert but exhaustion overcame her and she drifted into a deep sleep.

****

The night air was still humid and a fine sweat broke out on Will's forehead. He opened the passenger door and pulled a package of cigarettes out of the glove compartment. He'd given up smoking a few years ago but needed one every so often when a job dug deep under his skin. Lighting a cigarette, he leaned against the wall of the truck bed, inhaling deeply. All in all, things were going well. Sure, his truck had a few bullet holes and the rear window littered the backseat. But on the upside, Emma and her son were inside and would soon be on their way to South Dakota. Too bad he didn't know more about the other guys.

Dropping the cigarette on the parking lot, he crushed it with his shoe, and pulled his metal case out of the truck. With any luck at all, Emma would be asleep and not notice it. The longer it took her to realize that he was armed, the better.

He went inside and placed the metal case next to his bed then kicked off his shoes and lay down. Tomorrow was going to be a long day.

****

Emma woke to the smell of coffee. Her hair fell in her face and she lifted it to see Will sitting in a chair holding a cup and reading the paper.

"Morning, Princess. I wasn't sure you were going to wake up."

She sat up, slightly disoriented. "What time is it?"

"Eight-thirty."

She swung her legs to the floor.

"I got some coffee and breakfast for you two. I'm going to take the truck and get the back window fixed. Wait here for me. Hopefully I won't be too long." Will got up and tossed the newspaper on his bed.

"Yeah, sure." She started for the bathroom. Will reached out and grabbed her arm. "Oww. Let go of me." She jerked her arm, but he held his grip.

"Promise me." His eyes narrowed as they bore into hers.

"Promise you what?"

"Promise me you won't take off."

She stopped struggling. "Why? What do you care?"

"We need to stick together. Promise."

His gaze still held hers and it unnerved her. "How do you know you can trust my promise?"

"Because you told me you keep your word and I believe you. Now promise."

This was irritating as hell. Who did he think he was ordering her around? Her plan had been to ditch him as soon as possible, but he was right. She did keep her word, so she wouldn't give it. She gave him a defiant glare. "And if I don't?"

He let go of her arm and picked up her suitcase.

"You wouldn't."

"Why not? It's my insurance."

"You know it's all I have."

His mouth lifted into a smile that didn't reach his eyes. "That's why it's so perfect."

"You're a fucking pig." It was pointless to argue with him and she knew she couldn't physically wrestle it from him.

"Thank you. I'll be back in a few hours."

She walked into the bathroom as she heard the motel door shut. She turned to check, already knowing he had taken her luggage.

"Son of a bitch."

She took a shower and since Will had all their worldly possessions, she was forced to put on the clothes she slept in. Jake woke up and they ate their breakfast in silence. She clicked on the television, thankful for Nick Jr. Jake devoted his attention to the television, unfazed, as if the previous evening hadn't occurred. He watched his show while she counted the money in her wallet.

"Jake, I think we should think about leaving Will and figuring out where to go."

He glanced up, surprised. "We're not done with him."

"What?" Emma threw the trash in the trashcan with more force than necessary. "What do you mean we're not done with him yet?"

Jake turned back to the television. "We still need him."

"I don't care what you say. We're not staying with him." She didn't have a plan. Should she leave without the suitcase? She had her purse, the gun, and fifty-six dollars in her wallet. How far would that get them?

"We have to. You need him." Jake was calm but firm.

Why was she taking orders from a five-year-old? She let out a loud sigh. "Can you tell me why? Please Jake, give me something."

He looked up again, his large blue eyes full of innocence. "I see us with him, driving during the day."

"Okay, so maybe what you see doesn't always come true. We could try to change things again."

"We've tried before. It never works." He sounded bored.

"So how long do we have to stay with him?"

"I don't know."

An argument was about to ensue when she heard a key in the door. She moved in front of Jake as Will walked in the door.

"You look like I've caught you in the middle of something." He grinned and arched an eyebrow.

"Where's my suitcase?"

"Don't worry, Princess. It's in the truck."

She headed toward the door. "Did you ever think that I might need it? Jake and I need to change clothes and I couldn't even brush my teeth."

Will blocked the door. "That was kind of the point, remember? I'll get it, just settle down. You two get ready, and I'll check us out. Then we can go eat lunch and figure out what to do next."

Emma turned to Jake, who nodded his head. "Fine," she grumbled.

****

"Any preference for lunch?" Will asked as they left the motel twenty minutes later.

"Chicken nuggets," Jake answered.

"Chicken nuggets it is."

Will noticed that Emma was uncharacteristically quiet. Instead of getting back on the interstate, he continued on the main road. He glanced at her, expecting a protest, but she ignored him.

He drove a couple of miles until he saw the café he'd driven past earlier that morning. He pulled into the parking lot. "Is this okay?"

Emma didn't answer.

They were seated immediately in a booth by a window. Will faced the door and Emma and Jake climbed in the opposite side. Will noticed she placed Jake next to the window. A waitress came and took their drink orders.

"This looks like the last place Mommy worked." Jake said as Emma and Will read the menus.

Peering over the top of the menu, Will raised an eyebrow. "Really? What did she do?"

"She was a waitress until we had to leave again."

"And you had to leave because of those guys who chased us?"

"Yes, the Bad Men." He nodded his head. His short curls bounced.

"Jake, enough." Emma's voice was harsh.

Jake turned to her. "He needs to know," he said, soft but direct.

The waitress returned and took their order. As she walked away, Emma turned to the boy. "Jake, I'm warning you. Don't trust him."

Jake studied Will as he seemed to evaluate his trustworthiness. Will gave him a disarming smile.

Jake kept his eyes on Will. "He needs to know, Mommy."

She scoffed. "I think this is a bad idea." Crossing her arms over her chest, she turned to face the kitchen.

Jake looked at Will, waiting.

"Who are the Bad Men?"

"I don't know."

"Why are they chasing you?"

"They want me."

Will glanced up at Emma to see if she would confirm what Jake said. Her mouth was set in a thin line, biting her lower lip.

"How do you know when they are coming?"

"I can see them."

"See them? How?"

"In my head. I see things."

Jake stated it so matter-of-factly, as though seeing things in his head was perfectly natural. Will wondered if he was joking.

"You can read minds?"

Jake's tongue peeked out of the corner of his mouth as he thought about the question. "Well, not exactly. I see things, things that will happen. Not all things, just some things, usually only bad things." His blue eyes clouded in distress. "But lately, I can touch people, and see more."

"Like read their minds?"

"Gah, enough with the read-their-minds shit." Emma rolled her eyes. "He already said he can't read minds."

Will glared. "I'm trying to understand, Princess. You've had about seven years to figure this out. This is my first time."

"First of all, he's only five, so what you just said is impossible," she spit out, placing her palms on the table and leaning toward him. "Second, we didn't know until he was two that he had his *gift*." The way she uttered the word made it apparent she used it sarcastically. "Third, quit calling me Princess."

Holding up his hands, Will said, "My mistake." He looked at Jake. "Sorry."

Jake shrugged. "That's okay." He didn't appear as offended as his mother.

"I'm just trying to understand."

Jake nodded. "It's okay. We've never told anyone before."

"Really? Why not?"

"It's not exactly the kind of thing you go around telling people," Emma said, her anger partially tempered. "Think about it. It sounds crazy, so who's going to believe it. And then if they do…some people try to take what doesn't belong to them and stop at nothing to get it."

"That's the Bad Men? Right? Who are they?"

"We don't know who they are, or even why they want Jake. But Jake has always sensed they were coming and we always got away. The first time it happened I didn't know what he was talking about, so that time we barely made it. I always listened to Jake after that." Emma had a far-off look in her eyes, remembering, before her face hardened. "We used to be able to stay somewhere for several months, but

DENISE GROVER SWANK 65

the last two times they have found us more quickly and with less notice. Before, we had several hours to pack and leave. This time we had about fifteen minutes."

"You know this sounds crazy?"

Emma narrowed her eyes. "I already told you it did."

"Why tell me? Why am I the first?"

"Because Jake says you need to know."

Will turned to Jake. "Why do I need to know?"

"I see you with us. You'd find out about me anyway, so might as well just tell you." Jake paused, staring into his eyes. "Soon you'll know what you're really protecting."

His stomach twisted. He felt like a snake, deceiving a child. But he supposed he was, in an indirect way. He wasn't there to protect Jake. In essence, he was protecting Emma, but only because he was required to bring her alive. Nevertheless, this was why he didn't work with kids. Kids didn't deserve the shit that life handed them. Their parents, on the other hand, usually did.

"What do you see me doing?"

A frown formed on Jake's face. "You don't need to know what you do. It will happen anyway. You don't even need to know we need you, but Mommy does. And if I tell you, maybe she'll trust you more." He gazed at her again. "In the end it wouldn't matter, no matter what she does, we'll end up with you. What I see is what happens."

"You can't change it?" Will didn't like the sound of that. He sure didn't plan to be stuck protecting this kid.

Jake shook his head. "No, I've tried. Sometimes it doesn't happen how I saw it, but it does happen."

"What do you mean you try to change things?"

"When I was little and in daycare, I saw a girl fall off the slide and break her arm."

"In your head?"

"Yes, like a movie in my head. So that afternoon, I saw her on the play set and I talked her out of going down the slide. But she fell off the picnic table instead and she still broke her arm. I tried to change what I saw, and it happened different, but it still happened."

"Did you ever try to change anything else?"

"Sure, I thought maybe that was just one time. I tried to change other things, like my babysitter burning her hand on an iron, and a boy in a store getting smashed by a shopping cart. I changed how I saw it, but in the end it happened. I didn't really change anything, so I stopped trying."

The waitress brought their food and they fell silent. Jake ate his chicken nuggets while Emma picked at her food.

Will decided it was time to broach their plan. "We need to talk about where we're going."

Rolling her eyes, Emma took a bite of her hamburger.

"Why are you planning on staying in Dallas?"

She shrugged. "It turned out to be the city you dumped us in."

"So why don't you come with me to where I'm going?"

Her hand stopped halfway to her mouth with a French fry. "Where exactly are you going?"

"South Dakota."

She started laughing and coughing at the same time. "I'm sorry, I thought you said South Dakota."

Will grinned. "You heard right."

"And why are you going to South Dakota?" she asked, still laughing.

"I told you I'm a consultant. I have a consulting job up there."

"So what are you doing in Texas?" She squinted at him, her disbelief evident.

"I just finished a job in Houston. I'm not due in South Dakota for a few days so I'm taking my time."

"Why would I go to South Dakota?"

"Why not? It's far from here; they're less likely to find you up there."

"South Dakota? Their winters are heinous. There's no way I'm going there."

"So go with me and I'll drop you off somewhere along the way. Oklahoma, Kansas, Nebraska. See? Three other states to choose from."

She looked torn.

"We go with Will," Jake said, dipping his chicken nugget in ketchup.

Emma scowled but didn't protest. Will relaxed a little. After the initial bumpiness, things were going pretty well.

CHAPTER FIVE

AFTER lunch, they got back on the highway. Stuck in her melancholy mood, Emma watched Dallas and its suburbs whiz past through the windows. As though being homeless, carless, and penniless weren't enough, she had an uneasy feeling in the pit of her stomach. Something wasn't right. Something was off. She turned to Will as he watched the highway in front of him. He seemed the likely reason, but there was something else. Something bigger.

"This is where we lived before, didn't we, Mommy?" Jake sat in the backseat, gazing out the window.

Emma bit her lower lip before she answered. "Yes, baby, we used to live here."

"Until the Bad Men came?" Will asked, glancing at Emma.

"Perceptive, aren't you? Yes, until the Bad Men came." Her tone was hateful but she didn't care. She hated that Will knew so much. *Goddamn it Jake, why did you have to tell him?*

"How long did you live here?"

"It's not any of your business. The less we know about each other, the better. We're not going to be together very long, so what difference does it make?"

"It's a long way to South Dakota, two days. We might as well get to know each other."

"I say we just listen to a CD. Got any Tim McGraw? You seem the country type." A gnawing in her stomach made her insides churn. She ran her hand over her forehead. God, she really shouldn't have eaten all those greasy fries. Emma jerked her head back to Jake, who was playing with a toy car she found in her purse.

Will scrutinized her through narrowed eyes. "Are you okay?"

Forcing herself to stay calm, Emma scanned the cars around them, looking for any black SUVs that appeared suspicious. "Jake, do you sense anything?"

He looked up in surprise. "No, Mommy. We're fine."

"What's going on?" Will straightened up in his seat and checked his mirrors.

"Something doesn't feel right." She lay back on the seat, hand over her stomach. "I guess I'm just not feeling very well."

Will's posture relaxed. "If you throw up in my truck…"

"I'm not going to throw up in your fucking truck." She closed her eyes and took some deep breaths. Everything was fine, at least for now. She had a good few weeks before she had to worry about the men showing up again. The panicked feeling began to subside and the movement of the truck lulled her into an uneasy sleep.

****

Will wasn't sure what happened with Emma, but he could tell she was pretty spooked. It surprised him she went to sleep so quickly. He shifted his gaze to the rear view mirror and saw Jake staring back.

"You doing okay, little guy?"

Jake nodded his head.

"So, what are you, like in kindergarten?"

Jake laughed. "No, it's summer time."

Will shook his head. "Yeah, I guess it is. It's been a while since I was a kid."

"My mom home-schools me anyway. I already know how to read and I can add and subtract," He paused for a moment then added, "I bet you were nice when you were a little boy."

It had been awhile since Will had thought about his childhood. "Yeah, I guess I was. I was a pretty quiet kid." He was lucky his childhood had been so ideal, at least when he was little. Of course, his father had missed most of it. He suddenly wondered how his parents were doing. He hadn't thought of them in quite a while. The last time he saw them, when he came home from Iraq, his father made it very apparent that Will was no longer welcome.

"Did you have a dog?" Jake asked.

"A dog? Yeah, I had a dog. Rusty, some old mutt that showed up one day and my mom let me keep."

Jake's mouth formed a pout. "I want a dog, but Mom says I can't have one because we move so much."

"It would be hard for a dog to move so much. Maybe you can get a dog if the Bad Guys stop following you." Will wasn't sure what Jake and Emma's future held. Why was he making friends with this kid when he was getting ready to hand Emma over to the people who hired him? Why did they want her? He had never put himself in a position to ask questions. Frankly, he never cared. "Jake, has your mom ever done anything bad?"

Will watched Jake's confused face in the mirror. "No, Mommy's never done anything bad."

Just because Jake said she hadn't didn't make her innocent. A desperate woman trying to protect her son might have stole money from someone. The only thing she had now was a suitcase. How did someone rebuild from that? If she'd been in this position before she could have taken money and pissed someone off. And now they were collecting their debt. Only these people were pretty powerful. Will felt an unusual nagging, startled by the unfamiliar prickling of guilt. It had been a long time since he felt any accountability for what he did. He quickly pushed it away; he was just doing his job.

Jake laid his head down on the seat and fell asleep. Will drove over the Texas border into Oklahoma.

****

Emma woke up feeling a little better, but still had a twinge of uneasiness that something was wrong. She looked in the backseat and found Jake sleeping. Obviously, he didn't sense anything. "Where are we?"

"Just outside of Oklahoma City." Will's left hand was slung over the steering wheel.

"How far are we going today?"

"Up into Kansas I think. We'll see how it goes."

They rode in silence until it overwhelmed her. He didn't even have the radio on. "Never found that Tim McGraw CD?"

Will laughed. "Sorry, you pegged me wrong. I'm not into country."

"So tell me about your consulting job."

He raised his eyebrows. "Decided to make some small talk after all?"

"Unless you'd rather play the alphabet game. So what kind of consulting do you do?"

He shot her a wicked smile. "I'd be more than happy to demonstrate if you like."

"I thought I wasn't your type, with my baggage and all." She raised her hand and waved to the back seat.

"Ouch," He pressed his hand to his chest. "That hurts. Maybe I've decided to be an equal opportunist."

"Do you ever lay off the crap or is it all bullshit, all the time with you?"

He laughed. "I work with computers. Networking stuff, nothing very exciting."

"So you make up for it with your crappy pickup lines?"

Cocking an eyebrow, a slow smile spread across his face. "I can assure you, I'm not all talk. The offer to demonstrate still stands."

Emma rolled her eyes. "Thanks, I'll pass."

They passed an exit. "Do you need to stop anytime soon? Use the bathroom?" Will asked.

"No, I'm good. Since Jake's sleeping, I say just keep going. Unless you have to stop."

"I've been trained to travel for long lengths of time without needing a bathroom stop."

"Oh yes, that previous military training. I still think you're bluffing on that one."

Will winked. "I guess you'll never know. So now, your turn. You have to tell me something about you."

She didn't want to tell him anything. Whatever she told him needed to be fairly benign. "I used to be an accountant before all of this happened. A CPA."

His eyes widened in surprised. "You? An accountant?"

A smug grin lifted the corner of her mouth. "Don't see me as the accountant type?"

"Not any accountants I ever knew. They teach you how to drive in accounting school?"

"Not hardly." She scoffed. "I learned how to drive like that when it became a necessity. Believe it or not, I used to be a very boring person."

"Princess, somehow I doubt you were ever boring." The way he said it made it sound like an actual compliment. "So why aren't you still an accountant?"

"It's hard to find a job in the professional world when you keep leaving without notice. Employers frown on that."

"Yeah, I suppose you're right. You keep leaving because of the Bad Men?"

Emma realized she had been too unguarded. She straightened up in her seat. "Jake might feel it necessary to discuss it with you but I don't."

"Fair enough."

Will's sudden niceness unnerved her. He had to be up to something. "So did you learn your consulting skills in the military?"

He paused then belly laughed. "Yeah," he choked out. "I guess you could say that."

"What did you do in the military?"

His cocky attitude returned and he gave her a lazy smile. "I could tell you but then I'd have to kill you."

She groaned. "Seriously? Is that the best you can do? It's such a cliché." Emma closed her eyes again. This was going to be a long trip.

"Ever live here?" Will asked as they drove around the outskirts of Oklahoma City.

"Fishing for information?"

"What do I care where you lived?"

"Exactly. Then why bother to ask?"

"Mommy, you need to be nicer to Will." Jake sat up in the back seat, tears streaming down his face.

Her heart lurched. She leaned over the seat to wipe the tears from Jake's cheeks. "I'm sorry. I'll be nicer, okay?"

Will grunted.

She narrowed her eyes with a glare. "Don't push me."

"Mommy, please be nicer. *Please*."

His face was so earnest that guilt hit her like a tidal wave. Why did he care if she got along with Will? Maybe Jake liked Will, saw him as a father figure. God forbid. Whatever the reason, she knew she needed to respect his feelings.

"I'm sorry, baby. I'll try, okay?"

Jake nodded his head but worry still etched his face. Emma stroked his soft cheek with her fingers. Why did he look worried? "What's wrong, Jake? Do you see the Bad Men?"

His tear-filled eyes held hers and he slowly shook his head no.

Emma caressed his cheek one last time and turned around, the gnawing feeling in her gut returning with a vengeance. Something wasn't right.

****

Will wasn't sure what to make of Emma and Jake's exchange. Jake was obviously a sensitive kid. Against his better judgment, he was starting to like him, freak show and all. He'd make a better effort not to antagonize Emma, even if she made it hard to resist. He passed a road sign stating that Wichita was seventy-five miles ahead.

"We should hit Wichita around rush hour time. We can stop for dinner right outside the city limits and try to miss some of the traffic."

"Sure." Emma answered, looking out the window. She had clutched her stomach since Jake's meltdown.

"There's a rest stop just up ahead. Why don't we stop for a few minutes? Jake, you have to go to the bathroom?" Will called over his shoulder.

"Yes."

Will glanced at Emma again. She bit her lower lip, lost in thought. "You okay?" he asked, softly.

His tone must have surprised her. "Yeah, I'll be fine," she said, but the uncertainty in her eyes was clear. Will liked the feisty Emma better. While a feisty Emma was definitely more fun, it was also easier to dismiss. Something was wrong.

He pulled off into a rest stop. A large building with restrooms on either side stood centered on the edge of the parking area. Vending machines lined the building and concrete picnic tables were scattered off the side. The parking lot held only a few cars this late in the afternoon. He pulled into a space in the middle of the lot, separated from the other cars. Emma got out, grabbing her purse. She held it close to her body as she helped Jake out of the backseat.

"Afraid someone's going to snatch your purse?"

Emma's expression was as puzzled as it was guilty. "No, don't be an idiot."

Will got out of the truck and walked to the front, waiting for Emma and Jake. She was up to something. As he tried to decide how to handle the problem, Jake ran up and slipped his hand into Will's. Will jerked in surprise, but Jake held on tight.

"I want to go to the bathroom with Will." Jake told Emma in a tone that left no room for rebuttal.

"Jake, I don't think it's a good idea right now. Just come with me and you can go with Will next time." Her usual anger was gone, replaced with an anxious tone.

Will tensed. "Is everything okay?" He did a quick scan of the parking lot, but saw nothing unusual.

"Something doesn't feel right." She clutched her stomach again while maintaining her death grip on her purse. "Jake, are you sure you don't see the Bad Men?"

Jake tightened his grip on Will's hand. "No, Mommy. Everything is fine."

Will had a sinking feeling that Jake wasn't being truthful. Looking around again, he put a hand on the small of Emma's back and gently pushed her toward the restrooms. "Let's just hurry up with our business and get out of here." He checked over his shoulder as they walked across the parking lot. Both of them were acting weird, and if he didn't have to pee so bad he'd skip the stop altogether.

Jake's hand still had a death grip on his when they got to the building. Emma reached out to Jake. "Come with me, Jake."

"I'm going with Will."

"Jake, please, we don't have time for this," she pleaded.

Will saw fear in her eyes. "Emma, what's going on?"

"I don't know. I just have this awful feeling that they're following us. I've had it all afternoon, but Jake says he doesn't see them and I don't see anything…"

Jake's hand had more strength than Will thought possible in such a small boy. Obviously, Jake wanted to go with him and Will was curious why. "Emma, just go to the bathroom. I swear I'll take care of Jake and make sure nothing happens to him." Will stared into her eyes as he promised, surprising himself in the process. This wasn't like him.

Emma looked from Jake to Will and relented. "Just hurry, okay?" She scanned the lot again before going into the restroom entrance.

A man and his two sons walked out as Will led Jake into the bathroom with him. Will did a quick check around the restroom and determined that no one else was there. Jake let go of Will's hand and headed for a stall while Will walked over to a urinal.

"I'll wait out here for you."

The tile wall in front of Will did little to hold his attention so his mind easily wandered to Emma and Jake.

Why did Emma seem so concerned, when Jake didn't? He was sure Jake was hiding something.

Jake emerged from the stall as Will finished up. They stood in front of the sinks and turned on the faucets. Will decided to see if Jake would spill some information. "How do you know when the bad guys are coming?"

Jake carefully rubbed his hands together. "I can see them. I see them sitting in their truck watching us, or chasing us."

"The next time you see them, will you give me some warning?"

Jake shut off the water and turned to watch him, water dripping from his hands onto the concrete floor. "I know about you." His unblinking eyes bore into Will's.

The blood drained from Will's face. He broke away from Jake's gaze and leaned over the sink, rinsing his hands. "What do you mean?"

"I see who you work for. When I was asleep, I saw you."

Looking up in the mirror, Will saw Jake's reflection, his piercing eyes staring at him in the mirror. He waited to see if Jake was going to say anything else before Will cleared his throat. "You mean my computer company?"

"No. The other bad men."

Will froze. How could a five-year-old make him feel like he'd been caught? He reached for the paper towels and handed a couple to Jake. He began to wipe his hands. "Jake, that must have been a really bad dream. Why would you think that?"

"I know the truth about you and now you know that I do." Jake stood still, his hands still wet and clutching the unused paper towels, his face expressionless.

Will knelt down in front of him, unsure how to handle this. Should he continue to protest? Should he call Jake crazy?

"I'm not going to tell Mommy." Jake's small voice echoed off the cinder block walls.

Will narrowed his gaze, his face less than a foot from Jake's, and lowered his voice. "Jake, if you think I'm bad, why wouldn't you tell your mom?"

A tiny smile lifted the corners of Jake's mouth. "I never said you were bad."

Will opened and closed his mouth, trying to figure out how to respond.

Jake spun to leave. "Mommy's scared and waiting for us. Let's go."

"Jake," Will called as he stood up.

Jake looked back over his shoulder.

"You didn't answer my question about the Bad Men. Will you tell me if you see them coming?"

Jake's face remained expressionless as he threw his paper towels in the trash can and walked out the door.

CHAPTER SIX

WILL walked out of the restroom and found Jake holding Emma's hand.

"How could you let him walk out alone?" Emma spit out through gritted teeth the moment he emerged.

Will eyed Jake with wariness. "He just ran out. Next time I'll handcuff him to me." His tone was shorter than he meant, but the bathroom incident still replayed in his head.

"Next time? There won't *be* a next time." She hurried toward the truck, dragging Jake behind her.

"Good." Will had no desire to be alone with him anytime soon.

They climbed in the truck and got back on the highway. Emma was in a foul mood and Will had one to match. He checked the mirror and saw Jake smiling at him. Will looked back toward the road, the hair on his arms prickling.

Jake knew. Maybe he was bluffing. Will cast another glance toward Jake, but he knew he wasn't. Why would Jake let him take them to South Dakota if he knew the truth? Maybe the people in South Dakota weren't bad. There was the possibility the South Dakota people would protect them.

I never said you were bad. Jake's words reverberated in Will's mind like they had against the dirty bathroom walls. Boy, was that kid wrong. The last ten years of his life were drenched in filth. The things he'd done...some on the orders of other people, some on his own. There had been a time when he was good, back when he was the little boy with a dog named Rusty. Life was so simple when he was a kid. Will had believed in fairness and justice. He had believed in right and wrong. When he was a little boy, he believed in heroes. Then he went to Iraq. He had joined the service to be a hero, just like his dad. But he came back a pariah, with the dishonorable discharge to prove it.

In Will's world, there were no such things as heroes.

****

Something happened between Jake and Will in the bathroom, but damned if Emma knew what it was. Jake acted like nothing was wrong. He played with his car and stuffed dog in the backseat, occasionally pointing out an amusing road sign or a road kill that caught his attention. Will, on the other hand, was in a dark mood. He alternated griping and wringing the steering wheel with both hands. He hadn't said a single word since they left the reststop and Emma didn't dare talk to him. Not that she had anything to say. Regardless, she didn't want her neck wrung instead of the steering wheel.

Traffic increased as they got closer to Wichita. Will turned off an exit and pulled into the parking lot of a Cracker Barrel, still silently fuming. After they got out of the truck, Jake smiled and took Will's hand. Although Will seemed reluctant to hold Jake's hand, he accepted it anyway. Anxiety twisted in Emma's chest as she watched Jake attach himself to Will.

The wait for a table was ten minutes so Jake asked Will to look around with him. Will raised his eyebrows at Emma for approval. She gave a reluctant nod and Jake pulled Will to the back of the store, leaving Emma to tag along.

Jake wandered to a pile of stuffed animals. He let go of Will's hand, moving his fingers from animal to animal, lightly touching them. "I have a stuffed dog," Jake said. "Since I can't have a real one."

"It's not all fun, you know. Real dogs take a lot of work." Will picked up a stuffed elephant and held it in his hands.

"Did Rusty take lots of work?"

"Sure, I had to feed him and water him and take him for walks after school."

Emma was surprised to hear that Jake knew anything about Will having dog. They must have discussed it when she slept earlier. She wondered what else they had talked about.

"But I bet he loved you. Did he sleep on your bed?"

Focusing on the back wall, Will's eyes glazed over. "Yeah, he did. He was a good dog."

Will's face became softer, more open. Emma had a hard time imagining Will as a little boy, but she was sure she caught a glimpse of what he must have looked like. She felt uncomfortable seeing this side of him, like a bystander overhearing a private conversation.

"If I had a dog, I would take really good care of it."

Will put the stuffed animal down in the bin and ruffled Jake's hair. "I'm sure you would."

The color rose in Jake's cheeks as he glanced up at Will, his eyes bright and shining. "I like you, Will."

Will's mouth opened and his eyebrows raised. The intercom overhead announced their table was ready and Will cleared his throat. "That's us."

Smiling up at Will, Jake took his hand, and led the way to the hostess. Jake's short legs stretched to match Will's strides. Emma followed behind them, wondering if she imagined what had transpired.

The hostess took them to a table in the back of the restaurant. Will sat down and Jake quickly slipped into the chair next to him. Emma sat on the opposite side, worried at Jake's sudden attachment to Will. Jake had never been interested in any adult other than her.

The waitress took their drink orders and Emma realized she only had forty dollars left after lunch. She ordered water for her and Jake as he began to color on his kids' menu.

"Jake, we're going to share something, okay?"

Jake's gaze lifted, crayon in mid-stroke. "But I want chicken."

Leaning over, Emma lowered her voice. "We can get chicken. We just need to share."

Will looked up from his menu. "How much money do you have?"

Her cheeks grew warm as she bristled with embarrassment.

Will saw her hesitation. "Emma, let him get chicken strips. I'll buy your dinner."

"Thanks, Will, but that's not really necessary. I can take care of it."

Will winked then leered at her with his cocky smile. "No worries. I can collect on it later."

Emma should have been offended, but the image of Will talking about his dog while rubbing Jake's head ruined it. It occurred to her that perhaps Will was a lot of bluff. "Yeah, I bet you'd like that, wouldn't you?"

He smiled and raised his eyebrows. "Are you accepting my offer?"

"Not hardly." Emma rolled her eyes and hid behind her menu.

Pushing the menu down, he leaned toward her. "I'm serious, Emma." He sounded sincere. She wondered why he was being so nice.

Emma gave him a cautious grin. "About the dinner or the payback?"

Will laughed and sat back up. "Dinner, of course. You have baggage and all." He leaned his head toward Jake who devoted his attention to their conversation.

"Will, really…"

The waitress came back and Will ordered his own dinner and Jake's chicken and a glass of chocolate milk. He turned to Emma. "And the lady?"

She ordered salad and handed the menu to the waitress. As she walked off with their order, Will asked, "A salad? Really?"

"Maybe I like leafy green vegetables."

"I hope so. It's too late to impress me with how little you eat after watching you inhale lunch."

Emma scowled. Jake put his crayons down and asked Will to play the golf-tee-peg game.

"You ever played this game before?" Will asked as he grabbed the triangle and moved it between them.

"A couple of times."

"I'm pretty good, so don't expect me to be easy on you."

"Okay, I'll go first."

"Fair enough"

Jake bent over the triangle studying which peg to move. He moved a peg and looked up at Will. "Your turn."

After Will examined the board, he performed a series of moves and removed several pegs.

Jake's mouth dropped in surprise. "How'd you do that?"

"Strategy."

The tip of Jake's tongue peeked out of the corner or his mouth. Classic Jake trademark look of concentration, Emma thought to herself. He removed a couple of pegs and sat back, watching Will with an eager gleam in his eyes.

The corner of Will's mouth lifted slightly. He removed six more pegs, giving Jake a wink as he sat up.

Emma worried that Jake might get frustrated by Will's slaughter, but he seemed more determined to beat him. Jake removed a single peg. Will finished him off on his next turn.

"How'd you do that?" Jake gaped.

"I told you, strategy."

"Will you teach me?" Adoration shone from his eyes.

"Ah." Will hesitated. "I guess."

They reset the pegs in the wooden block and Will tutored Jake on where to move his pegs to get the most moves. After they finished the second game, Jake begged to play again. Emma watched, surprised by Will's patience and tolerance. The food arrived in the middle of the match, not that it slowed them down.

"Jake, that's the last round and then you need to eat."

His mouth pursed in a pout.

"Your mom's right. After you finish eating your chicken, we'll play another game."

Jake's face brightened and he dug into his food.

Will and Emma ate in silence, his foul mood now gone. She almost regretted yelling at him earlier. Jake could be impulsive and Lord knew when he decided to do something, he did it. He probably just ran out without Will. Plus, Jake hadn't sensed the Bad Men, even if she felt uneasy. Jake crammed dinner in his mouth, trying to hurry so he could play.

"Slow down there, big guy. I'm not going anywhere," Will laughed.

Jake slowed down, but not much. "Done!" he mumbled through a mouthful of food after stuffing the last piece in his mouth.

"I'm not, so you still have to wait."

Emma expected Jake to pout again, but instead he fingered the pegs, practicing moves. Will's mouth lifted into a small grin as he shifted his eyes to catch a glimpse of Jake.

"Thanks," Emma mouthed.

Will winked. "I'll collect later."

Shaking her head, she turned her attention to her food.

After another round, Will paid the bill and Emma tried to ignore the shame that burned in her gut. They walked through the store on the way out and Will headed to the toy area. Jake and Emma tagged behind.

"Where are you going?"

Will didn't answer. Instead, he found a packaged peg game and handed it to Jake. "Here, I'll get you one of these and you can practice. We'll see if you can beat me next time."

Jake broke into a huge grin. "Really?" He threw his arms around Will's legs, nearly tackling him. "Thank you, Will!"

Will's mouth dropped then he rubbed Jake's head with a couple of swipes and looked away. "Hey, no problem. Why don't you pick out something else to play with, too? Tomorrow's going to be a long day of driving."

Guilt washed through Emma in waves, lapping at the little confidence she had left in her mothering skills. While grateful for Will's generosity, it only reinforced that she couldn't provide for her own son. "Will, you really don't have to do this…"

"I'm doing this for me," he growled and turned to watch Jake searching the shelves. "I'm worried he'll bug the shit out of me if he doesn't have something to do."

"Can I get a book instead?" Jake asked, thumbing through a basket.

"Yeah, sure. Whatever you want." His tone was short. "Just pick it out and let's get out of here." Will stormed off toward the register.

Emma worried Jake's feelings would be hurt by Will's sudden mood change, but Jake didn't seem to notice, his eyes shining with happiness.

****

He wasn't sure what to make of this kid. One minute he freaked Will out; the next he wormed his way into Will's softer side. He was just as surprised as Emma that he bought the peg game and book for Jake. This kid was getting to him.

This was why he didn't work with kids.

His bad mood returned. He glanced over at a confused Emma. His mood was flip-flopping like a woman with PMS. *Get a goddamned grip.*

Emma moaned lightly. Her face was strained when he shifted his gaze over to her. "Are you okay?"

"I don't know. Something's wrong."

Will glanced over his shoulder. "Jake? Do you sense anything?"

Jake had been practicing the peg game and looked up surprised. "No."

Maybe Emma was a hypochondriac. Jake seemed to be the guy in charge, still a hard concept to swallow. He didn't seem worried, so Will didn't see any reason to worry either.

Will checked his GPS. "Salina's only an hour and a half away. We can spend the night there."

"Sure, whatever," Emma mumbled, her face turned to the window.

They drove the next hour in silence. Jake played with his peg game in the backseat until he announced he had to go to the bathroom.

"We're almost there. Can you wait?" Will asked.

"I dunno." He sounded unsure. Will decided it was best to pull over at the next stop. He sure didn't want the kid peeing on the backseat. He exited, driving past the truck weigh station and to the rest area. The setting sun cast long shadows across the almost empty parking lot.

"Something's wrong," Emma said, her voice tight.

"Jake?" Will whipped his head over his shoulder.

Jake shook his head, confused. "I don't see anything."

"Can you park in a space in front of the bathroom? *Please?*"

"Sure, why not?" He drove closer to the restroom entrance and parked in a space. "How's this?"

Emma looked around the parking lot, her eyes wide and her mouth drawn. "Thanks."

Emma's really losing it. Will opened the door.

"Jake's coming with me this time."

"Fine by me." He had no desire to spend any more quality time in the restroom with Jake.

Clutching her purse to her side, she grabbed Jake's hand.

"Let's make this quick." Will leaned against the truck and watched her drag Jake into the restroom entrance about twenty feet away. He opened the back door, reached under the backseat and pulled out the metal case, deciding it was better to be prepared. He reloaded his rifle and tucked it beneath a blanket under the seat. The gun on his ankle was loaded, ammo under the driver's seat.

A family emerged from the restrooms and wandered back to their car. Will turned to watch them get in their car. A black SUV appeared out of the corner of his eye on the passenger side. He tensed. There were a million black SUVs out there. Seeing one didn't mean anything. Then another pulled in behind it. Will grabbed his rifle.

"Emma!"

The Navigators advanced toward them as the car with the family pulled away. Will cast a quick glance toward the bathroom entrance. Emma stood in the doorway alone, the color drained from her face. "Jake says they're coming!" she shouted.

No shit. So much for Jake as an early warning system.

Will would have preferred having Emma and Jake run out to the truck, but the SUVs were too close. They were probably better off behind concrete walls.

"They're already here. Stay there!"

"We have to get out—"

Will shut the back door, his rifle now where Emma could see it. "Stay in the bathroom!" He lowered himself behind the front of the truck and raised his rifle over the hood. He checked the doorway, but she had disappeared.

Will really didn't want a shootout with his truck in the middle, but he didn't want to abandon it, either. He ran to a sheltered vending area about fifteen feet from the building and hid, rifle aimed. The SUVs pulled up parallel to the buildings and lowered their windows. Handguns pointed out the window and gunfire exploded into the evening. Will felt compelled to yell to Emma to take cover, but she seemed experienced enough to take care of herself. Will took out one of the men in the rear SUV. A couple of men came from behind the cars. He had to make sure they didn't get to the restroom.

His best guess was there were six to eight bad guys. He was outnumbered, but he'd been in this situation before. One of the men hiding outside the SUV darted toward the restrooms. Will took him down with one shot. Patience was the key. As long as they weren't moving toward him or Emma, he could wait all night. He only got paid if he delivered Emma alive and he'd be damned if he lost his money now. Two of the men moved toward the restroom entrance. He shot one but the other darted to the safety of the building.

Son of a bitch.

CHAPTER SEVEN

THE sight of Will pulling a rifle out of the truck scared Emma, but there wasn't time to think about it with the SUVs approaching. She ran into the bathroom and pushed Jake into the last stall. Emma sat him on the back of the toilet and shut the door behind them.

Gunfire echoed in the parking lot. She pulled her own gun out of her purse and unlocked the safety. While she worried why Will had a rifle, but the sounds of a gun battle told her he must be on their side. Sitting on the toilet, she placed her body in front of Jake's and pulled her feet up off the floor. Her hands trembled as she pointed the gun at the stall door.

"It's going to be okay, Mommy." Jake rubbed her shoulder with his small hand. She wanted to burst into tears.

This is so bad. "Are you sure, Jake?" This was all backward. She was supposed to reassure him.

"Yes. Will's going to help us."

Emma wished she were more sure of that fact. The sound of the gunshots slowed down. What if they shot Will? Panic crashed through her.

Jake's hand rested on her shoulder, a burn searing her shoulder blade.

It's okay Mommy. We'll be okay.

She heard Jake's words in her head and jerked around in shock. A small smile lifted the corners of his mouth, then quickly faded.

A Bad Man's coming.

The gun quivered in her hands as she turned back to the door. Soft footsteps echoed off the bathroom tile and mingled with the slow drip of water from one of the faucets. Maybe it was Will.

No. It's a Bad Man.

Not only could she hear his voice in her head, he heard her thoughts as well. She didn't have time to dwell on this revelation. A stall door slammed open and the partition walls shook. Emma tensed. There were four stalls, and they were in the last one. Her breaths came in short bursts she tried to control. *Calm down, Emma. Get a grip.*

The fluorescent light flickered overhead as the second stall door slammed. The dull thud of metal hitting metal interrupted her thoughts. Her chest constricted, making it difficult to breathe. Jake's hand on her shoulder radiated a heat through her body, spreading slowly, slightly calming her.

You can do this, Mommy.

The third door slammed open. The walls shook violently. A round of rapid gunfire went off outside.

Their stall was next. She braced her elbows into her sides to help steady the gun, her finger on the trigger. *Oh God, what if it's Will?* Tears filled her eyes, blurring her vision.

It's not.

The door slammed open. She squeezed the trigger and held it down. Several shots burst out of the gun. The eyes of the man in the doorway flew open in surprise as he stumbled back. His gun fell and bounced, clacking on the tile floor. He hit the wall and slid down, leaving a bloody streak on the tile behind him. Emma stifled a sob.

Oh, my God. I killed him.

****

Will needed to get over to the building without getting himself shot. A row of dumpsters stood about four feet away. If he could get behind those, he could dive behind the building and break open the small window in back. He let out a volley of shots and dove behind the bins. Other than a few scrapes from the concrete, he remained unscathed. He dashed to the far edge of the dumpsters, realizing that the entrance to the restroom was unguarded. Just then several shots echoed in the bathroom.

Shit. His heart lurched to his throat.

He sprinted the short distance from the dumpster to the back of the building. Back to the wall, he smashed out the window out with the butt of his rifle, then turned, holding it up and ready. One of the gunmen sat on the floor, slumped against the wall, blood pulsing from his chest. From the amount of blood, he had to be dead. Emma's head jerked up in alarm, turning the gun in her hand toward him, her face ashen. The gun tip lowered.

"Are you okay?" He didn't have time to ask where she got a gun.

She nodded.

"Where's Jake?"

Jake poked his head from behind the stall door. His eyes were wide, but he seemed unscathed.

Will knocked the remaining glass from the frame and hopped through. He dropped down and picked the gun off the floor. He checked the clip and handed it to Emma. "Obviously, you know how to use one of these."

She took it, her trembling hands catching him by surprise. He pulled his keys from his pocket and handed them to her. She stood frozen, staring at his hand.

He knelt down and pulled a gun out of an ankle holster. "I want you and Jake to get to the truck. Put Jake in front on the floor. I'm going to cover you two. Once you get in the truck, pull up to where I am. I'll get in and we'll go. Okay?"

Emma peered down at him, her wide dark eyes a sharp contrast to her unnaturally pale face.

Will stood and grabbed her face with his free hand. "Emma, snap out of it. Stop being a goddamned baby. I need you to focus." His fingers dug into her cheeks. "Are you ready or not?"

Anger burned in her eyes. She jerked her face out of his hand. "Yes."

Will moved to the restroom entrance. "Stay behind the wall while I keep them busy, then take Jake and run as fast as you can to the driver's side and get in. Put Jake on the front floor. Okay?"

"I heard you the first time," she spat.

"Just remember to come back and get me." He winked, crouched at the opening, and started firing.

****

Emma put the second gun in her purse and pulled Jake behind her along the concrete wall. Anger replaced her fear. Will was an ass and his flippant attitude pissed her off. Maybe he was used to gunfights, but she wasn't.

She saw the truck parked in front of the building about twenty feet away. Will ran out of the doorway, away from the truck, shooting with both guns. Emma inched closer to the edge, her gun pointed forward, ready to use if necessary. She took several deep breaths.

Her heart pounded furiously as she grabbed Jake's arm in her left hand. "Stay behind me, Jake."

"They won't hurt me."

Maybe not, but she wasn't taking any chances. She ran for the truck, her gun aimed toward the SUVs. One of the gunmen saw her and pointed his gun at her, but fell to the ground before he could fire. Will must have shot him.

It was surreal watching men die, but she told herself she'd deal with it later. Emma pulled Jake behind the side of the truck, opened the door and pushed him in. Her adrenaline kicked in. Behind the wheel of a car, she knew how to fight the Bad Men.

"I hope this thing has four-wheel drive," she mumbled to herself.

She put the truck in reverse and then forward, running over one of the gunmen in her path. His body flopped onto the hood and flew off to the side. She didn't let herself dwell on the fact that she probably just killed someone else. The truck jumped the curb and she bounced in the seat, gripping the steering wheel to remain in her seat. *Stupid.* She hadn't stopped to buckle her seat belt. The truck skidded to a halt behind the vending machine, and she leaned over and opened the passenger door. Will got in, scrambling over Jake's hunched body on the floor, and slammed the door behind him. He threw himself into the back.

"Go!"

Emma tore through the grass, cutting over to the road. Gunshots fired behind them. Will opened the back window and thrust his rifle out. "They're going to follow us. I need you to do some of that fancy driving."

Emma maneuvered the truck onto the parking lot surface. "Any particular direction?"

"Surprise me."

Emma glanced in the rearview mirror. An SUV followed them. At least there was only one. Jake sat cross-legged on the floor, staring up at her, his face lit by the parking lot lights. She was amazed that he didn't look frightened.

The entrance ramp to the highway was ahead. She floored the gas pedal as she merged into more traffic than she expected at this time of night, the highway probably full of summer vacationers. She hated to think she was playing Pied Piper to a gun toting SUV.

A line of cars loomed ahead of her. The cars were spaced far enough apart that she could weave around them, but the line appeared endless. This didn't look good. She reached over and grabbed the seat belt and buckled herself in. Her gun lay tucked under her leg to hold it in place.

"They're catching up," Will said.

Emma checked the mirror. The headlights of the SUV were getting closer. She continued weaving, but the pack of cars got tighter and she found herself blocked in the right lane. A guardrail ran down both sides of the highway. The SUV swerved over to the right shoulder, ramming the edge of the back bumper. Emma fought to gain control of the truck and prevent it from crashing into the car in front of her

"Son of a bitch!" Will cursed. "Get us out of here!"

"I'm trying!"

A car occupied the left lane next to her. Emma laid on the horn and swerved in their direction. They hit the brakes, honking their own horn as she shot into the opening they created.

"I'm gonna have to get us off this highway."

"Whatever you have to do."

The SUV darted into the spot they had vacated. Cars around them responded to the erratic drivers in their midst. Some slowed down, others pulled to the side of the road.

"I don't see any exit signs. I don't know how soon we can get off."

Will leaned over the back of the front seat and pushed buttons on his GPS. "Son of a bitch. The next exit is six miles ahead."

The SUV hit the back of the truck, pitching Will forward. His head hit the dashboard. "Shit!"

"Are you okay?"

Will touched his head. His hand came back covered in blood. "Not for long if we stay on this highway." He slid into the backseat.

The right lane opened up. Emma straddled the center line, weaving back and forth, trying to keep the SUV from getting alongside them. Another pack of cars appeared up ahead. Both sides of the road were still surrounded by guardrails. Emma hit the hi-beams. Once they got over the bridge ahead, there was a gap between the end of the guardrail and a line of trees on both sides. She glanced down at the GPS.

"Hang on. I have an idea," she told Will. "This thing *is* four-wheel drive, right?"

"Yeah."

"This is going to be bumpy." She jerked the steering wheel to the left. The truck shot off into the grassy median. She backed off the gas, slowed down then wrenched the steering wheel in a tighter turn. The uneven terrain made the truck harder to control as she turned to face the opposite direction, trying to keep from flipping over. Pitching wildly, the truck plunged down the hill to the two-lane road under the bridge. Emma turned right and floored the gas pedal as she hurtled into the darkness.

****

As soon as Will stopped bouncing around in the backseat, his first thought was to kill her. The wild ride caused him to hit his head on the back window frame and he now had a raging headache. But when he sat up, he realized what she had done and changed his mind.

"Did we lose them?" she asked.

He looked out the back window and heard the squeal of tires from the cars on the highway above them. The headlights of the SUV appeared in the median. "No."

"Shit."

"That's okay. You slowed them down and got us away from all the traffic. It will be easier to deal with them out here in the middle of nowhere." Will leaned forward again to check the GPS. "There's pretty much nothing ahead of us but corn and wheat fields for the next fifteen miles. This is brilliant."

Will glanced down at Jake. "How are you doing? Did you get banged up back there?"

The dashboard lights cast eerie shadows across Jake's face. "No, I'm okay."

Will eased into the backseat and reloaded his rifle and his revolver. Only one Navigator following them. Good. The headlights were still off in the distance and he knew the truck and SUV could probably maintain the same speed. They could drive like this until one of them ran out of gas. Or the police showed up.

"Emma, I want you to slow down."

"*What?*"

"We can play cat and mouse like this all night, but I'd rather just be done with it. We let them catch up and then I shoot either them or their tires. Or both. Either way, they won't follow us anymore."

She looked over her shoulder. "Can you do that? Take care of them so they don't follow us?"

"Yes."

She turned around and gripped the steering wheel with both hands. "Okay. Tell me what to do."

"Slow down, but not too much or they'll know it's a setup."

The truck slowed slightly and the headlights behind them grew larger. "That's good, keep that speed."

Will eyed Jake down on the floor. "Stay down. There's going to be gunshots but as long as you stay down, you'll be fine."

There weren't any oncoming headlights in the road in front of them. He stuck his rifle tip out the back window. The silhouettes of crops rushed past on either side. Only a few houses and barns dotted the landscape, for which he was grateful. Witnesses were always bad.

The Navigator headlights got closer as the vehicles raced down the county road. The gunshots Will expected weren't far behind.

"Emma, try to keep your head down."

"Yeah, a little hard to do when I'm driving here."

"Either keep it down or get it shot off. Your call, Princess." He hoped to take care of the gunmen before they became a real threat to her.

More shots echoed, but none had hit the truck yet. Will's rifle still lay across the ledge of the open back window.

"Are you going to shoot that thing or just let them catch us?"

He smirked at the irritation in her voice. "I'm still weighing my options." He grinned when he heard her snort.

Will ducked below the window. They were getting close enough that their bullets could actually hit them. He aimed at the windshield behind him and squeezed the trigger. The SUV swerved and the bullet went into the center of windshield but didn't shatter. It didn't surprise Will that they had bulletproof glass, but it put him at a disadvantage.

A man's head leaned out the passenger window, the tip of a gun with it. Will ducked down as the glass of his back window rained down on his head. "Son of a fucking bitch!" Those assholes had blown out his back window twice. Now he was really pissed.

"Keep your head down, Emma!" His voice was angrier than he meant. He wasn't about to get this far and get her killed.

"I am!"

He stuck his head up, peering over the bottom edge of the window. The SUV weaved across the lanes as he aimed the rifle. He shot at the driver's side of the windshield again, but the road was covered in potholes and the truck bounced. His shot missed.

He aimed again and hit the window dead center where the driver's head should be, but the glass still held together. There was no telling how many shots it would take to finally break it. One more or twenty, he grew tired of waiting. Will squeezed the trigger and released a round of shots into the windshield. It finally shattered and the SUV swerved to the right side then righted itself. A torrent of bullets hit the back of the truck and Will ducked.

"They're trying to pass us!" Emma shouted.

Will tried to sit up to see, but the truck lurched to the side and jerked as it ricocheted off a hard object. The crunching of metal told him it was the SUV. Emma must be trying to run them off the road. He righted himself and looked out the back window, which was now completely open. Will leaned out the opening and released a round of shots into the half-open passenger windows. He pulled back inside the truck just as another round of fire shot at the back window.

The truck swerved across the highway from the force of the SUV pushing it, the nose of the SUV reaching to the middle of the truck. They probably had a good shot at Emma but so far hadn't taken it. He didn't want to push his luck.

"We're gonna need something fancier than this. What else you go up your sleeve?"

Emma's head shook as she looked around. The SUV forced the truck onto the gravel shoulder. Her hands held the steering wheel like a vice grip. "An open two-lane road, our options are pretty limited."

"Come up with something."

"I hope you have insurance." She mumbled as she jerked the wheel and rammed the truck in to the SUV. The truck shook and Will heard metal scratching. "I'm going to try to ram them into those mail boxes ahead. Can you do something to them after that?" Her biceps flexed as she strained to hold the wheel.

"If you can manage your part, I can do mine."

The SUV rammed back. The two vehicles locked in a tug-of-war over ownership of the road. Emma needed to get them over to the shoulder, but she strained to hold the steering wheel. Will leaned forward over the seat back. He pressed his chest into her back as he placed his hands above hers on the steering wheel.

"What are you *doing*?" Her voice rose.

Her already tight back muscles tensed against his chest.

"I'm helping you."

She relaxed a little and her hair tickled the side of his face. He turned to see the SUV next to them. The muzzle of a gun pointed out the side window.

"Hit the brakes!"

Emma spun her head to the side to see. "Let go."

Will released the steering wheel and threw himself backward into the backseat. He picked up the gun and lowered the back driver side window as Emma slammed the brakes. The SUV's brakes squealed, seconds after Emma's. The maneuver sent the SUV surging slightly forward of them, but clipped the front end of the truck in the process. Emma fought for control as Will shot at the SUV's back tire. The smell of burnt rubber filled the air as they heard the tire explode. The SUV swerved back and forth as it fought for control. Emma braked hard. Will braced himself against the back of the seat, the squeal of the tires deafening his ears. The SUV swerved precariously in front of truck. She jerked the wheel to the left, barely missing the Navigator's tail end. It crashed into a fence on the side of the road. Splintered wood flew into the air as the nose of the SUV dipped and came to rest in a ditch as Emma raced down the road.

CHAPTER EIGHT

WILL told Emma to drive for another hour, turning onto multiple country roads and trying to put distance between them and the accident. Jake climbed into the front seat and fell asleep while Will stayed in the back giving her directions. He finally told her to turn onto a gravel road tucked between two cornfields. She parked under the canopy of a massive oak growing at the edge of one of the fields. Emma shut off the engine and relaxed for the first time in hours, slumping over the steering wheel.

"Let's get out and check the damage," Will said as he pushed open the back door with more effort than it usually required.

Emma rolled down the windows so Jake, still asleep on the seat, would get air from the soft breeze. She opened the door and climbed out, following Will.

"Holy shit," Will mumbled. Scratches and deep crevices dented the side of the truck, starting at the driver's door and angling to the back. Bullet holes riddled the body of the bed. "We're lucky we could open the door."

"Sorry." Emma stood behind him taking in the damage.

Will ran a hand through his hair and winced. "Better the truck than us."

"Let me see your head."

Will turned to face her and winked. "I bet you'd like to see…"

"Shut up. I was talking about your forehead." The light of the full moon illuminated the dried blood that ran down his cheek. "Let me look at it." She moved closer to him and reached up to touch his cheek.

"Careful, Emma, I'll think you're trying to seduce me."

"As if." Her thumb brushed the hair off his forehead revealing a half-inch gash. "We need to clean this up. Do you have a first aid kit?"

His reached up and wrapped his fingers around her wrist. "Can't you just kiss it and make it better?"

Two hours earlier his comments would have pissed her off, but her view of him shifted. He just risked his life to save her and Jake.

Emma laughed and pulled her hand away. "I don't think so. Do you know how many germs are in human saliva? I'm sure you have a first aid kit somewhere. A big boy like you carrying guns around should have Band-Aids for when things get a little too rough."

He tilted his head and narrowed his gaze as he studied her, then dropped his hand. "I have one in the back." Walking past her, he opened the gate to the bed of the truck and hopped in.

"Keys?" he asked, reaching out his hand.

They were in her hand, out of habit, and she handed them to him over the side.

Emma leaned her arms on the truck side and watched him lean over and unlock the metal box attached to the back of the cab. He opened the lid and Emma stood on her tiptoes in an effort to see its contents.

"You do know that curiosity killed the cat?"

"A cat has nine lives. I've still got a few left."

"Princess, after spending the last twenty-four hours with you I suspect you've used them all." He rummaged in the storage box and pulled out a first aid kit and a couple of bottles of water.

She walked to the end of the truck bed and waited for him. He sat on the open tailgate door, legs hanging over the edge.

"Thirsty?" He handed her a water bottle and opened his, taking a long drink.

"I'll look at your forehead first." She put the water bottle down on the tailgate and opened the small first aid box. She paused, studying the contents of the box. "Will, what do you really do for a living?"

His silence hung in the air and it surprised her when he answered, "I told you, I'm a computer consultant."

Emma fingered a stack of band-aids. "Who happens to carry around a full assault rifle? And can fight off half a dozen armed men?" She shook her head and glanced up at him. "What do you really do?"

He studied her, all teasing gone. "What does it matter, Emma?"

What did it matter? Tomorrow they would reach South Dakota and part ways. She knew she should be cautious of a man she hardly knew driving around with a truck full of guns, but he'd proven he was on her side. And Jake said to trust him.

"Why would your risk your life for us? You don't even know us."

He took another drink of water before he answered. "All that honor and duty crap. You know."

"Damsel in distress?"

"Yeah."

Emma climbed up into the truck bed and knelt beside him. She opened her water bottle and poured some on a gauze pad from the kit. "I need to clean this." She began to gently wipe dried blood from his cheek.

"I'm tough. You don't have to be so careful."

"No reason to be rough either."

He looked at her from the corner of his eye, raising an eyebrow. His voice lowered huskily. "Maybe I like it rough."

Emma got a new gauze square, doused it in water and dabbed his face. "Why do you do that? Why do you pretend you're such an asshole when you're really not?"

Will's hand jerked up and grabbed her wrist, his fingers digging into her flesh. His eyes penetrated hers. "Don't underestimate me, Emma."

Her gaze held his, her arm still in his grip, gauze on his cheek. The moonlight cast shadows across his face but allowed enough light for her to see emotions vacillate in his eyes. Anger, surprise, fear. *Fear.* What did Will have to be afraid of? Emma realized he was uncomfortable, but he refused to turn away so she broke away first and looked down. "Got it."

Releasing her arm, he grabbed his water bottle with both hands, twisting it back and forth in a barely perceptible movement.

Emma continued to wipe the blood closer to his cut. "Does this hurt?"

"No." His tone was gruff.

They had actually been getting along. It disappointed her that their truce seemed to be over. "Thank you."

"For what?"

"For helping us. For saving us. Thank you."

He closed his eyes and let out a slow, ragged breath. Obviously she upset him, but his reaction was far from what she expected. Sarcasm, yes. Hostility, no. Will's jaw clenched and unclenched as he seemed to wrestle with what to say. Finally, he opened his eyes.

"You're welcome," he choked out.

****

What the hell had just happened to him? He never lost control, always kept his cool, yet he practically snapped her arm off, along with her head. *Way not to look suspicious, dumbass.* Yet Emma took it in stride, staring at him like he sprouted another head but was too polite to say so. What the hell happened to *her*?

She's grateful. Gratitude made her feel indebted to him. A slow grin curved his mouth as he realized he could use it to his advantage. He turned a fraction of an inch to watch her as she bent over the first aid box. She was pretty, but either she didn't realize it or tried to hide it. Perhaps from all her years of hiding and trying to stay unnoticed. She used her abrasive exterior to keep people out. From what little he had seen, he knew it had to be effective. He realized she only let her guard down because she thought she could trust him. The tiny stab of guilt he felt over that puzzled him, but he ignored it. There was something else, something he couldn't quite put his finger on. It came to him as she opened a bandage and placed it on his cut with a bewildering gentleness. Emma had lost her anger. Just as he rediscovered his.

Emma closed the lid to the first aid kit and turned her head and smiled, the smile she saved for Jake. The pureness of it caught him off guard and his heart tripped. She studied his face, her eyes holding his in a thoughtful gaze, mesmerizing him. The dark pools promised some unnamed consolation he had forgotten he craved. Until now.

He clenched the water bottle in his hands, fighting the urge to touch her, yet unable to drag his eyes away. Her smile deepened with a look of tenderness and he had to suppress the impulse to suck in his breath. Emma lifted her hand to his face, placing her fingers on his temple and stroked his cheek with a feathery touch. She leaned over and her lips brushed his cheek, her breath hot on his face, hotter than the summer night's air. He found himself drowning with a need he couldn't name. His eyes closed involuntarily; this wasn't lust, a sensation he was all too familiar with. This was something else. And it scared him.

"See, I kissed it and made it better," she whispered in his ear. Will wondered how she could speak at all, much less with the teasing tone she used. He was still trying to remember to breathe.

"Um, I have to go to the bathroom."

It took him a moment to realize it was a question. "Ah," he cleared his throat. *Get it together, idiot.* "We're going to stay here for the night, so that's our bathroom." He gestured to the oak tree.

If the news upset her, she hid it well. "Do we happen to have any toilet paper?"

Will got up and dug through the storage box. He handed her a couple of napkins. Her fingers grazed his as she took them, reigniting his desire. *Moron.*

"Thanks." She walked toward the tree and turned to see him still watching her. "Turn around, Will."

"Free country, Princess," he said, grateful for his returned bravado.

Her face scrunched in disgust and she walked behind the tree trunk. "Seriously, Will."

He made a show of turning away from her, but was thankful to have a moment to recover.

She emerged from behind the tree several minutes later, holding the napkin gingerly in her fingers. "Got a trash bag?"

"Aren't those biodegradable?"

She pursed her lips and raised an eyebrow, the napkin dangling from her hand.

Will groaned and retrieved a plastic bag from the storage box. He hopped down from the truck bed and walked toward her. "Here you go."

She took the bag from him, looking up into his face. Moving this close to her was a mistake. His breath caught in his chest and the fire he tempered earlier now roared back to life. His fried brain told him to reach out to her. Instinct told him to stop.

"I've got to go, too." He turned abruptly and walked toward the tree to get a moment away from her. The sound of the truck door opening and closing blended with the sound of crickets and the rustle of corn. When he finished he found her sitting on the truck bed, her legs dangling. Her arms braced her as she leaned back, searching the clear starry sky. Her long dark hair blew in the soft breeze behind her back. She heard him approaching and twisted her head and smiled. The sincerity of her smile astounded him.

He sat next to her on the edge of the tailgate, a foot away, careful not to touch. "What are you looking at?"

"The stars. When I was a little girl I used to wish on the stars." Her voice was wistful with memory.

He copied her, leaning back braced on his arms. "And what did you wish for?"

"A father."

Her answer surprised him. Will tried to remember what his little sister wished for. Dolls, ponies, Prince Charming. He studied her still upturned face. There was no self-pity on her face, only contemplation.

"Did your life turn out how you expected it to, Will?" Her voice was soft against the rustle of the stalks in the cornfields.

He didn't expect that one either. "No."

She sighed, accepting his answer without explanation. "Me neither." She looked into his face. Her eyes were like magnets, making him incapable of breaking contact. "But for some reason tonight, I can forget my life sucks. I can forget that my sleeping son has a miserable excuse for a mother. Tonight, I can sit here under the stars and just be."

"Why?" he asked softly.

She turned back to the sky. "I don't know. It's really strange, something just feels different. I feel safe."

"You're not a miserable excuse for a mother."

Emma's head twisted back to him. Her eyes narrowed, as if she suspected a false motive, then she shook her head. "A good mother would protect her son. A good mother would provide a stable home. A father." A small, bitter laugh escaped from her throat. "Ironic, isn't it? The only thing I wanted as a child I failed to give to my own son, not that the sorry excuse of a man who fathered Jake has the right to call himself one."

"Where is Jake's father?"

"Where he belongs, no part of Jake's life."

She laid down on the bed of the truck and sighed, closing her eyes, her hair pooling around her. Will watched her, entranced. *What the fuck is wrong with me?* He resisted the urge to shake his head to clear it. The need to be close to this exposed Emma stymied him. He definitely was not himself tonight and he had no idea why.

"What did you want when you were a little boy?"

Uncertain how to answer, he remained silent. Why were Jake and Emma constantly making him think about his past?

Emma sat up and leaned close. "It couldn't be a dog. I know you had one of those." She put her hand on his shoulder. Her touch sent a jolt through him. Had she felt it too? He turned slightly and saw her eyes momentarily widen, confusion clouded her eyes before she continued. "What one thing did you think would make you happy?"

"I wanted…" A snide remark stopped on his tongue as he stared into her eyes. Did she know what she was doing to him? The innocence on her face answered his question.

Indecision nipped at his conscience. What he wanted most was to kiss her. She was so close. All he had to do was lean a little closer. She smiled, a sweet smile full of the promise her eyes held earlier. But the still-decent part of him knew she deserved better. Despite what Jake said, Will was not a good person and he had plenty of evidence to prove it.

Will cleared his throat, disappointment clinging to him like the anchor that tethered him to his sins. "I'm tired. I'm going to sleep out here in the back of the truck. You can sleep inside on the backseat."

"I'd rather sleep out here under the stars."

"I don't have a pillow. At least the seat is cushioned."

"And covered in glass."

"I'll clean it up for you."

She studied him again. "A chivalrous Will, who would have thought?" she said with a silky laugh. "Thanks, but I'd rather stay out here."

The missing *with you* only confirmed she was off limits. If Emma gave him a sign she wanted him, he wouldn't be able to stop himself. He hesitated, hoping she'd give him one. When it didn't come, Will got up and pulled a blanket out of the storage box. "I've only got one blanket."

"I don't need one."

"I was going to use it for a pillow, but you can use it."

"That's okay. I can use something else."

Digging through the box again, he found a t-shirt. After he handed her the blanket, he lay down next to her, putting the wadded shirt behind his head.

"Thank you." Her voice was still soft and warm, tugging at his resolve.

They lay on their backs, mere inches separating them. Will felt the heat radiating from her body.

"I should probably stay awake and keep watch," he said, studying the stars above. Out in the country with no city lights, there were thousands more than he was used to.

"That's not necessary. We're safe here."

"You don't know that."

"Somehow I do."

Will remembered she'd felt sick before the men in SUVs showed up. "Emma, do you usually sense the Bad Men before they come?"

"No, that's Jake, remember?"

"But today, you did. You knew something was wrong and you felt sick. You sensed them but Jake didn't. Has that ever happened before?"

"No." The softness was replaced with concern.

"What does it mean?"

"I don't know."

He felt her tense and against his better judgment, he worried the moment would be lost until he heard her slow even breaths.

They watched the sky as the sweet smell of the cornfield washed over the truck bed. "Do you know any constellations?" Will asked, not ready to let her go yet.

"Yeah, I know a few." He heard the smile in her voice. Her arm reached up and pointed. "There's the Big Dipper and if you follow that star there in the corner, you can see the North Star." She moved her arm as she pointed, then lowered her arm and turned to him. "But I'm sure you already know that. You were in the military."

She was silent for a moment before she said, "Orion's my favorite, but you can't see it in the summer."

"Why Orion?"

"I don't know...I just always have," she paused. "Will?"

"Hmm?"

"Will I always see the face of the man I killed?"

He could soften his answer, but it seemed unfair. Still he felt badly for her. "Yes." He sensed her sudden despair. "But it'll fade with time."

"When I close my eyes I see him. I see the surprise on his face and the pain. And I know I did that. I killed him." Torment enveloped her words.

"You had no choice. He would have killed you and Jake. You did what you had to do."

She laid her arms over her head, as if surrendering to it. "It doesn't make it any easier."

He thought of the countless faces whose lives he had extinguished. "No, but it will get better."

She sighed again and he fought the urge to touch her and give her comfort. Where the hell were these feelings coming from? He couldn't remember the last time he cared about someone other than himself. He wanted to blame it on the gunfight earlier, the near-death experience, but he knew better. This vulnerable Emma reopened dreams he'd had long ago. Earlier, Will couldn't answer what one thing he wanted when he was little because he had forgotten it. He'd stuffed it away with everything else. Now he remembered.

He wanted to be like his dad.

But he lost that dream along with all the others the day he came home and saw the disappointment and disgust on his father's face. After the humiliation of his court martial and the self-deprecation he'd heaped on himself, his father's disapproval was the final blow to his salvation.

Emma represented the possibility to love and be loved. He wondered what it would be like to see her sweet smile every day. The need to protect her from the men who hunted her overwhelmed him with a surprising intensity. *Where did that come from?* A heavy sigh of acceptance seeped from deep within. He was a fool. She wasn't what he craved; it was the promise of the life he'd thrown away years ago and could never have. The blood of too many innocents had rotted his soul.

CHAPTER NINE

EMMA woke to the chirping of birds, the sun low on the horizon of swaying cornstalks. She rolled over to check on Will, but he was gone. Her back was stiff from sleeping on the hard truck bed and she pushed herself up, her arm still numb from lying on it. After a quick glance around, she found Will sitting under the tree with his back against the trunk. His tipped head and closed eyes told her he was asleep. The memories of the previous evening rushed back and her face burned with embarrassment. Last night the feeling of safety made her unreserved, like a stupid high school girl. She hadn't felt that safe or free since before Jake and she reveled in it, letting her guard down, saying too much. But the cold light of day brought reality back, front and center. Will had acted so strange the night before. He was probably horrified by her behavior, but she sensed it was something else.

Emma crawled across the truck bed to look through the open window. Jake was still asleep, curled up on the front seat, cuddling his beloved stuffed dog. She suddenly felt stiff and agitated and scrambled off the truck, walking several feet down the gravel road as she watched the sunrise.

The sun inched higher and an anxious knot grew in the pit of her stomach. She closed her eyes, filling her lungs with deep breaths in an attempt to calm her jumbled nerves. The undeniable reality that they had almost been killed the night before meant the rules had changed. This was no longer a game of cat and mouse. Jake was in real danger now and Emma had no idea what to do about it. Her eyes burned with tears and she struggled to keep them from falling. Had their time run out? Years of running led to what? The end? Obviously she couldn't accept that, but she didn't know how to fight it either. After years of being several steps ahead of the men after them, she was no longer in control of the situation. The realization slammed her hard and her fear erupted in a stifled sob.

"Emma?"

She turned to find Will next to her. His brown eyes were dark with worry and he hesitated before resting his hand on her arm. "What's wrong?"

"Just leave me alone, Will. Please," she choked out, her words muffled as she covered her face with her hands in humiliation.

"Maybe I can help," Will whispered in her ear and his hand moved to her back, stroking slowly, in a soothing circular motion.

"No one can help me." Saying the words aloud made it even more real, pushing her to the brink of panic. "Please, just go away. Please."

She sensed his indecision before he wrapped his arms around her and pulled her close. Her first impulse was to resist, but as soon as her cheek rested on his chest, her eyes closed and she sank into him. In spite of her anguish, she marveled how right he felt, how perfectly she fit in his embrace. She felt safe, and that bewildered her even more. His hand reached up and stroked her hair while the other encircled her waist and the feelings of safety gave way to a rush of protection. Will made her feel safe. The thought simultaneously thrilled and terrified her; thrilled someone was capable of making her feel protected, yet terrified that Will was the one to provide it.

Will was unreliable.

But, there was something else. Feelings buried long ago now erupted, catching her by surprise. Every nerve ending tingled with anticipation, of what she wasn't sure. Will's embrace awakened the emotional part of her she had ignored for so many years, the need to be held, to be touched, to be loved. She'd been alone for so long she had forgotten this ache for something more. Succumbing to his embrace filled her with a sense of belonging, a feeling even more dangerous than the perception of protection.

Emma pressed her hands against Will's chest with the intent to push him away, but when she looked up at him, she froze. His eyes studied her face with a gentleness that caught her off guard. Arrogance, even a snide remark, she expected, but not gentleness. Their eyes locked and her stomach dropped. She knew it was ridiculous, she hardly knew him and what she did know was unflattering, yet there it was anyway. This need for him.

Without breaking his gaze, he moved his hand to her cheek. She sucked in her breath at the contact. He leaned closer and hesitated, his mouth inches away from hers.

Her insides fluttered and she waited.

Will released a heavy sigh and closed his eyes, leaning his forehead against hers. His heart beat rapidly under the palm of her hand and she stood in his arms confused. He leaned back up, his smartass grin spreading across his face. "Who knew you'd be so easy?"

Emma gasped and reached up her hand to slap him. His hand stopped hers in midair and he laughed.

"You're so predictable."

She grunted in frustration and jerked her hand from his as she stormed off toward the truck. Against her better judgment, she looked back over her shoulder only to see him walk toward the main road.

****

Will resisted the urge to run. There was no way in hell he could let Emma see how much she affected him. He walked about twenty feet down the gravel road and turned around to see her leaning against the tailgate, clearly upset.

Why did it bother him so much to hurt her? She was nothing to him. A job. Nothing more, nothing less. Women came and went in his life. There was never any hint of permanency and definitely no thoughts of a relationship. But even more disturbing was the sentimental bullshit that still burned in his gut. Last night he chalked it up to temporary insanity. But this morning, here it was. It was bad enough he couldn't resist touching her last night and resorted to sleeping under a tree, but when he heard her crying his impulse was to go comfort her. *What the hell?* Holding her in his arms was nearly his undoing, but thankfully, some deep-seated self-preservation instinct stopped him from kissing her just in time. Even if he hurt her in the process.

The sooner he got rid of Emma, the sooner his life got back to normal.

****

Emma leaned over the tailgate trying to calm down. The truck bed was damp and greasy under her hands, matching the slimy feeling that coated her soul. How did she let that happen? Memories of a night from long ago replayed in her head, memories she'd tried so hard to shove to the recesses of her mind. She groaned and shoved herself away from the truck, irritated she let herself get distracted by him. She laughed wryly. *Distracted.* That didn't quite cover it. Her son's life was being threatened and she was about to make out with Will. Riddled with self-disgust, she fought to focus on coming up with a plan to survive.

It's going to be okay Mommy. Jake's voice said in her head.

Emma jerked around. Jake's head popped up in the back window. She gaped at him, numb with shock. How could he do that?

Things are changing.

"How do you do that?" She had forgotten that he had spoken in her mind in the restroom the night before. Visions of the man she shot, the surprise on his face and the blood smeared on the wall, snuck into her mind, startling her with their vividness.

You had no choice.

The scene replayed in her head. In the stark daylight, she was no longer so sure. "That's what Will said," she whispered.

He's right.

She shook her head in frustration. "Stop talking in my head. You're freaking me out!" On top of everything else, it was too much.

"It's okay, Mommy. I'll stop."

Emma was on the verge of losing it, a feeling she was not acquainted with, and it terrified her. Everything grew fuzzy. As she fought to regain control, she realized Jake had gotten out of the truck and stood next to her.

He reached out and put his hand into hers. "I'm sorry, Mommy." His eyes were glassy with unshed tears and he looked so devastated Emma reached out and pulled him into a hug.

"Oh baby, it's okay." Her love for him washed through her. Emma sat down on the ground and pulled him onto her lap, resting her cheek on his head. She held him tight, breathing in his little-boy scent of baby shampoo and sweat. This was what was important, the little boy in her arms. "When did you find out you could do that, talk in my head?" she asked.

"Yesterday, in the bathroom."

"But how did you know?"

He leaned back, looking confused by her question. He shrugged. "I don't know. I just did."

Was he telling her the truth? Part of her didn't think so and she wondered if he would ever tell her everything he knew.

Only what you need to know.

He was right. Things were changing.

****

Will stopped and turned around after he walked about a quarter mile. He sure as hell couldn't walk away from Emma, so there was no point in going any further. His irritation settled into a palpable level and he developed a plan. Get back to the truck, drive to South Dakota and drop Emma and Jake off as soon as he possibly could.

By the time he got back to the truck, he convinced himself he overreacted and that Emma meant nothing. That is, until he saw her sitting on the ground, holding Jake on her lap. The way she looked at Jake reminded him of her softness the night before.

Son of a bitch.

Will walked up and cleared his throat. "Well, now that everyone's up, we should take off before a farmer shows up and prosecutes us for trespassing." He climbed up into the bed, wadded up the blanket and stuffed it in the box. Jake glanced at Will over his shoulder, his mouth pinched in a brooding pout.

Jake was quite the enigma. Will had to admit he was cute, but something was off with that kid. Sure, he was freaky, seeing things in the future one minute, talking about wanting a dog the next. But Jake seemed to know more than he let on, apparently even to his own mother. Will worried what he knew and didn't share would get them killed. Will shook his head and groaned. This was another reason he didn't do kids. They always messed with his head.

Will had all the glass cleaned off the back seat by the time Emma and Jake returned from going to the bathroom. Jake climbed in while Emma waited outside, her back to the truck as Will climbed out and walked around to the driver's side. Emma got in, sitting at the far edge of the seat looking out the window. Will headed for the road, eager to get this trip over with.

****

They drove in silence for almost an hour before they came to a town that offered any type of facilities open before eight o'clock. Will pulled into a McDonald's for breakfast and Emma took Jake into the bathroom to change clothes. She turned around to see Will standing next to the truck as he watched them. His face was stoic but quickly shifted to a smirk before he turned and walked to the back of the truck.

Emma and Jake walked out of the bathroom to find Will waiting for them wearing a different shirt. They ordered breakfast and sat in silence as they ate. Will kept watching the truck through the window.

"How do you feel?" he asked Emma, finally breaking his silence.

"I'm fine." Her answer was short.

"Are you sure? Will you tell me if you feel anything?" He turned, his eyes guarded yet holding a hint of a glare.

She nodded wondering why he was mad at her when she was the one who should be offended. She tried to shake it off. He wasn't worth the effort. Instead, she focused on the questions he raised. Why Jake didn't have more notice the day before? Maybe his new mind-reading talent was the reason. With her head lowered, she glanced from Jake to Will and wondered if Jake could read Will's thoughts. Could he talk to Will, too?

No. Jake said in her mind, taking a bite of his hash browns.

"Stop it!" she hissed.

Will turned and stared with a dark expression. "Stop what?"

She shook her head. "Nothing."

His eyes narrowed with uncertainty. "Are you sure you're all right?"

"I'm *fine*." She gave him the nastiest look she could muster, then returned her attention to her food.

After they finished eating, Will pulled into a gas station for gas and disappeared inside, coming out with several bottles of water and a bag of snacks. He handed the sack to Emma.

"I thought Jake might get hungry on the road. The stops might be sparse in Kansas." He glanced over his shoulder. "I need to replace the window again. I want to head up to Great Bend. It's a bigger town and we'll have more luck getting it fixed sooner."

She wasn't about to argue with him so she nodded and stared out at the passing scenery. The drive to Great Bend was only thirty minutes, but Will grew even moodier with each mile, not that she thought it possible. He found a repair shop and pulled into the lot, leaving Emma and Jake in the truck while he went into the office.

As soon as Will started walking across the parking lot, Emma spun toward the backseat. "Jake, why didn't you know the Bad Men were coming yesterday?"

Jake's mouth dropped open and his eyes widened. "I did. I told you when I saw them."

"As soon as you saw them?"

"Yes." The earnestness in his eyes told her he spoke the truth.

This was definitely bad news. They had lost their advantage.

"But Mommy, you knew they were coming."

"What?"

"That sick feeling was a warning they were coming. You have it now."

Emma shook her head in disbelief. "No, how can that be?"

Jake shrugged and seemed unconcerned. "You're the one who knows they are coming now."

Emma's eyes widened in horror and she covered her face with her hands. "I don't understand. I've never sensed them before." She turned to him. "I felt bad twice yesterday, but we only saw them once. Why did I feel bad in the morning?"

"They must have been watching us."

Her mouth dropped open. "What? How do you know that? Why didn't we see them?"

"Because they were just watching us. We weren't in danger."

"But we were the second time!"

"And you felt bad. Plus, I told you they were coming."

"Not soon enough, Jake! We could have been killed."

"But we weren't. I told you as soon as I knew."

Emma narrowed her eyes and glared. "Jacob, I order you to tell me when you know *anything* about the Bad Men."

Before Jake could answer, Will walked back to the truck. He cocked his head. "What's wrong?"

"Nothing." Emma didn't mean for it to sound so hateful.

He looked from Jake to Emma and scowled. "There's a whole lot of nothing going on this morning."

Emma pursed her lips in a glower.

"You both can get out. They can take in the truck right now and you can wait in the waiting room."

Cars filled the parking lot. Emma expected a longer wait. "How'd you get us in so quickly?"

"Money talks," he grunted.

A game show played on TV, barely holding Emma's attention. Her nerves were too far gone. Not only did she have to worry about how they would survive on less than fifty dollars, but how they would survive, period, especially in light of the news that she was the warning system now. Emma got up a few times and checked out the window. Will paced in the parking lot, in spite of the heat. He must really be irritated with her if he wouldn't even come inside. Her anxiety increased. That was just something else to worry about, his exasperation with her and her sudden attraction to him earlier. *It was nothing.* She had felt weak and vulnerable and she simply fell into the damsel-in-distress mentality. That was all. It was a moment of insanity. Besides, in the scheme of things, it seemed the least of her worries.

An hour later, Will came in and told them it was time to go. He ignored them, driving in silence until they reached Russell, the town bordering I-70, when he announced they were stopping for lunch.

"But we just ate breakfast," Emma said.

"I don't know how long it will be before we find civilization again in Kansas, so we better eat while we can." He pulled into a restaurant's half-empty parking lot.

"But..."

Will gripped the steering wheel, staring straight ahead. "Jesus Christ, Emma. The only goddamned thing you can say today is *nothing* and *but*. Get a fucking dictionary." He got out of the truck and slammed the door.

Emma turned to Jake, who stared at her with softened eyes while he patted her shoulder. "He'll be fine, Mommy. He's just confused."

"Confused about what? And how do you know?"

"Don't worry, he'll figure it out," he said as they got out, ignoring her second question.

Will stood in front of the truck, wringing his hands through his hair. Emma was afraid to approach him, but Jake walked over and pulled down Will's arm, tucking his little hand into Will's before Emma could stop him. Emma's insides twisted. Jake had begun to idolize Will and that was a problem. She didn't need any more problems.

They sat in a booth by a window. Jake scampered into the seat next to Will before he could protest. Will slid to the far edge and hunched over the table, studying the napkin dispenser as though it held the secret to life.

An attractive young waitress walked to the table, bringing them menus. She asked for their drink orders, keeping her eyes on Will. She suddenly caught his attention and he sat up straight, plastering on his grin.

"Good afternoon, darlin'."

Emma looked at him in confusion.

"What can I get for you and your…" she glanced at Emma's left hand, which lay on the table. "…wife?" she finished, uncertainty in her voice.

Will gave a throaty laugh. "You've got it all wrong, sweetheart. She isn't my wife. She's just a friend. I'm doing her a favor. That's all." He topped it off with a wink.

The waitress's smile widened and she leaned closer to him. "Well, aren't you the nice guy, helping out a poor woman like that?"

"That's me, Mr. Nice Guy." He cocked his head to the side and smirked.

"I'll have an iced tea and Jake will have milk," Emma interrupted.

Will lifted his eyebrows at Emma with an amused expression. "I'll have water."

The waitress turned to get their drinks and Will ogled her as she walked away. Emma's eyebrows rose. "What the hell is that?"

"Just appreciating the view."

"Yeah, I can see that. Maybe you could wait until I leave the table next time."

His eyes narrowed. "What's it matter to you?"

She glared at Will and they locked in a momentary staring contest. Anger boiled in her chest and she broke the gaze first, turning to Jake, who played with his toy car and seemed unmoved by the discussion. He was right. What did it matter if Will flirted with every waitress in the entire fucking town? She slumped in her seat, crossed her arms and frowned at the window.

The waitress returned with their drinks, taking her time to lean over and set Will's water on the table in front of him. Will gave her a sly smile and Emma rolled her eyes.

"What can I get you?" the waitress asked, the question directed to Will.

"What I want doesn't seem to be on the menu."

His response pleased the waitress who preened, a blush fanning her cheeks. Emma wondered how a woman with her obvious experience could muster a blush.

"I'll have a club sandwich," Emma volunteered, handing her menu to the waitress. She pointed to Jake. "He'll have chicken nuggets and he'll," she pointed to Will, "take a cold shower."

Will laughed. "Make that hamburger and a hot order—"

Emma snatched the menu out of his hands and thrust it at the waitress. "Just give him some fries. Thank you."

The waitress narrowed her eyes at Emma before turning around and walking to the kitchen.

Will leaned back, arms crossed over his chest, a huge smile spread across his mouth, but his eyes were dull. "Jealous?"

"Jealous? *Jealous*?" Her voice raised an octave. "Hell, no. Disgusted? Annoyed? Sullied? Yes. Jealous? No."

"Don't worry, Princess, you're the one I'm bringing with me."

"Not likely if you keep this up. It's insulting."

His smile faded. "It's not like you have a choice now, is it?"

Emma's anger spilled out. "Don't tempt me, Will. Russell, Kansas or God Forsaken, South Dakota. It's all the same to me. I won't be there longer than a few weeks anyway." It occurred to her maybe that was his intention. Maybe he wanted her to stay behind.

They sat in sullen silence while Jake played with his car. The waitress came back with their food, attempting to flirt with Will again, but he ignored her and turned his attention to his plate. Emma could hardly eat, her stomach twisted with apprehension. What was she going to do? Where would they go? A homeless shelter seemed like the logical choice , but that squeezed her stomach into a tighter knot. She looked over at Jake, trying to imagine taking him to a shelter. It couldn't be much worse than the last motel they stayed at. She wondered if a town this size even had a homeless shelter. She pushed her plate away, the smell of the grease making her nauseous.

"Do you feel sick?" Will asked, suddenly alert.

Their eyes locked and she tried to read his emotions. He didn't seem angry, only concerned.

"It's not like yesterday."

"Are you sure?"

She sighed, trying to calm her nerves. "Yes, I'm sure."

Will didn't look convinced. "Let's hurry up and get out of here." Will got the waitress's attention, not a difficult task since she stalked their table after Will's abrupt change of attitude. He paid the check while Emma and Jake went to the bathroom. When they finished, Emma saw him through the windows outside, pacing in long, quick strides on the sidewalk. She pushed open the door and he stopped, turning to face her. Lines of worry and tension wrinkled his forehead, but they softened when he saw her. Emma realized he was trying to hide it from her. He might be an ass but there was no denying he owed her nothing, yet he risked his life for them twice now. It was unfair to put him in more danger.

"Will." She held Jake's hand and squeezed it tighter as she drug Jake toward him.

He stared down at her, his hands stuffed in his jean pockets.

"I think this is where we should part ways."

His eyes widened and his mouth gaped, making it clear that wasn't what he expected.

"We've already asked far too much of you. You were almost killed last night and your truck was damaged because of us, and while I appreciate everything you've done for us, I think this is where we should say goodbye."

Jake's hand wriggled in hers and she released her unintentional death grip.

The color drained from Will's face.

"Mommy…"

"Jake, enough." Her tone was firm. The wind blew with remarkable force and she reached up to control the hair whipping into her face, never breaking eye contact with Will.

"Emma," Will said in a ragged breath as he pulled his hands out of his pockets. He started to reach for her, but stopped.

"We'll be fine. We always have been." Her voice softened and she hoped Will heard her gratitude. She couldn't believe Jake hadn't tried to intervene again.

Will snapped out of his daze. "Emma, don't be an idiot. Just get in the truck."

"Will…"

"What? You want an apology? Fine. I'm sorry. Okay? I was a complete ass. There. Now let's go." He wrapped his arm behind her back, pushing her toward the truck. Jake followed behind.

Emma stopped and turned to face him. "Will, that's not it." His apology caught her off guard and his delivery made it clear it wasn't something Will frequently did, but that wasn't what she was looking for. "I think it's time we went our separate ways. I obviously annoy you, and that's okay. You don't owe us anything. You don't have to drag us around anymore."

Will swallowed hard, and spun away, running his hand through his hair. He appeared upset, although Emma couldn't understand why. Finally, he turned back to her, his eyes full of worry. "I'm not ready for you to go yet."

"Will…" His reaction baffled her. There was no way he could really want them to go with him. His actions all day told her the opposite.

He grabbed her hand in his, holding it with a gentleness she didn't expect. "Not yet, okay? Just come with me."

She searched his dark brown eyes trying to figure out why he was doing this, but they gave nothing away. She hesitated. Common sense told her to ditch Will now, but a part of her was still drawn to him and she didn't understand it.

"All right."

A sigh escaped him as he ushered her to the truck. Emma sensed he was trying to get her in before she changed her mind.

They sat in the truck in silence. Tension hung in the air as Will peered out the front window, his hand draped over the steering wheel. His eyes narrowed as they focused ahead.

"Will…" Emma hesitated. Maybe he changed his mind.

He hung his head for a moment, confusing her even more. Slowly, Will tilted his head toward her, defeat in his eyes. "Change of plans. We're going to Colorado."

CHAPTER TEN

WILL told himself it made sense to take the long way. It occurred to him maybe her enemies knew where to find her because they knew he was taking her to South Dakota. If that was true, then he should be able to elude them by detouring through Colorado. It sounded good, but in the back of his mind he had to admit he was also postponing her handover.

"What are you talking about?" Emma shook her head, incredulous.

"I think we should take the long way to South Dakota and see if we can lose the guys after you and Jake." Will started the truck and turned onto the road.

"It doesn't really matter where you go. They'll still find us. Besides, what about the job waiting for you?"

"I don't have to show up for a few days. I'd rather try to lose those guys."

She agreed in the end, to his relief. After her stand in the parking lot he didn't want to push his luck. He had almost pushed her too far with the waitress incident. Hell, he wasn't even interested in the waitress. It had been a combination of automatic reflex and his need to prove he wasn't interested in Emma. The fact that it irritated her was pure bonus. But in the parking lot, as she calmly announced she was parting ways, he realized his job wasn't the real reason he convinced her to stay with him. He really wasn't ready to let her go.

Jake napped in the back seat as Will and Emma rode in silence, although it was more comfortable than the morning. His earlier anger was tempered, but his nerves were still on edge. He snuck glances at Emma, who found the rusted oil rigs, pumping in their monotonous circular motion, more entertaining than the small talk he tried to make. The dilapidated pumps, dispersed among large bales of hay and scattered black cattle, littered the flat green fields of western Kansas. He might have bought her fascination if he hadn't known she spent so much time in Texas. Not that he blamed her for avoiding him.

Jake woke from his nap unusually subdued. He laid his head against the side window, gazing out through the glass with a vacant stare as the landscape blurred past. When he didn't shake his lethargy, Emma became concerned. She reached back and brushed the curls off his forehead, using the age-old mother's thermometer.

"Jake, are you alright?"

"I'm okay, Mommy. I just have a headache." He offered a forced smile and tried to push her hand away. She stroked his cheek, lingering.

"I don't have any children's Tylenol." Will heard the self-recrimination in her voice. If she hadn't confessed concerns about being a bad mother the night before, he never would have caught it. Then again, before last night he wouldn't have paid attention.

"Emma, I can stop for some." His voice was gentler than usual and she turned and looked at him, distrust in her eyes.

"Mommy, I'm fine. I feel better already." Jake sat up and smiled, though even Will could tell it was only to get Emma to leave him alone.

Emma relented, and sat back down in the front seat, biting her lip as she snuck glances at Jake.

They stopped outside Denver to eat. Will bought a Colorado map from a convenience store when he stopped for gas and a bottle of children's Tylenol. Studying the map while they ate, he determined which direction he wanted to go from Denver. He considered heading north since it was closer to South Dakota, but it was peak tourist season and the Estes Park area was the closest northern mountain range. It would be crawling with people. South seemed like the better choice.

"Where are you planning to go?" Emma asked, peering over the top of the map.

"I want to head into the mountains." If the gunmen were tracking them, he thought they might have planted a tracking device on his truck. If they had, he hoped the poor radio transmission in the mountains might lose them.

"Tonight?"

"Yeah, it won't take more than a couple of hours to get to where I want to go."

Jake picked at his food with his fork, pushing the macaroni and cheese on his plate around in circles.

"Jake, you want something else to eat?" Will asked. Emma suggested Jake get something other than chicken and he could see the guilt on her face. She wouldn't ask to get Jake something else since he was paying for it.

"No, I'm not hungry."

Emma put her hand to his forehead again.

"I'm fine, Mommy." He lifted his luminous blue eyes to Will, pleading for help then stabbed several noodles and put the fork in his mouth. "See?" He mumbled with his mouth full of food.

Denver evening traffic was still heavy when they left. They inched their way around the city and headed south, the Rocky Mountains grew larger framed by puffy, towering white and purple lined clouds.

"Jake, have you ever seen mountains before?" Will asked over his shoulder. Jake's silence was beginning to concern him.

"No," he answered with an exaggerated sigh.

They drove into the mountains and Jake remained eerily quiet while Emma fidgeted in her seat. Anxiety hung in the air like a thick cloud of smoke, choking Will with a dread he couldn't pinpoint. He questioned if he was doing the right thing, heading this direction.

"When you get a dog, what will you name him?" Will asked Jake.

Emma's head whipped up.

Jake looked up to face Will's reflection. "I don't know. Maybe Rusty." A small smile lifted at the corner of his mouth and his eyes glistened with unshed tears.

Will's stomach dropped. "Jake, you'd tell me if you saw something, right? You'll tell me if the Bad Men are coming?"

"Does Mommy feel bad?" Jake hesitated a fraction of a second before responding, but it was enough to confirm Will's fears.

Will turned to Emma. She shook her head, biting her lip.

"Then there's nothing to worry about," Jake answered and turned back to the window. Will wasn't convinced and neither was Emma.

"Jacob, I insist you tell me if you see the Bad Men!" Emma's voice constricted with fear.

"I don't see them, Mommy."

"Don't lie to me, Jake." Her tone was harsh.

Will had never heard her raise her voice to him.

"Mommy, I've never lied to you. You know that." He sounded weary, more weary than a five-year-old should sound.

What about a lie of omission? Will was positive Jake wasn't telling them everything.

"Jake, last night we were really lucky to get away," Will said softly but direct. "You have to tell us the minute you see something."

Jake held Will's gaze in the mirror. "I'll tell you when we're in danger." He finally answered, closing his eyes.

The highway turned into a two-lane road that began to twist and wind as the incline increased. Trees grew dense, giving Will a sense of claustrophobia. Sky visible in the thin strip above the road became overcast and gray, and the smell of rain hung in the air. Will found it difficult to shake off the feeling of foreboding.

They drove through a small town with a few motels lining the street. Will decided to risk staying in a motel, although he would have preferred camping in an out-of-the-way spot. But he didn't have any camping gear and the threat of rain remained. A rundown cabin rental office came into view and Will pulled off.

Emma and Jake waited in the truck while Will went to check them in. He returned with the cabin key and a bag of marshmallows.

"The guy at the desk said there's a fire pit outside the cabin. I thought you might like to roast marshmallows, Jake."

Jake graced him with a real smile. "I like to roast marshmallows."

The motel consisted of about fifteen small cabins staggered along a curvy winding gravel road that wound back along the side of the mountain. The parking lot held more cars than he would have preferred, but it was summer and they were in a tourist area. But their cabin was in the back in a secluded area, and he parked the truck out of sight.

Emma and Jake went inside, Emma carrying their suitcase. After Will carried in his bag and the metal gun case, he grabbed some newspaper in the cabin and took it to the fire pit, bringing his rifle with him. Will grabbed several logs from a nearby firewood stack and started a fire. It crackled and sputtered before flames erupted, spreading across the stack with a burst of yellow and orange. Jake emerged from the cabin, appearing more animated than he had all afternoon. Emma followed behind him and they sat on one of the benches encircling the pit. The sky had quickly darkened and their faces glowed in the firelight. Will sat on an opposite bench, watching them in silence as the fire roared to life.

Emma's eyes glazed watching the fire, and she looked lost in terrifying thoughts. She bit her lower lip, looking more haunted than he had ever seen her. Will wanted to ask her what she saw in the flames that caused her such distress, but he knew she wouldn't answer. Instead, he decided to distract her.

Will stood up. "Jake, let's get some sticks and roast some marshmallows."

"Okay," Jake's new enthusiasm remained, to Will's relief. He knew if Jake was happy, the chances of Emma being happy increased.

Will handed the first stick to Jake then sat down next to Emma and stuffed a marshmallow on the end of the twig. Jake's face radiated as he neared the fire.

"Jake, be careful." Emma warned.

Jake seemed invigorated by the blaze, his eyes mesmerized by the flames. They widened in a sudden burst of energy and his face lit up in marvel. If Emma was lost in a nightmare, Jake looked lost in an epiphany. His marshmallow caught on fire, but he didn't seem to notice, his gazed focused on the dazzling sparks.

"Jake, your marshmallow's on fire," Will said.

Jake's face glowed, the illumination of the flames dancing on his face. He took a step toward the fire.

"Jake!" Emma called out, standing up from the bench.

"Huh?" Jake shook his head in confusion. He stared down at the flaming marshmallow. "Oh," He pulled the stick out of the fire but watched the ball of flames begin to spread down the branch.

Will took it from him and handed Jake his. "Be careful, big guy. You don't want to get burned." Will blew out the flames and swiped the burnt marshmallow on the ground. He observed Jake, wary of his change in demeanor.

Emma sat back down on the wooden bench. Will was sure she hadn't seen Jake's face. Otherwise, he knew she wouldn't be so sedate with her shoulders hunched over, her elbows on her knees. Her eyelids drooped.

"Emma, why don't you go ahead to bed. Jake can stay out here with me if he wants."

Emma hesitated, darting her eyes between them both.

Jake stood up straight and turned to Emma. "Mom, go inside." His voice was deeper than Will had ever heard from Jake and he spoke with an authoritative tone. The hair the back of Will's neck stood on end.

Will expected Emma to reprimand him for his order, but she simply stood up and went inside. He watched in disbelief as she walked into the cabin, never turning back to even check on Jake. No instructions for Will about how long he could stay out, no chastisement to put on a jacket. She just disappeared.

"What just happened there?"

Jakes spun around, his face stoic, his eyes cold. "I told her to go."

Will narrowed his gaze at Jake, although he wasn't sure this was really Jake. Something happened to him in front of the fire.

"Sit down, Will." Jake's voice was short and cold and he sounded years older than five.

Will sat on the bench, his instincts screaming in protest.

Jake held his eyes in an unblinking gaze as he moved to stand in front of him, their faces a foot apart. "I have a lot to tell you, Will, and not much time."

"Why not? Why don't you have time?" Will tried to sound calm.

Jake laughed condescendingly. "Will, if you listen, I'll tell you what you need to know." Jake's face glowed with the light of the fire and his eyes glistened with power. *Power.* That was how he was different. Will unconsciously scooted backward on the bench.

"I won't hurt you, Will. At least not now. Someday we won't be friends, but it isn't today. *Things are changing.*" Jake's face hardened. He was Jake, but he wasn't. He seemed possessed.

"What are you talking about, Jake?" None of this made sense. Will started to get up but Jake pushed him down with more force than a normal five year old had.

"For now, you must listen. I need to make sure you are The One. I'm pretty sure you are because everything started changing, but for my mom… I need to be sure." His eyes softened.

"What…"

"Will, you have to *listen*. Will you let me be sure?" Jake's gaze pierced his with a painful intensity.

Will's mind reeled. "What are you talking about, Jake? Be sure of what?"

"I need to touch you. I need to read you to be sure you're The One."

"What do you mean read me? What do you mean The One?"

Jake sighed with impatience. "I'll touch you and I'll know. Whether you give me permission or not, I'll be sure before..." his voice trailed off. "It'll be easier if you agree. It won't hurt. Then I'll explain it all to you."

Will wondered if he was hallucinating. He'd known guys who finally cracked under the pressure and saw things that weren't really there. After everything he had gone through with this job, maybe that was what was happening now.

"You're not hallucinating, Will. This is very real."

Will's eyes widened. "How did you know what I was thinking?"

"I can read your thoughts," Jake said with a playful smirk.

"Your mom told me you couldn't read minds. She got completely pissed when I kept asking if you could read minds."

"It's new. It's part of the changes. I only found out about it yesterday."

"What do you mean just found out about it? Can you talk to your mom in her head? Can you talk to me?"

"I can speak to my mom but not you, not yet. I can only hear you."

"Why? Why are things changing?"

"Because of you. Now will you let me read you?" The flames of the fire silhouetted Jake, making him even more intimidating.

Will was terrified. He was out of his element.

Jake smiled, his expression softening. "I'm sorry, Will. I didn't mean to scare you. I'm not used to this power yet. He said it would come with fire; I just didn't realize this was how it would happen."

Will's eyes narrowed. "Who told you?"

"I don't know who he is but since you showed up in the parking lot that first night, he visits me while I sleep. He told me that I would get power from fire. When I stood in front of the fire tonight, I felt it. I'm having trouble controlling it."

Will shook his head. "What else does he tell you Jake?"

Jake's face grew stern again. "He says you are The One, but I need to know for sure."

Agreeing felt like stupidity, but Will found himself nodding anyway. "All right."

Jake took a deep breath, leaned his head back and closed his eyes. He reached out and touched Will's forehead with his left palm and placed his right hand on Will's left forearm. An electric power surged through him. He fought to break contact, but his body refused to move. Panic spread through him, following the wake of electricity. It crashed with a suffocating intensity. He gasped for breath, drowning in terror. Both surged in waves, rippling from head to toe with decreasing intensity until it became a dull undercurrent. Heat poured through his arm, searing his flesh. Emotions and sensations churned and separated as if being sorted through a sieve, measured. Anger, sadness, happiness, love swirled in a cesspool of pain and death. An avalanche of emotion suffocated him. Jake's strained voice echoed in the night, speaking a language Will didn't recognize, but understood in his mind.

> *The land will fall desolate and cold*
> *As it waits for the promised ones.*
> *God resides within the queen*
> *While she hides among the people of the exile land*
> *Hunted for that which she must lose*
> *One who is named protector, The Chosen One,*
> *Shall be a shield, counselor, companion*
>
> *The elevated one will arise from great sorrow*
> *In the full moon after the summer solstice*
> *His powers will be mighty and powerful*
> *He will rise up to rule the land*
> *The supplanter will challenge him*
> *But only one will be overcome*
> *By that which has no price*

Jake withdrew his hands. Will's forehead and arm tingled from the broken contact. Sweat beaded his brow. Will's consciousness convulsed as he struggled to regain control. His chest heaved, sucking in deep breaths to clear his head, as if it were possible. Jake stood before him, his eyes dark and wild. An aura of pale red light surrounded him. Jake's gaze bore into Will's and a slow smile erupted.

"You are The Chosen One."

Will's arm throbbed. He lowered his head to see dark markings on the flesh of his forearm. He rubbed it with his thumb but it didn't smudge.

"It's your mark."

His head jerked up to face Jake. "What?"

"It is the imprint of The Chosen One."

The fire cast a dim light, making Will narrow his focus on the marking. He could make out the outline of a three-pointed spear with a short curved handle. He rubbed it again, the mark tingling with a residual current.

"Yes, it's like a tattoo. It'll prove that you are who you claim to be."

"I don't claim to be anyone. I'm not a chosen anything. No one asked me."

Jake sighed. "Of course no one asked you. You were *chosen*. It's your destiny."

Will held his arm out. "Take it back."

"I can't take it back, Will. It's done."

Will stood up and backed away from Jake and the fire, dried leaves and pine needles crunching under his feet. "I don't know what's going on here, but I'm not having any part of it. I'm not chosen for anything but pain and death." Will's voice choked. His emotions, still tangled in knots, unfurled in spasms. "You say you know who I work for yet you say I'm not bad. You wouldn't say that if you really knew. You have no idea what I have done, what I am capable of, what I'm doing *right this minute*." His voice broke and Jake's outline became hazy through his tears. "If I'm chosen, it's not for anything good, I goddamn guarantee you."

"Sometimes the choices we make are part of the path that takes us to where we need to be." Jake said softly. "Those choices are in your past and you can't change them. It's what you chose to do with what you have now."

He clenched the fist of his marked arm and held it toward Jake. "I don't choose anything. I sure as hell don't choose this."

"Even not choosing is a choice. You can fight it all you want, but it's still your destiny."

"You're five years old. What the fuck do you know?"

Jake smiled, a mixture of tolerance, kindness and power crossing his face. His hands raised from his sides, palms up to the sky, fingers splayed. As they rose, the fire behind him rose higher, crackling and sputtering in protest. His arms rose over his head causing the flames to do the same, arcing off with a burst of power. Heat engulfed Will, making him stagger backwards. He fell on his ass in the dirt, twigs digging into his legs and pine needles poking his palms. Dark clouds in the sky tumbled, rolling upon themselves as though trying to escape the onslaught of energy. Thunder rumbled and roared.

"I have power that I never knew I was capable of possessing." Jake's eyes narrowed, piercing Will as he lowered his arms. "You did that. Your presence released it. I'm Jake but I'm not. I've changed into something else. A war is brewing and we'll be on opposite sides, but not tonight. Tonight I need to show you who you really are."

Will's emotions were still a snarled mess. The sins of his past replayed in his mind, putting him on trial all over again. Tears streamed down Will's cheeks. "Do you have any idea what I've done?"

"Yes, I've seen it all and some of what it is to come. Good, bad, they're just words. Who's to decide what is good or bad? In the end, only the consequences matter." Jake walked toward Will. He leaned over and put his hand on Will's shoulder. "You're destined for great things. Your life will be full of pain but glory as well." Jake's eyes softened. "And you will know great love." He sighed and dropped his hand. "It'll be easier for you when you accept your fate."

Will shook his head in disbelief. "This isn't real."

"It's more real than you know. You have much to think about but little time to accept it all. The prophecy will always be implanted in you, use it as your guide. Beware of those who choose to ally themselves with you, they are not all who they seem to be."

"I don't understand what's going on." Will's voice lowered. He watched the fire, still dancing out of control.

"A war has begun. It's lain dormant for centuries waiting for prophecy to be fulfilled. Tonight it begins."

Will shook his head. "Jake, you're just a little boy. What do you know of war? I've seen war. I've wallowed in the utter misery of it. I won't do that again. You don't want that, Jake."

"I may be a boy but the power you just saw is only the beginning. It'll grow stronger than you can imagine. We have no choice. It's destiny." Jake's voice was heavy with resignation.

"Jake, this is crazy. Let me help you." Will risked grabbing Jake's upper arm even though he knew Jake had the power to hurt him. "Let's go talk to your mom. We'll figure this out."

Jake's eyes filled with tears. "There's nothing to figure out. Don't tell my mom. Please. I'll tell her when it's time."

Will sighed. Emma needed to know this, although he had no idea what her reaction would be. It couldn't be good. "I'll give you until tomorrow night, and if you haven't told her then I will." Will's voice was sterner than he felt. Jake scared the hell out him, but without this new power, he was still just a little boy.

Jake nodded, and Will pulled him into a tight embrace. Jake stood stiff but eased into Will's contours after a moment. He laid his head on Will's shoulder. Will felt his shirt dampen from Jake's tears and Will laid his head on top of Jakes and closed his eyes. From sheer terror one minute to his heart melting the next. This kid would be the death of him.

"I thought you told me it wouldn't hurt." Will said into Jake's hair, the words muffled.

"I didn't hurt me." Will heard the smile in his voice. Jake pulled away, his face softened with regret. "I wish you were *my* dad, Will."

Will shook his head. "I'd make a terrible dad, Jake. You deserve better."

The corner of Jake's mouth lifted with the hint of a smile. He turned and walked to the cabin, waving an arm at the roaring fire. It abruptly folded in on itself, leaving a pile of glowing embers.

Good night, Will. Pleasant dreams. It was only after he watched Jake disappear into the cabin that he realized that Jake spoke in his head.

CHAPTER ELEVEN

AFTER Jake went inside, Will collapsed on a bench and watched the glowing embers in the fire pit, trying to make sense of what happened. By the time the cinders grew cold, his mind still tumbled in confusion and anxiety churned in his gut. Exhaustion finally overtook the emotions let loose by Jake's encounter. He crept into the cabin, leery of running into Jake. The living area was dark and quiet. Will's tension eased slightly as he entered the vacant bedroom and locked the door behind him. He stripped and fell into bed, tossing and turning until he fell into a troubled sleep.

Will's dreams were turbulent. Scenes from his tour in Iraq revolved endlessly with images of Jake by the fire until they melded into one. Will raced down the hallway of a long darkened building, screams barraging him from the doors he ran past. Heavy black smoke filled the hall and he coughed violently, fighting for air. First he ran from someone, but just as quickly the dream spun around and he ran to save someone. *Jake.* Will screamed his name, pulling on the locked doors in vain. The thick smoke swirled around him and he fell to his knees, still calling for Jake between gasps for air. The next moment cool, fresh air filled his lungs as he knelt outside the building, now consumed in fire. Jake's emotionless face watched him from a window before dissolving into the flames.

Will sat up in bed with a jerk, a cold sweat beading his forehead. He slowed his rapid breaths. It was all a nightmare. Had he dreamt the event with Jake too? Dim sunlight filtered through the partially opened curtains and Will held out his arm, looking down to prove himself crazy. The black mark contrasted against his tanned skin, mocking his disbelief. Will groaned and swung around to put his feet on the rough carpet, resting his elbows on his knees. He lowered his face into his open palms. He was losing his grip on reality.

Sounds came from the living area. Relief swept through him, making him grateful he wasn't the only one awake. He wasn't eager to face Jake but he couldn't deal with being alone with his thoughts either. He pulled on his jeans and walked out of the bedroom.

The living area was one small room with a sofa and a couple of chairs on one side, a small kitchenette on the other. Emma stood in front of the sink with a glass of water, gazing out the window. He stopped and drew a deep breath, caught off guard at the sight of her. The softness of her face made her look young and vulnerable. Her eyes focused on some faraway sight, deep in thought, her hips leaning against the worn counter. Her hair hung in dark waves, skimming a bare shoulder that peeked through the oversized neck of her t-shirt. The shirt she wore was too large and hit her mid-thigh, making him wonder what she had on underneath.

Emma turned her head toward him with a look of surprise. Her uplifted chin caught the soft morning light, emphasizing her profile and the contour of her neck. Her mouth lifted in the barest of smiles but it was enough to send him over the edge. He suddenly wished he hadn't come out of his room. Every time she smiled at him he felt like an ice pick chipped away at his soul, leaving him raw and exposed.

"Good morning. You're up early." The sound of her voice jolted him from his daze.

"I could say the same of you." He shoved his hands in his pockets and walked closer. The need to be close to her overrode all reason.

"I couldn't sleep." She turned back to the view. "I've never been to Colorado before. It's kind of peaceful here."

The memory of the previous night came to mind. "I guess it might be for some people."

"I've been trying to figure out what to do. You know, when we get to where we're going."

It surprised him she was discussing this with him. She'd kept her past and her plans so private. But talking about her future reminded him of his mission, racking him with guilt and uncertainty. He cleared his throat. "Come up with anything?" He stood next to her now, mere inches apart.

"No," she sighed and set the glass down. "I want to apologize for the way I acted the other night, by the cornfield." She scrunched her nose as she searched for words. "I'm sorry I acted so... weird. I just felt so different... so safe." Closing her eyelids, her face relaxed with the memory and he held his breath, mesmerized. She opened her eyes, a sheepish expression on her face. "I've never felt that safe, ever really. I know how crazy it sounds." She paused. "I was foolish, talking about stars and wishing...Anyway, I know I freaked you out and I just want to tell you that I'm sorry."

"Yeah," his voice was unnaturally low and he cleared his throat again. "Umm..." He lost himself in the dark brown depths of her eyes. There he saw the real Emma, the Emma she hid from everyone else. Opening herself to him made his agony even worse. He ached to hold her and to kiss the lips she gnawed in her nervousness. He wanted her to feel safe every day, not just one night, but instead he bit his tongue. The rational part of him knew he stood on a precipice. If he touched her there was no going back and he wasn't willing to pay the price. Two nights ago he didn't touch to protect her. Now he stopped to protect himself.

"I'm going for a walk," he said. He turned and walked to his room, grabbed his shoes and went outside, without even stopping to put them on. He only knew he needed to get as far away from Emma as possible.

****

Emma watched as horror spread over Will's face before he ran from her. She couldn't help wondering what she had done this time when he shot past her and out the front door without giving her a second glance. She didn't know why, but his revulsion hurt.

After a long shower, she dug around the cabin searching for food, but the cabinets were empty. Since Jake was still asleep, she walked outside and sat on a bench by the fire pit, the peace of the mountains calming her nerves. The morning mountain air was cool and a light mist hung in the air. Emma wrapped her arms around herself and rubbed in an attempt to warm up. She would have gone in to get a jacket if it weren't for the fact she didn't own one anymore. The thought should have depressed her but the morning was too beautiful to wallow. Her misfortune would wait. It sure wasn't going anywhere.

Lost in her thoughts, she saw Will emerge from the woods next to the cabin. He stomped out into the clearing, scowling. He carried a long branch in his hand and as he left the forest, he whacked the stick into a tree trunk, cracking the stick in half. He looked up, startled to see her.

Words of greeting caught on her tongue. For the first time she saw what all those other women saw. He hadn't brushed his hair yet and the waves were unruly. His eyes were dark, darker than usual, and the hard angles of his scowl contrasted with the softness of his cheeks. His shirt was stretched taut against the muscles of his chest and arms. She saw a tattoo on his left forearm, why hadn't she noticed it before? He watched her scrutinize him and his scowl softened.

"Will…" She stopped not sure what to say. Obviously, he was mad at her but for the life of her, she couldn't figure out why. She only knew she didn't want him mad at her anymore.

Will looked torn, wrestling with something. Suddenly, he threw down the stick in his hand with a violent toss. It took only a few strides before he stood in front of her. He reached down, grabbed her upper arms and pulled her to his chest in one swift movement. Too shocked to protest, Emma's heart raced instead. Will held her arms in a vise grip while he searched her face. His smoky black eyes captured hers. It never occurred to her to fight him. His grip loosened. She thought he was about to release her until he groaned. His left arm pinned her back, his other hand cupped the back of her head and pulled her mouth to his.

The violence of his kiss surprised her, his mouth rough as he possessed hers. His stubble scratched her chin but she didn't notice, only the undeniable pull she felt. She lifted her arms up and around his neck, pulling him closer. He groaned again into her mouth, holding her tighter, claiming her mouth with his tongue. Dizziness washed through her as her stomach tightened, overwhelmed with an intensity that frightened her.

His hand knotted in her hair, holding her mouth to his but she had no intention of pulling away. A long extinguished flame combusted to life and she hungered for it. If she hungered, Will craved.

His hands roamed her body in wild abandon. Emma clung to his neck, afraid to let go, afraid she couldn't stand. His cold hand reached under her shirt, fingers skimming her ribs. She stiffened at the contact, not that Will noticed. His hand pushed on, finding her breast. She gasped, exciting him more. His mouth ravaged hers. His free hand pressed against the small of her back, pulling her hard against him, proving without a doubt he wanted her. His hands grabbed the bottom of her shirt. In one movement, he jerked it up, over her head and upstretched arms, only breaking contact with her lips for a brief moment. They found hers again, rough and frenzied. His hands circled her waist, sliding up her sides. They stopped beneath the swell of her breasts, her every nerve taunt in anticipation.

His hand reached up and grabbed the hair on the back of her head, pulling her mouth from his. Her eyes fluttered open in surprise. Will's face loomed over hers. His eyes burned with passion and something else. Anger. Her stomach dropped and her eyes widened in fear.

"What are you doing to me?" he growled as he studied her face. He didn't wait for an answer; instead dropped his face to her neck, her hair still in his hand. He pulled her head back, giving his mouth complete access. She moaned, in spite of herself. Her chest rose and fell as she struggled to catch her breath. Will's mouth worked its way toward her breasts. The heat in her belly raged.

"Will," she begged.

His mouth found hers again, wild and primal. He moaned, moving his lips away from hers. "God, help me. I want you." One hand still gripped her hair, the other circled behind her waist. His body shook as he caught his breath.

"Mommy?"

They both froze. Emma turned to see Jake standing in the cabin doorway, her cheek next to Will's chest. She felt his head twist and his arms tightened around her.

Jake took in the sight of them, then went back into the cabin. Emma's eyes closed in embarrassment and Will's embrace loosened. He placed his hands on her shoulders and pushed himself away from her. He squeezed his eyes shut and ran his hands through his hair as he struggled to catch his breath.

Emma stood before him, arms by her sides. The cold air hit her exposed flesh, giving her goose bumps, but she resisted the urge to cover herself. She didn't know what he was thinking, but she refused to look embarrassed, even if she was.

Will opened his eyes, hands still threaded in his hair. Terror flashed in his eyes before he lowered his hands to cover his face. Emma waited, a blush spreading despite her inner resolve. She couldn't believe she gave into him so willingly, so *eagerly*. Will was a player. She had just been played. *What an idiot*. Her embarrassment turned to anger as the cool morning air dulled the remnants of passion. She put her hands on his chest and shoved with all her weight.

"What the hell was that?" she spat at him.

He hadn't seen her coming and he stumbled backwards, almost tripping on the fire pit. She followed and reached to shove him again. He was ready for her this time. He grabbed her wrists. His smartass smirk was back.

"Didn't hear any complaints a minute ago." He leered with a lopsided grin.

She jerked her hands free and swung her right hand toward his face. He stopped her again, grabbing her wrist in mid-swing.

"Get your fucking hands off me," she snarled.

"Again, no complaints earlier."

He winked but even in her anger she could see the amusement didn't reach his eyes. He twisted her wrists around and down, pulling her body up against his.

"Sorry we can't finish what we started here, Princess." He looked down at her and she saw confusion flicker across his face. Her anger faded as she realized he might have actual feelings for her.

Will dropped her hands and backed away from her, then turned and walked toward the truck. "I've got to get out of here."

Emma watched him drive away and she realized she stood outside in only a pair of jeans. She picked up her shirt off the ground with a shaky hand and went inside.

****

Will drove on the mountain road away from Emma. He sucked in deep breaths trying to clear his head. *I am fucking losing it.* He couldn't believe he'd attacked her like that. But when he saw her sitting there, the look of sadness and expectation on her face drew him to her. Not one molecule of his existence could have stayed away from her. He literally had no control.

"Motherfucking son of a bitch!" He slammed his fist on the stirring wheel as he drove down the winding mountain road. *Not the smartest move, asshole.* No sense getting himself killed over a piece of… He stopped himself. Even in his anger, he wouldn't let himself think of her that way.

He should have known how she'd react. She'd made it perfectly clear from the moment they met what she thought of him. Of course, he'd done a pretty good job playing the asshole card. Why would she expect any less from him? What was he thinking? Something happened to him that night in the cornfield. Sure he found her attractive before, but it was as if some switch in his brain had been tripped and she was the thing he needed to make his life complete.

He snorted at the ridiculousness of the thought, but there was no denying the draw to her was stronger than his resolve. Will was a man used to being in control and he had officially lost it. He groaned in frustration and anger. And, he hated to admit, fear.

A picnic area rounded the bend fifty feet ahead so he pulled over and got out of the truck, thankful no one else was around. He leaned over a concrete table. His palms scraped against the rough concrete and his head hung between his arms. Emma had to go. The thought of turning her over made him ill, but the reality was he had no choice. The people who hired him had money and power, two things you didn't fuck with, and he'd already wasted time stalling. If he didn't turn her over, they would send someone else after both of them. He had no idea why they wanted her but it wasn't his business to know. Or care. He was hired to do a job. After all these years he had never been anything but professional. Until now.

The sounds of a car approaching interrupted his thoughts, reminding him that he left his gun at the cabin. A minivan drove around the curve, its brake lights flashing as it continued down the road. Will turned back and the tattoo on his arm caught his eye. He stood up and held out his arm, studying the mark Jake had given him. It was black and about three inches long and two inches wide. It looked like a three-tipped sword, similar to a trident, with curves shooting off the tips. The base was a short handle with more curves.

The memories of Jake and the fire felt like a nightmare. If that damn mark wasn't on his arm he would swear he'd hallucinated all of it. But there it was, embedded in his skin. He'd tried to scrub it off during his walk in the woods until he realized that it wasn't going anywhere.

Anxiety constricted his chest, making it difficult to breathe. How did Jake get that kind of power? What was he capable of?

The Chosen One. What a bunch of fucking bullshit. The tattoo might be part of him but he had no intention of acting the part of a hero. He'd tried that one before, and look how it ended. He scoffed at the memory. The prophecy began playing in his head like a recording, taunting him.

"Okay! Enough!" he shouted in anguish to the trees surrounding the picnic area.

Enough.

****

Emma worked herself into a state worrying about Will. She'd been so sure his only motivation was to get laid. Not that she protested much. Okay, at all. But now, she wasn't so sure. The horror and confusion on his face didn't look like a guy trying to get laid. But then, it also wasn't the look you wanted to see on the face of the guy who just made you forget your own name.

She should be horrified with herself for letting him kiss her, for wanting it as much as he did, but she wasn't. How long had it been since she kissed a man, let alone... her mind went back to the night Jake was conceived. She wouldn't go there. She couldn't. That night was firmly locked away where it belonged. Instead, her mind wandered back to Will, the longing in his eyes when he told her that he wanted her. She wondered what would have happened if Jake hadn't interrupted.

Jake didn't appear affected by what he saw. If anything, he seemed elated. Emma attempted to discuss it with him but he was uninterested, only saying he wanted her to be happy. But she was far from happy.

After Will had been gone an hour, she began to worry he might not come back. But he was going to leave her in South Dakota today, anyway. Did it really matter whether he left her now or later? She wasn't ready to say good bye to him yet. At least not this way.

He showed up half an hour later, carrying a small bag of food. His anger was gone, replaced by a quiet resolve. He set the bag on the small kitchen table and disappeared into his bedroom. Emma handed a breakfast sandwich to Jake, her stomach too tangled to eat more than a few bites. Will came out of his bedroom and disappeared in to the bathroom, the sound of the shower running a few moments later.

"He'll be okay," Jake said.

"Jake, you don't know what you're talking about."

Jake's eyes softened and the corners of his mouth lifted into a small smile, making Emma wonder if somehow he did.

Will came out of the bathroom about ten minutes later, his hair dripping water onto his t-shirt, his face taut. He looked exhausted and worried. Emma longed to comfort him but knew she was probably the last person he wanted sympathy from.

"Go ahead and pack up. We'll leave as soon as you're ready." He disappeared into his bedroom and shut the door.

There wasn't much to pack so it didn't take her long. Jake became quiet again, but she was so concerned about Will she didn't pay much attention. She was ready for this to be over with.

CHAPTER TWELVE

WILL carried Emma's suitcase out to the truck along with his bag and metal case. Emma and Jake followed behind, Jake kicking stray rocks in his path. Will loaded up the luggage in the back seat while Emma watched. She clenched her fists, unsure what to say. The damaged side of the truck taunted her, accusing her of taking him for granted.

"Will?" she hesitated.

His expressionless eyes turned to meet her gaze. "I'm sorry about this morning. It was completely inappropriate and it won't happen again."

"Will..." She started to reach for his hand but he pulled it away.

"Emma," he sighed. "Just get in the truck."

Defeated, she climbed in the front seat. Jake sat in silence, staring at the fire pit. Emma didn't blame him. It was safer to stay out of the line of fire although at this point it seemed to be a war of silence. Will turned in the cabin key at the office then headed onto the mountain road back to Denver. Emma leaned her elbow on the window frame, resting her chin on her hand watching the endless parade of trees pass by. She couldn't shake her feeling of dread.

A haze hung over the road casting an eerie pall and it matched Emma's mood perfectly. There was no hope of anything between her and Will, but she hated to part this way. Her head hurt thinking of it all and her stomach began to revolt from the few bites of breakfast sandwich she'd choked down.

"Will, pull over."

"What?" Her words shook him out of his contemplation and he looked over at her in confusion.

"Pull over, I'm going to be sick."

"*What?*"

"Are you freaking deaf? I'm going to throw up!" It came out harsher than she intended but she didn't know how long she could hold it.

The road was a tangle of curves, and Will cast a worried glance her direction. "I'm trying."

A short straight stretch of road appeared after the next curve, but a steep incline bordered the narrow shoulder.

"Stop there!"

"Emma, you'll fall down the hill if—"

She suppressed a gag and covered her mouth with the back of her hand. Will whipped the truck over and Emma had the door open before he completely stopped. She tumbled out the door on the shoulder, already losing her breakfast as she fell out. Balanced precariously on the edge of the drop-off, she bent over at the waist. *God, this is embarrassing.*

"Are you okay?" Will asked, his head leaning out the passenger door.

Her hair fell around the side of her face and she looked up at him, trying to push it back. "Do I *look* okay?"

"Do you want me to do something?"

"Yeah, wanna come hold my hair?" She regretted her snippiness but another round of nausea hit her and she vomited again. She pitched forward and her footing slipped. Her body tumbled over the ledge and she found herself rolling down the twenty-foot hill. Emma cried out as her body was assaulted by sharp rocks. As the bottom blurred into view, her forehead smashed against a rock, the pain obscuring all the others. She heard Will yelling her name as she reached the bottom and lost consciousness.

****

Will's heart skipped a beat as he watched Emma fall over the side of the mountain. He scrambled out the door and stood on the shoulder, looking down the hill. At the bottom, the ground leveled out for about five feet then blended into a thick forest of elm, pine and birch trees. Clouds overhead darkened and churned. They tumbled furiously over one another until angry gray streaks shrouded the sun. The air turned cool as gusts of wind burst out of nowhere.

"Emma!" He started racing down the hill.

"Will," Jake called.

Will stopped, irritated at the interruption.

"Don't forget your gun." Jake held the rifle out the window, the tip pointed toward the sky.

Only a few feet down, Will turned around and climbed back up, grabbing handfuls of brush to aid in his climb. He wondered if it was worth the effort, but he knew he shouldn't leave his gun again. The ascent was steep and he briefly wondered how he was going to get Emma back to the top. He reached the truck and grabbed the gun.

"Please take care of my mom." Jake's intense eyes pierced into his.

"Don't worry, Jake, she'll be okay." Will knew he was trying to convince himself more than Jake.

Jake's mouth lifted into a small smile and his eyes shimmered with tears. "Thank you," he whispered.

Will looked back over his shoulder at Jake before he descended toward Emma's still body. If Jake was worried…Will's heart beat wildly, scared of what he'd find at the bottom of the hill. He almost fell several times in his haste and he wondered again how he would get her back up.

"Emma?" She lay on her side, hair covering her face. He touched her shoulder and she moaned in response. He laid his gun down and knelt, carefully sweeping her hair off her cheek. Her eyes were closed. Blood trickled from a gash on her temple, down her cheek and into her hair. A purple knot was already forming under the cut.

She moaned again, her eyes fluttered open and she tried to sit up. He eased her back down.

"Just rest for a minute. Are you hurt anywhere?" His hands ran along the length of her legs and ankles checking for swelling.

"Never one to miss an opportunity to feel a woman up," she said in a raspy voice.

Some of the tension released from his shoulders. If she was mocking him, she couldn't be hurt very badly. He continued onto her arms. They were covered in cuts and scratches and a deep gash slashed across her left upper arm. "Well, you know me, ever the opportunist. Of course, it's not every day I have a woman falling for me." He didn't feel any obvious broken bones on her limbs but the wound on her head and the cut on her arm worried him.

"Maybe I was falling to get away from you." Her mouth lifted into a smirk.

"A bit extreme, even for you. Do you want to sit up now?"

She groaned as she struggled to get up. Will reached an arm behind her back and eased her to a sitting position. She sat up, legs extended in front of her.

"Do you hurt anywhere?" His arm lingered on her back.

"You mean other than my pride? Yeah, my head is killing me." She reached her hand to her temple and flinched.

"Did you pass out?"

"I don't know, maybe. I remember hitting the bottom and then nothing until you were feeling me up. But I'm okay now." Her head swayed and her face was pale.

"You don't look like you're okay. Let's just sit here for minute, okay?"

He sat next to her. His arm was still wrapped around her back for support. He pulled her head to his chest.

"Ever the opportunist." She mumbled, but relaxed into him.

"Of course. Would you expect anything less?"

Her hair covered her face and he gently pulled it back away from her gash. The strands were soft and silky and he admonished himself for noticing.

"A little late to be holding my hair back now, don't you think?"

He suppressed a laugh. "Better late than never."

"Hmm..." Her breathing slowed and her body grew limp.

"Emma, are you sleepy?" Her dark lashes lay against her pale cheeks.

"Yeah, a little."

His chest tightened. "Don't go to sleep, okay?" He held his hand up in front of her. "How many fingers do I have?"

She focused on the three fingers he had raised. "Well last time I counted, you had five. But right now you're holding up three. See? I'm okay. Let's get back up that hill and get out of here. Jake's up there all alone."

Will glanced up at the sky. The turbulent clouds swirled overhead. There was no telling how long it would be before all hell broke loose. He grabbed his gun and stood up, extending his hand down to her. "Can you stand?"

She leaned against him and swayed as she regained her balance. "I'm a little dizzy but I think so."

Will held her arm as they stood at the base of the hill. "Take it slow. I don't want you falling down again. You go first and I'll follow behind you."

She stepped away and took a deep breath. "Okay, I can do this."

Will heard the sound of a car approaching on the road above. He tensed in apprehension, but he told himself there was nothing to worry about. This was a public road. Of course, there would be other traffic.

The clouds darkened to a smoky gray. A bolt of lightning streaked across the sky and thunder rolled, shaking the ground under their feet.

Things are changing. Jake's voice whispered in his head. Will's stomach dropped.

"Jake." Will's eyes widened in alarm. He charged forward and began to scramble up the hill.

Emma stood on the clearing behind him. "Will?" Her voice rose in fear. He turned to see confusion on her face.

"Emma, go hide in the woods!" He shouted as he continued to climb, rifle in his hand. "Jake! Get out of the truck!" He shouted as a burst of wind assaulted him, making him lose his foothold and he fell down several feet. His words were lost, carried away with the gust, which just as quickly ceased.

On the road above, the tires screeched to halt. Car doors slammed closed, the sound magnified, echoed off the mountain walls. The steep incline prevented Will from seeing who was above him, but he didn't need to see. He already knew.

"Jake!" Emma screamed. The terror in her voice felt like a knife in his gut.

Will froze in indecision, torn between saving Jake and protecting Emma. He looked up at the truck. Jake was unprotected and Emma was completely exposed on the hill. He couldn't save them both.

Your job is to protect my mom. Jake's voice reverberated in his head.

"*Jaaake!*" Emma lunged for the hill. Her hands dug into the earth, trying to find a handhold. Her body convulsed with sobs. "*Jaaake!*"

The cocking of guns echoed in the mountains. Emma ignored it and continued crawling. The sound of her weeping hung eerily in the air. The clouds seethed, shooting off a lightning bolt that slashed nearby and struck a tree. Cracking wood and the explosion of thunder followed milliseconds behind, chased by the sound of gunfire. Will's head jerked up. *Emma.* Without thinking, he dove for her, covering her body with his. He pried her hands from the brush and dragged her down the hill.

"Let go of me!" she screamed, hysterical. She bucked, trying to shake him off.

Will ignored her and pulled her toward the trees behind them. She continued to fight and he wrapped his arms around hers. "Emma, you don't have a gun. We've got to take cover," He grunted in her ear. He pulled her behind a thick pine tree and hid behind one close to her. Her tears mixed with the blood that ran down her cheek. Her face was so pale he worried she would faint.

From behind the tree, Will saw a black SUV at the rear of the truck. Two men dressed in jeans and black t-shirts walked toward the truck carrying rifles in their hands.

"I need to change positions and get a better angle. Stay there." He darted to the tree next to him to get closer to the back of the truck, then glanced back at Emma. She leaned around the tree, crouching, on the verge of running up the hill. "Emma! Don't do anything stupid!"

She looked up at him, her eyes crazed with fear, and in that instant he knew she would do anything to get to Jake. Emma bolted for the hill just as Will ran to intercept her. She made it to the opening of the clearing when he wrapped an arm around her waist and pulled her back to the safety of the trees.

She flailed in panic, hitting and scratching his arm, "Let go of me!" The words escaped in a high-pitched shrill.

Thunder roared. The air felt ripe with electricity.

He heard two more shots. The men had seen Emma in the clearing and now shot into the woods. The SUV had pulled to the front of the truck and sat idling. Its brake lights glowed in the dusk created by the storm. The men had also moved to the front giving Will better aim.

Emma began to kick Will's legs in protest and he tightened his arm around her waist. "Emma, if you run up that hill they will *kill* you," he growled in her ear. "You won't be able to save Jake. *Let me do this.*"

She stopped struggling; her breath came in short bursts. "Oh, God, Will, please." She twisted around in his arm to face him, pleading. The desperation on her face tightened a vise squeezing his heart, catching his breath in his throat. "*Please* save him. I'm *begging* you." Her legs buckled and she sank into his chest, sobbing.

He closed his eyes for a moment, holding her close, wishing it would all go away. But he knew it wouldn't. It never did. He pulled her away from him and cupped her cheek in his hand. "I'm going to save him. But you have to stay hidden. Promise me."

She nodded, her body shaking from fear. He looked down at her tear-stained face and to his amazement realized he wasn't doing this because of his job, he was doing this for her. He finally believed in something other than himself. Without thinking, he leaned down and kissed her, a quick kiss offering her comfort, what little he had to give.

Will placed Emma behind another tree. "Stay here, okay?"

She nodded.

A slow, steady roll of thunder filled the woods, the rumble constant and building. The smell of rain hung heavy, clinging with the scent of pine and the decay of the forest floor.

He darted to a tree closer to the front end of the truck and gripped the rifle handle, his hand still wet with Emma's tears. Two men stood in front of the truck. Their posture told him they didn't consider him a threat. He realized they didn't know he had a gun. He needed to use that to his advantage. One of them pointed into the woods, and the other turned back to the SUV, shouting orders, but they were lost in the wind. Will suspected the gunmen were planning to come after them. He raised his gun and took careful aim at the man who had pointed. His finger squeezed the trigger and the man fell limp to the pavement. The other man watched his friend collapse, and before he fell with Will's next shot, he threw a small round object toward the truck. The tires of the SUV squealed as it pulled away.

Will tensed. Déjà vu washed over him and he froze, reliving long-suppressed nightmares. Dread crept up his spine and nestled at the base of his neck. He'd lived this experience before. He knew what to expect.

"Jake!" he cried out in horror.

The sound of the explosion burst through the air with a deafening roar. The force of the blast knocked Will to the ground, hitting his back on a tree on the way down. He pushed himself up to his knees and searched for Emma. She was sprawled on the ground several feet from the tree but was already scrambling to her feet. They spun toward the road.

A fireball of flames engulfed the truck. The heat of the blaze scorched Will's face and his breath stuck in his chest. Flaming embers rained down the hill, minute pieces falling through the tree canopy.

Emma dropped to her knees. "*Noooo!*" She wailed. "*Nooo! JAAKE!*" The wind carried her screams into the forest and they echoed off the trees. She fell, burying her face into the forest floor. Will crawled to her and lay across her back. His touch jolted her and she shook him off. She pushed herself to her feet and rushed to the hill.

Thunder boomed as rain spilled from the sky, sizzling as it hit the flames.

Will caught her and pulled her back to the edge of the forest. The heat of the fire burned his exposed flesh yet the raindrops instantly soothed the pain. "Emma, it's too late," he whispered in her ear. She tried to fight him, but he was stronger.

"Jake!" she screamed.

"Emma, he's gone."

"No," she moaned as she twisted to face him, shaking her head. Her eyes were wide in horror, dark orbs sunken into her deathly pale face. "No, no, no." She turned back toward the hill, clawing at Will's arm around her waist. "*NO!*" She collapsed, folding over his arm, her body heaving with sobs. He lifted her up, pulled her against his chest.

"I'm so sorry." Will's voice choked.

Her body shook as she buried her head into his wet shirt. Their rain soaked clothes clung to their bodies. "*Nooo....*" She clutched his shirt, hanging on with clenched fists.

Movement up the hill caught his attention. He his head jerked up. The SUV was back and three men emerged from the back doors, carrying guns. They headed to the edge of the drop-off, one shouting orders to the other two.

Will grabbed her arms and pulled her away from his chest. "Emma, we have to go."

She shook her head violently. "No, no, no..." Her hands gripped his shirt, eyes clamped shut. Her tear and rain drop covered face, smudged with dirt, was so ghostly white it startled him. He reminded himself she had just fallen down a cliff about ten minutes earlier and she probably had a concussion.

"No..." she moaned as she tried to pull away. "Jake..."

"Emma he's gone," he said gruffly. "We have to go. They're coming."

The men descended down the hill. They were out of time. He wrapped his arm around her waist and pulled her into the woods. Emma dug her feet into the ground. "I can't leave Jake. I can't leave Jake. I can't leave Jake," she repeated over and over.

Will would have gladly welcomed a bullet through his head at that moment, but he had to protect Emma. He continued pulling her into the woods even though she resisted with every step. The men were almost down the hill and it wouldn't take long for them to catch up. Emma fell to the ground sobbing.

"Emma, we have to go!"

She ignored him and refused to get up.

He reached down to pull her up. Her body was slick from the rain, making it hard for him to hold onto her, and while she didn't fight him anymore, she didn't help him either. Her body convulsed with her tears and Will wished there was time to comfort her.

One of the men entered the opening to the forest and Will shot him, hitting the man in the chest. That one was pure luck. He and Emma were too close to the clearing. They needed to get deeper into the forest.

"Emma, get up. We have to run."

She lay on the ground, refusing to get up.

There were at least two other men, maybe more on the way and Emma obviously wasn't going to cooperate. Will picked her up and threw her over his shoulder. He noticed several trees clumped close together about ten feet back. If he could get her hidden behind those trees, then she might be safe and he could focus on the bastards in front of him.

Will lay her on the ground and waited for a clear shot. His heartbeat coursed through his ears, every sense alert.

Next to him, he heard Emma's muffled cries. The hard raindrops pattered on the forest floor with the roar of the fire in the background. Birds flew out of trees overhead, startled by the sudden movements deeper in the forest. The musty smell of pine, mold and smoke filled his nostrils. He was thankful he had years of military training on which to rely.

Will sensed the man who crept through the trees before he saw him. The man heard Emma's cries and when he turned in Will's direction, Will took the easy shot. There should only be one more gunman, but other voices filled the forest. His heart sunk. Emma's crying was going to give away their cover, not that he could do anything about it. His only hope was to outrun them.

He threw her over his shoulder, checking to make sure the men weren't close behind them, and took her further into the woods.

CHAPTER THIRTEEN

WILL decided he was out of shape. He doubted Emma weighed that much, but he didn't make it very far before she got heavy. Although the men following them hadn't caught up, they couldn't be far behind and had to be moving faster. He had to come up with a plan.

The woods were dense, but the terrain was fairly flat here, considering they were in the Rocky Mountains. But he knew the flat land couldn't last long, and he couldn't climb and carry her weight. Water gurgled ahead of him and he decided to head that direction. Will approached the top of a short bluff, about six feet tall. If he could get Emma down to the bottom, she'd be protected until the gunmen passed. The creek was deeper and wider than he expected considering it was in the mountains. He laid Emma down at the top of the bluff, assessing the best way to get her down. She appeared unconscious, which concerned him because of her head wound. Once he had her on the narrow creek bank he checked her pulse and breathing. Thankfully, both seemed good.

"Emma?" He rubbed her cheek, trying to wipe off some of the dirt that covered her face. She didn't respond.

They were far enough away from the fire that it was a dim roar. The crunch of leaves and twigs above let him know they weren't alone. The rain still fell and although the dense canopy overhead protected them from the torrential downfall, they were still soaked. Will climbed back up the side of the bluff, trying to get a solid foothold. A small bush hid his head from the four men approaching, who were spread out over a good thirty feet. Between the tree growth and the clouds above, this section of the forest was dark. Dark enough to make him unsure if there were more men.

He waited, hoping they would pass, but he knew that would be too easy. The men continued to approach the creek bank, slowing now, more cautious. Will still had the element of surprise and he didn't want to blow it. He had to make sure they were close enough to get a clean shot, yet not close enough they could rush the bluff.

They were caught off guard when he fired his first shot, but spread out and quickly recovered. He took out the two to the left before the two on his far right took cover. His mind quickly went to other possible options and escape routes, if it came to that. Without Emma, he could easily get away and if she were mobile, it would still be possible. But his options were limited with her current condition, and even if she were conscious, she wouldn't be lucid.

While he waited for the gunmen to make another appearance, he took in his surroundings. Behind him, on the other side of the creek, the mountains began to climb. The gunmen hiding in front of him made that route impossible unless he could dispose of them. He cast a glance to the creek behind him, realizing it might be his only option. It wasn't deep but it was swift. If he had something to float on, they could float down creek faster than the men on the ledge could chase them. The creek flowed straight for about thirty feet, then curved away from the bluff, blocked by a dense growth of trees. The decision to use the creek solidified when he saw movement in the distance. More men had shown up and they were spreading out. The only ammunition he had was what was in his rifle. Irritation nagged him as he realized he had no idea how many shots were left. He was getting lax. He probably didn't have enough bullets to take them all out, even with the gun strapped to his ankle.

Shit.

He really didn't want to jump in an icy creek and he wasn't sure how he was going to keep Emma from drowning. A thick log on the creek shore, about ten feet downstream caught his attention. If he could get Emma to the log, maybe they could get away, but he needed a distraction to give them a head start.

He looked around, not coming up with anything when his time ran out. There was movement in the trees. The gunmen were advancing. He shot one man, wasting another two bullets. Beginning to get nervous, Will knew it was time to figure out his diversion. If he got off a round of shots, they might fall back, giving him time to get Emma in the river and down the stream. He decided it was his best option. He removed the handgun that was still strapped to his ankle. He waited until he saw the men try to advance again then shot with his rifle until the clip was empty. He wasn't as careful with his aim and he wasn't sure how many found their mark.

He threw his rifle down, hopped off the side of the bluff, and dragged Emma to the log. He pushed it out into the edge of water, and pulled her on top of it. He was taking too long and couldn't afford to be so gentle with her. With Emma on the log, he pushed off, trying to hold her on with one arm and his revolver with the other, and waded into the icy water. Shock from the cold crashed through him. He suppressed a gasp as he continued to push into the middle of the creek, watching the bluff. He knew it would be too easy to get away without a skirmish and he was right. Two men appeared on the ledge pointing their guns in Will's direction. Emma lay on top of the log, but the shock of the cold hitting her limbs began to wake her. Will knew he had to get her out of their gun sights.

"Sorry, Princess," he said more to himself than her. He hated what he had to do. The creek was deeper than he expected and he used it to his advantage. He dove to the other side of the log keeping his gun above the water. In one quick jerk, he pulled her off and under water, along with most of his own body, only keeping his head behind the log and his hand with this gun on the side. Seconds later, bullets hit the water and the log. The shock of the cold and being held under water revived Emma and she fought him. The current was swift and the curve was up ahead a short distance. If they could make it around the curve, they would be out of reach of the gunmen. More bullets hit the thick tree trunk and whizzed over Will's head. Emma continued to thrash. He had to let her up soon, but they weren't around the curve yet.

One of the men suddenly appeared on the bank, closer to Will. He knew the man had a clear shot at them. Will couldn't get a good shot while continuing to hold Emma down. The gunmen raised his gun and Will reacted. He released Emma and aimed. The current moved the log, making the gunman's aim off. But Will's wasn't. The gunman fell just as they hit the bend in the river.

Emma. He scanned the water for her. *Where is she?* He hoisted himself up on the log to get a better view of the water and saw nothing. Had she gotten shot? Was she still under water? He began to panic as he rounded the curve. The current picked up and he still hadn't found her. He dove under the water, looking, and found nothing. His heart raced. The stream became wider and shallower ahead. He worried she would get beaten up by the rocks in the creek bed.

He looked over the log and spotted her, face down in the water a few feet away. He dove and swam to her, somewhere in the process dropping the gun. He turned her over and pulled her to the log, pushing her up so her upper body leaned across. Her lips were blue and she wasn't breathing.

Even though a clump of trees jutted out, blocking their view, Will wished they were further away from the gunmen. He had no choice but to take her to the creek bank. As soon as he could touch the creek bed, he dragged Emma to the shore and began CPR. After only a few compressions and a blow of air in her mouth, she sputtered and coughed. Will turned her head to the side as she vomited water.

"There you go." Relief flooded him as he swept her hair from her forehead, careful to miss the lump with its gash. *It really should be stitched.* But he knew that was the least of their worries. He pulled her shivering body up and held her in his arms as she regained consciousness.

****

Emma woke cold, wet and confused. She felt arms pulling her to a cold body. "What happened..." her voice trailed off. She buried her face into the chest and gripped a t-shirt in her fists trying to steady herself. She had no idea where she was.

"Emma, we have to go back in the water," Will said, regret in his voice. Will. Reality slowly eased back in. Will, the Bad Men. *Something about Jake.*

"Jake..." Her voice was soft with confusion. She shook her head trying to clear it, instead setting off sharp pains and a wave of dizziness. Her body shook from the cold.

Will pulled her to her feet and started walking, her hands still clinging to his shirt. A creek roared in front of them. *How did we get here?*

"Where's Jake?" She heard her voice in the distance, everything was foggy.

He ignored her question and dragged her into the creek. The icy water shocked her as it lapped her feet. She jerked back in defense. Will pulled her more forcefully.

"We've spent too much time here already. I'm sorry, Emma, we have to go back in."

She gasped as he pried her fingers off his shirt and put her arm over a log.

"Hold on. Hopefully we can get out of the water soon." He pushed off and the log floated downstream.

She looked at Will's grim face. "Where's Jake?" She began to cry, not knowing why. Everything was all jumbled up. Why were they in icy water? Where was her baby?

Will hung onto the log with one arm and put his other around her back, holding her on. The pain in her head was almost unbearable and the blackness crept in the edges of her mind. "Emma, don't go to sleep on me now. You'll ruin my reputation." His voice in her ear was soft and warm, but not quite right. Nothing was right. Will stroked her cheek.

"I'm so tired…" She struggled to get the words out. They felt heavy on her tongue.

"Talk to me." She heard his voice, far away. "Where did you grow up?"

His question confused her. Where did she grow up? She couldn't remember. "I don't know…" she finally slurred out through the fog. She was so cold. She couldn't feel anything. She felt herself slipping down into the water.

"No, you don't." Will pulled her back up. "You've spent enough time under water."

Although she tried to hold on, her arm wouldn't cooperate. She felt Will holding her up.

"Emma." His voice was stern this time. "Look at me."

She wanted to obey him, yet her eyelids were so heavy.

****

Will worried that Emma had a concussion and cold water wasn't helping things. The temperature had dramatically dropped with the storm. There was no denying her body was cold, her skin tone a dusky gray. They had to get out soon. But then what? She'd be freezing in the rain and he was cold himself. He couldn't even warm her up.

Earthen walls etched out from years of rushing water enclosed the creek ahead, causing it to narrow. Ahead of that, the creek turned to rapids, with multiple boulders jutting above the surface. It would be difficult to get through by himself, let alone with Emma balanced precariously atop the log. He decided to wait until they got through the narrow part and then move to the bank, but it proved trickier than he expected. He kicked through the swift current until his feet got a foothold, then pushed Emma and the log to the bank. Her legs dragged along the rock-lined creek bed.

"Son of a bitch," he cursed under his breath. He was sluggish with cold, but he managed to pick her up and stumble up the muddy bank, slipping in the rain-soaked sand and rocks.

"Emma." He lay her down and rubbed her already battered arms, worried he would hurt her yet more anxious she wouldn't wake up. She moaned when he accidently rubbed the gash on her arm. He hated that he hurt her, but was grateful for the response.

"Emma, can you get up and walk? We need to get moving and try to find someplace dry."

Her eyes moved behind her lids.

"Emma, you'll warm up if you move around." He pulled her limp body into a sitting position. He sat on the bank and pulled her into his lap, wrapping his arms around her and rubbing her arms and legs. "Wake up, Princess."

She moaned again. "I'm so tired." Her words were thick and slow.

"I know, but if you get moving you'll warm up. Let's try, okay?" She didn't answer, but he decided to try anyway. "We're getting up now." He stood up, hauling her limp body with him. She was dead weight against him and the pebbles that covered her back and arms made it difficult to hold onto. "Come on, Emma. Stand up."

She moaned against him.

He had to make her move and being nice wasn't working. He sucked in his breath, hating himself for what he was about to do.

"Goddamn it Emma, don't be such a drama queen." He shook her, matching the rough tone of his voice.

She moaned again, but put more weight on her legs.

"You expect me to carry you? I don't think so. Get your lazy ass moving. I don't have all day."

Emma began to cry as she clutched his shirt for support.

He felt like a bastard, but it was working.

"I can't." Her eyes were still closed and her entire body shook with cold.

"Yes, you can. Now start walking."

Her feet shuffled, but her legs wouldn't support her weight. As she began to fall, he pulled her back against him. "I can't," she choked through sobs.

"Yes, you can. Don't make me leave you behind." But he kept his arm around her, holding her up as she clung to him.

"Don't leave me," she whimpered and opened her eyes, looking up at him.

His throat tightened at the sight of her. She looked like a ghost with her pasty gray face and blue-tinged lips. Her sunken dark eyes pleaded with him. He had never seen someone look so broken.

"Then get moving." A white-hot fire burned in his gut. He couldn't believe he was doing this to her, but she moved, one foot at a time. Will wanted to encourage her yet he didn't want her to stop moving. "Come on, you've got to do better than that." He would surely rot in hell for this.

Emma cried, but moved, maintaining her death grip on his shirt while Will kept his arm around her waist. The slope of the embankment proved difficult to climb. Once at the top, he looked around and realized he had no idea where they were. Mountain slopes encased them in a small valley. He had no clue which way to go, so they went forward.

He walked and half-dragged Emma deeper into the woods. The winding course of the river made him lose track of what direction was north, not that it would help with finding a road. Besides, given the circumstances, he wasn't sure finding a road was such a good idea anyway. Their last encounter on a road didn't go so well. The understatement made him think of Jake. He swallowed the bile that rose in his throat along with the thought. Thinking about Jake would not be helpful. At the moment, he needed to focus on finding someplace warm and dry.

Emma continued to cry, leaning against him but shuffling along. At least she was walking, albeit slowly. He took consolation in knowing that her blood was moving and hopefully warming.

After about fifteen minutes, Emma staggered, releasing his shirt and collapsing to the ground before he could catch her.

"Emma." He leaned over her.

"Please don't leave me, Will. Please don't leave me." Her eyes begged, brimming with tears. She looked even worse than earlier, if that were even possible.

He sat down and pulled her into his arms, rocking her. "No. I won't. I won't leave you." His hand cradled her head as she buried her face into his chest.

She clung to him, a fresh wave of sobs consuming her. "Jake's gone."

"Yes."

She cried in earnest. He could only hold her as she shook violently, from both cold and despair.

"We have to go Emma. We need to find someplace dry."

"I can't."

He stood up and scooped her in his arms, cradling her against him. She wrapped her arms around his neck clinging to him, still crying. Will didn't know how she could have any more tears left in her.

Will was freezing. His arms became dead weight, making it difficult to hold her for very long. When he finally caught a glimpse of a structure through the trees ahead, it turned out to be a small cabin, appearing in a clearing, deserted, with no cars or any other signs of habitation. He lay Emma down at the edge of the woods, behind a thick tree.

"I'm going to see if anyone is here, okay?"

Emma had cried herself into exhaustion. "Please don't leave me," she pleaded, barely audible.

"I'm not leaving you. I'll be right back."

Will approached the cabin with caution, feeling naked without a gun. Logically, he knew there was little chance of a threat here, but there was nothing logical about their situation. The cabin looked old and rundown, the paint on the siding faded and peeling. The surrounding landscape looked overgrown. His sagging spirits rose a bit. The place looked abandoned. He went to the front door and knocked, casting a glance in Emma's direction.

When no one answered, he pounded on the door. "Hello?"

Still no answer. Will tried the door and found it locked. Checking all the logical places for a hidden key turned up nothing, but it only took a couple of good kicks to get in. He stood in a living area with a small kitchen in one corner. He found no light switch, but spotted a couple of kerosene lanterns sat on a table covered in thick dust.

He went back outside to get Emma, picking her up and carrying her inside. The cabin was small with a living area, two bedrooms, and a bathroom. Grateful to find a bed in the first bedroom he came to, he laid Emma down. The curtains on the window were open, filling the room with meager light. He opened the dresser drawers and looked for clothes, finding a few t-shirts, some socks and sweats. He pulled out some clothes and went to the bathroom for some towels and a washrag.

When he went back to the bedroom, Emma's deathly pall startled him. "Emma, we have to take your clothes off. Can you do it?"

She was unconscious again. He pulled the bed covers back on the side Emma didn't lay on and began to remove her clothes. Will thought she might wake up and protest, which he would have welcomed. Any movement from her at the moment was a positive sign. But her breathing was slow and shallow as he stripped her clothes off as quickly as possible. He grabbed one of the t-shirts and pulled it over her head and scooted her over to the dry side.

He picked up the wet wash rag and began to wash the mud off of her face. Since the rag was cold, he tried to warm it between his hands first but it wasn't enough because she flinched when the rag touched her cheek.

"I'm sorry. I'm trying to clean your face."

It seemed to revive her, but her eyes were still closed and fat tears rolled from the corners of her eyes. He wiped them with the rag as he cleaned her face, his heart heavy. He washed her arms next, as gently as he could, but they were covered in cuts and bruises. She flinched several times and he murmured his apologies as he cleaned. The cold rag made her even colder and she shook when he finished.

He stripped his own clothes and climbed in the bed with her, throwing the covers over the top of them. He curled up behind her, lifting the back of her shirt so the skin of his chest contacted her back, his legs against the back of hers. He wrapped his arms around her stomach, under her shirt, giving her his warmth. What little he had to give. Exhaustion and sorrow overcame him and he fell asleep to the sound of the rain

CHAPTER FOURTEEN

WHEN Will woke, the room was dark. Emma's back pressed against his chest and she had stopped shivering. Her body had warmed a little, although she was still cold, and her breath was slow and even. He was thankful she still slept.

He eased himself out of the bed and put on sweat pants and a t-shirt he found earlier. Picking up their wet clothes, he carried them out to the kitchen and opened the battered back door, the fading sunlight signaling it was early evening. Once he'd lit the lantern, he shut the door and looked around to take in the room. The kitchen was a bare bones affair, with only the essentials, and the essentials in this case didn't include a stove, refrigerator or a microwave.

The cabinets were stocked with a few items. He found a couple boxes of cereal, a box of crackers and snacks, a box of quick rice, some oatmeal, coffee, and some bottles of alcohol. He could use those to disinfect Emma's wounds. The Spartan feel of the place helped him decide it was a hunting cabin.

The woodstove meant there probably was a woodpile outside, and sure enough, he found the stack by the back door. Once he had a fire roaring in the stove, he sank into a chair at the kitchen table, resting his head in his hands. On the bad-day scale, this ranked as one of the worst. And that said a lot.

Will's thoughts turned to Jake and he exhaled in frustration. *Jake.* The mark on his arm reminded him how he let Emma down. *A war is brewing and we will be on opposite sides, but not tonight.* Jake had been wrong about that. They couldn't be on opposite sides of a war if Jake was dead. *Jake is dead.* The reality of it hit him. It was too close to what happened in Iraq. The explosion replayed in his mind and he shook his head in anger. He refused to let himself think about it. He'd allow himself to think about Emma, but not Jake.

He started a pot of the rice on the stove, making enough for Emma if she woke up, but he hoped she didn't. She needed the sleep and when she woke, he knew she'd be a mess. Part of him couldn't deal with that right now. He felt like a prick admitting it to himself, but then again, there was no denying what he was. He became a prick years ago. Saving Emma today didn't change that fact.

While the rice cooked, he checked the rest of the cabin. He found a locked gun cabinet in the back bedroom and searched for a key, finding it hanging on a hook in the back. The contents proved to be beneficial: in addition to the four hunting rifles, he discovered a handgun. And ammunition. He felt better knowing he could defend them, but hoped it didn't come to that. He took one of the rifles and some ammo into the kitchen.

After he ate, he loaded the rifle and went outside to canvass the area. The cabin was tucked in a small clearing, deep in the forest, making it a perfect hiding spot. A narrow gravel road led into the forest, but it was too dark now to investigate. It would have to wait until the next morning, and he suddenly realized that the next day was his deadline for turning over Emma. He'd worry about that tomorrow too.

He went back inside, eager to check on Emma and feeling guilty for leaving her alone as long as he had. But she was still safe and asleep.

He took off his shirt and carefully pulled back the covers, sliding in next to her. She rolled over to face him, but the sound of her breathing assured him she remained in a deep sleep. He tentatively reached out a hand and placed it over her arm. She didn't stir and still felt cold. Pulling her closer, he pressed her body against his, her face to his chest. He wrapped his arm around her back, cradling her. Her hair tickled his chin and her breath warmed the center of his chest. He closed his eyes and settled into her, soaking in an overwhelming sensation he couldn't name.

****

Emma stood on the edge of the forest. The truck was in front of her, about twenty feet away. Jake's face peered out the back window, tears streaming down his cheeks as he cried out for her. Overwhelmed with fear, she tried to run to him, but something held her back. As she tried to break free, flames erupted in the truck. Jake beat on the window, screaming for her. She couldn't move.

"Jake!" she screamed as the truck exploded.

Fire and smoke rushed past her, then cleared and Jake stood in front of her in a swirling cloud of smoke, his clothes in flames.

"Jake!" she screamed hysterically, reaching for him while the force behind her held her back.

Jake's face was expressionless, as though he were oblivious that he was on fire. "Mommy, why didn't you save me?"

****

Emma woke to the sound of screaming. Startled, she sat up, disoriented. Arms wrapped around her, pulling her close to a warm body.

"It's okay. It was only a dream." Will's voice soothed in her ear, her hair stirred with his breath.

"Jake…" her voice trailed off. *Jake*.

"Shh…" He pulled her closer.

It wasn't a dream. It was real. "Jake…" she wailed, collapsing in his arms. Her body wracked with sobs and his hand stroked her hair with light caresses.

"It's okay," he whispered, but she knew it wasn't true. Nothing would ever be okay again.

****

She settled down after an hour of crying. Will had no idea how she had the energy to cry for so long. When her violent sobbing subsided, he handed her the glass of water from the bedside table.

She sipped a small amount, pushed the glass away, and fell back into his arms as he sat with his back against the headboard. The clouds had cleared off and the open curtains allowed the silvery light of the full moon to fill the room. He looked down at her tear-ravaged face. A stream of tears trailed down the sides of her cheeks into her hair, glistening in the moonlight, and he wiped them away with the tip of his fingers. He didn't know what else to do. For the first time in his life he had no plan, no instinct to guide him. He held her, hoping somehow he could absorb some of her pain.

She fell asleep again, in his arms. He stayed awake much longer, worrying about what to do for her. He came up with nothing and fell into a troubled sleep.

****

For the first time in years, he dreamed of the fire. He had shut it out of his mind so effectively that even his dreams obeyed the order to never think of it again. *Until now.* Will woke in a cold sweat, thankful Emma had rolled away from him. Pushing himself up, he sat on the side of the bed, staring at the floor in disbelief. *It was all coming back.* He couldn't deal with the memories along with everything else, but he knew why the door had opened. Jake. Emma. The explosion. It was all too close to home.

There was no going back to sleep, so he went into the kitchen. It was later in the morning than he thought, almost seven, and he needed a plan for the day. He found a sweatshirt hanging in a coat closet and stuffed his arms in the sleeves as he walked outside with the rifle. It was cold, but not as cold as the day before. Sunlight peered over the mountains to the east. Birds chirped in the trees around him, sounding more cheerful than he. They were stuck in the middle of the forest with no way out but their feet, and Will seriously doubted Emma would be up to the task of walking for miles. His cell phone had been soaked in the creek and the rain. Not that he knew who to call, anyway.

Definitely not the people who hired me.

Will knew now that he couldn't hand Emma over. But what to do with her? It wasn't like he could haul her around with him while he did his job. Shit, it's not like he'd have much of a job, anyway. His reputation would be shot to hell when word got out he didn't finish this one. He briefly considered trying to convince them that she died in the explosion with Jake, but there would be no body to confirm it. He sighed. Not only would they be looking for Emma, now they'd be looking for him too. They'd have to run.

As he walked down the gravel road to investigate, he shook his head at his circumstances. He couldn't believe he had turned his life upside down for some woman he met four days ago, let alone a woman period. If only he knew why they wanted her, not that they'd tell him. His job had been simple: find her, bring her to them and hand her over. What happened after that wasn't his concern. Until now.

Their best option was to hide out here for a few days, regain their strength, and hike out. But where? Emma might not even want to go with him. She might hate him, might hold him responsible for Jake's death. Not to mention that if she found out why he really helped her, she would never trust him. But there was no reason for her to find out. He would just let her believe they were running from the men who killed Jake. He sobered when he realized they would be running from them too. Shit, now he had two powerful enemies after them.

He was a half-mile down the gravel road now, with no end in sight. He had no idea how long the road went on, but they were embedded deep in the woods. At this moment, he chose to see it as a good thing. He turned around and started back toward the cabin, anxious to return to Emma. He didn't want her to wake up alone.

****

Emma woke screaming again, and Will's arms wrapped around her within moments. Her cries subsided and her mind drifted, focusing on the soft beams of sunlight filling the room. Dust danced in the rays, and her eyes strayed to a few specks floating in the light. Jake was dead and she stared at dust, yet she couldn't look away, mesmerized by the dance. It was something to focus on other than the pain that ripped her apart.

"Emma, I want you to try to eat something."

He pulled her to the edge of the bed. She felt herself moving, but it was like watching someone else, everything surrounded in a fog. Her bare feet touched the cold floor and cool air brushed her bare legs. She stood up and realized she had nothing on under the oversized t-shirt she wore, yet she didn't care. Her legs wobbled and Will's arm steadied her. He smelled of pine and dirty lake water. Or was that her?

"Here, you can sit by the stove and I'll get you a blanket." Will pulled her to an oversized chair by a wood burning stove and eased her down.

He disappeared into the bedroom and came back with a blanket, covering her lap. "Do you like oatmeal or would you rather have some rice?" He knelt in front of her, his eyes narrowed with concern, his hands rested on her knees.

His questions made no sense. "I don't know..."

He reached up and trailed his fingers along her cheek. He leaned forward and kissed her forehead with a gentleness she didn't expect.

"That's okay, I'll figure it out."

Emma lay back in the chair. The fabric on the seat scratched her bare legs. The sounds of banging metal vibrated in her head, accentuating the dull ache already there. The heat from the stove warmed her feet peeking out from under the blanket, the warmth and the cold wood floor creating an odd combination. The blanket felt heavy on her legs. Tears slid down her cheeks, the warm tears cooling as they fell. Her senses were the polar opposite to the numbness she felt inside.

Will's warm fingers wiped off her tears. She leaned into his hand, soaking in the compassion he offered.

"I made you some oatmeal."

"I'm not hungry." Her eyelids sank closed. It was too much effort to keep them open.

"I know, but I want you to try anyway. Okay?"

She nodded and felt a spoon on her bottom lip and opened her eyes in surprise. He was feeding her. He had pulled a kitchen chair next to hers and sat on it, holding a small bowl of oatmeal in his hand. Emma laid her head back against the high back of the chair. She couldn't remember the last time anyone had fed her, most likely when she was a small child. It made her think of feeding Jake as a baby and her tears welled up again, spilling down her cheeks.

"Shh, don't cry," he soothed, wiping her tears away again. He brought the spoon to her lips and she took several more bites.

"No more," she sighed, sinking farther into the back of the chair. If she sunk in enough maybe the chair would swallow her and everything would disappear. If she could disappear, maybe all the pain engulfing her heart would go away.

"Okay. But you have to drink some water now." He lifted a glass to her mouth and she drank several gulps. "Good," he whispered when she pushed the glass away.

Why was he being so nice to her? A new river of tears flooded through her eyelids. Will's thumb wiped them away. She reached and held his hand to her cheek.

"Emma..." he murmured, heavy with grief.

She opened her eyes, searching his face for an explanation. He knelt on the floor, his hand still on her face. His lips brushed her forehead. The warmth of his lips on her cool skin provided an unexpected comfort and new tears fell in gratitude. His mouth skimmed the side of her face, leaving a trail of tender kisses, each one a consolation in her abyss of pain.

"Oh, Emma. I'm so sorry," he sighed, his breath causing her hair to quiver against her cheek.

She slowly pushed him back and searched his face, amazed to see his eyes glisten with unshed tears. Emma reached her hand to his face, her fingertips skimming the stubble on his cheek. His eyes widened in anguish and surprise before he squeezed them shut. He inhaled sharply and pulled her into an embrace. His hand left her cheek and she felt herself drowning from the loss of contact, overwhelmed with a vehement need for his skin on hers, to drive away the suffocating agony.

She shook her head. "I can't do this. I can't survive this."

"Shh," he whispered in her ear. "I'm here."

Will is here. She clung to his words as if they were the air she breathed. *Will is here.* Why he was there, she couldn't fathom. His touch suppressed the tidal wave of grief that smothered her. She pressed her cheek to his and gasped in relief.

Will turned his face toward hers at the sound, his lips brushing hers. He pulled back, looking into her eyes with more tenderness than she believed possible.

She lifted her face to his and kissed his parted lips, tentatively, seeking the consolation they offered.

Will leaned back, his eyes widened in surprise. And fear. Why would Will be afraid?

She didn't stop to think about it. She only knew what she needed. *Him.* Reaching her hand up to his head, she pulled him back slowly, until his lips were on hers again.

This time he kissed her back until hers were no longer tentative, but urgent instead. He pulled away again, pressing his cheek next to hers and breathed in her ear, "Emma."

She heard the hesitation in his voice.

"Please." She turned her mouth to his and felt his indecision. "Please," she begged. "I need you." Her voice broke and she kissed him again, in sad desperation. He was the one who could save her from this pit of hell. He was her salvation.

Will groaned and his body sagged into her, lighting a fire of hope. He cradled her head in his hand and pulled her close, chasing away the nightmare in her mind.

He stopped. "Emma, I'm sorry." He pulled back, sounding horrified.

"No," she clung to him, and her eyes pleading with his. "*Please*." He kissed her, releasing a fresh batch of tears. This time he understood. He tenderly wiped her tears and followed with his lips, soft and warm. His lips were a double-edged sword. They filled the void, but only partially, leaving her with an ache for something more. She found his mouth, kissing him with a fervor that startled him. He groaned and stood, pulling her with him, his mouth still on hers, just as urgent, just as needing.

"Emma, are you sure?"

She knew she should care. She knew she should think of him, but the pain was too overwhelming to think of anything else. She responded with her mouth on his, eager and demanding. That was all the encouragement he needed. He scooped her into his arms and moved to the bedroom within a few steps. Will set her on the edge of the bed and stripped off her shirt. She lay back waiting and watching him as he hesitated again. Emma knew she had never needed anything more than she needed him right now. She reached up and grabbed his hand, pulling him toward her. He had his shirt and the sweat pants off in seconds and lay beside her in the bed.

Emma wrapped her arms around him for fear he'd change his mind. Her mouth was on his again, hot and needing. All hesitation gone, Will's need seemed to equal her own, making her dizzy with exhilaration. He rolled her on her back and straddled her, lifting her arms over her head and then running his hands down their sides, stopping at her breasts. He watched her face the entire time and she returned his gaze, amazed at the emotion she saw there. He leaned down and kissed her mouth again before moving down to her breasts and she reveled in it. Will eclipsed the pain. If only for this brief time, he was her savior.

She reached down and pulled his mouth back to hers, needing to taste him again. He moaned into her mouth as she reached down and pulled on his hips, showing him what she needed.

"God help me, Emma. I want you," he gasped. She cried from the odd mixture of passion, gratitude and consolation, only vaguely aware of the burning on her back, before overcome with her rising need. It didn't take long for her climax, with him right behind her. Will collapsed beside her and gathered her into his arms, pulling her close as she cried herself to sleep.

CHAPTER FIFTEEN

IF Will ever wondered if he was a bastard, he sure proved it this afternoon. *God, what was I thinking?* Obviously, he wasn't. It bothered him that it bothered him at all. He never cared before. If a woman was willing, why not? And Emma had been more than willing, she begged him. That got him off the hook. Maybe it was hard to convince himself because it forced him to admit that Emma meant something to him. And he wasn't ready to go there yet.

After she fell asleep, he rolled her away to get up. As he pushed her on her side, he noticed a tattoo on her right shoulder blade. He'd seen plenty of tattoos on women before, but this one caught his eye. About three inches tall and two inches wide, the center was composed of vertical flames of a fire. Elaborate waves of water ran horizontal across the bottom of the flames. But it was the intersection of the two that caught his eye. Chills tingled down his back. In the center was a miniature version of the mark on his arm.

Holy shit.

Will had no idea what it meant, but he suspected how it got there. He looked down at his arm again, trying to remember what Jake had said, amazed when it instantly popped into his head.

The land will fall desolate and cold
As it waits for the promised ones.
God resides within the queen
While she hides among the people of the exile land
Hunted for that which she must lose
One who is named protector, The Chosen One,
Shall be a shield, counselor, companion

If he were to believe any of that crap, and it was a big if, then he was The Chosen One. Jake told him that. He said he needed to be sure for his mother. The Chosen One was *protector, shield, counselor, and companion.* Will glanced down at Emma, now curled into a fetal position. He pulled the blanket up to cover her, but left her shoulder exposed. Did that mean she was the queen? *She hides among the people of the exile land.* He didn't know what *exile land* meant, but she had been hiding for the last three years. *Hunted for that which she must lose.* Jake. *Shit.* His chest tightened with anxiety. Jake knew he would be killed. He had to make sure Will would protect Emma. How long had he known? His stomach twisted when he wondered if Jake had known the first moment they met.

Shit.

The room closed in on him and he felt a desperate need for fresh air to clear his head. Will grabbed his clothes, processing this new information as he walked to the living room. That was why Jake insisted Emma go with him. That was why he didn't tell Emma whom Will worked for. Jake knew that Will wouldn't turn her over.

He sucked in deep breaths. Jake knew he would die. That had to be why he'd been so quiet the day before. But what about the morning he died? Will had been too busy in the middle of his own pity party to notice. Why didn't Jake tell him? And why did he insist he and Will would be enemies?

Will found a coffee pot and put it on the woodstove, then went out the back door, startled to see the sun had begun to set. He thought about the second half of the prophecy.

> *The elevated one will arise from great sorrow*
> *In the full moon after the summer solstice*
> *His powers will be mighty and powerful*
> *He will rise up to rule the land*
> *The supplanter will challenge him*
> *But only one will be overcome*
> *By that which has no price*

None of it made sense to him and he wasn't sure he even wanted it to. *What a fucking mess.* Irritation grated his nerves. This was just a job with a reward of a nice, fat paycheck. Since when did he turn away money, especially for a woman? Of course, turning her over wasn't even an option anymore. His willingness to throw his career and probably his life away for her still shocked him.

****

Emma stumbled through the dark forest. Crying, she searched for Jake, calling his name. The truck stood in front of her, on fire. Her screams filled the forest. She tried to run toward the truck, but something held her back. She twisted to see Will holding her waist. She tried to pry his arm away. "Let me go! Let me go!" but he held on tighter. Her screams grew louder.

"Mommy." Jake's voice whispered in her head.

Emma froze. The forest darkened and everything disappeared, even Will. Terror wrapped around her heart. "Jake?" she called out in a croaked whisper, frozen by the nothingness around her.

"Mommy." Jake's face, dimly lit, appeared several feet away. He walked toward her as the rest of his body appeared.

Emma fell to her knees in relief. Jake stopped about three feet in front of her. She reached out to him.

He shook his head, a frown appearing. "You can't touch me Mommy, I'm sorry. I'm lucky I can see you this way."

"I'm dreaming…"

Jake's mouth lifted into a slight smile. "You're dreaming, but I'm really here. I'm alive."

Emma fell face to the ground, sobbing with thankfulness. She couldn't believe he was really here.

"Mommy, please don't cry. I don't have much time," he pleaded.

Emma pushed up, still on her knees. "I don't understand… how…"

He smiled at her, the smile he always used when he understood things she couldn't. "I didn't die, but I'm gone. You have to stay with Will now."

"No." She shook her head. "No, I'll come get you."

His eyes dulled. "No, Mommy. You can't."

"Where are you, Jake? Tell me where you are."

"Mommy, it doesn't matter…"

"I have to know," she pleaded. "Please, Jake, tell me."

The corners of his mouth lifted up in a sad smile. "You have to stay with Will and forget about me now." He sounded firm and authoritative.

"*Forget about you*? How can I forget about you? You are my *life*." Her voice broke.

"You have a new life now, with Will. You need him and he needs you. It's your destiny."

"*You* are my destiny."

"Not anymore."

She shook her head trying to understand. "No…"

"Mommy, I couldn't see you hurt anymore." His calm voice soothed her pain. "I shouldn't have come to you, but I had to let you know you don't have to cry anymore." His voice broke and a tear fell down his cheek.

"I didn't even say goodbye," she cried.

"It's okay."

"I wasn't even very nice to you before… I can't remember the last time I said I love you." Her words cracked under the weight of her pain.

"I know, Mommy, it's okay."

"I love you, Jake."

"I know, Mommy. I love you, too."

Her body shook with sobs. "I'll come find you, Jake."

"No, Mommy. You must promise to stay with Will."

"But I can't leave you there."

"I have to go before they find out I'm gone. Promise me. I can't leave you until you promise you'll stay with Will."

He looked so devastated she had no choice. "I promise," she choked out.

"Please be careful, Mommy. And stay with Will. He'll protect you." He backed up and his voice grew softer.

"Jake!"

"I love you, Mommy." His voice echoed in the darkness.

Emma sat up in bed, completely naked, covered by a blanket. *Will*. She knew she should be embarrassed by her earlier behavior, but she was too overjoyed to care. She found the t-shirt she wore earlier, threw it on over her head and walked out of the room. Will stood in front of the makeshift kitchen.

"Jake's alive. He's alive, Will." Dizzier than she expected, she held onto the door to keep herself upright.

Will turned, startled. "Emma, you should probably sit down."

"You're not listening to me."

"I know you think…"

"I saw him. He talked to me."

Will stared at her like she had lost her mind, not that it surprised her. "Emma, the truck exploded," his voice lowered. "How could he talk to you?"

"He came to me in a dream."

"I'm sure you'll dream about him. I'd be surprised if you didn't." His arms slipped around her waist, pulling her to him. Her cheek rested on his chest, the soft murmur of his heart in her ear.

"No, it wasn't like that. He was there, really there."

"I'm sure it seemed that way, you *want* to see him," he said softly, stroking her hair.

Frustrated that he wasn't listening to her, she took a deep breath and pulled back to look at his eyes. "No, he was there and he told me I had to stay with you."

His mouth lifted into a grin. "I thought that was pretty clear."

"I have to go find him."

"Emma. You've just been through an ordeal. You're not thinking clearly."

"I have to go find him. Are you going with me?"

He sighed and pulled her to his chest. "We'll have this discussion, but not tonight, okay? It's not like we could go right now anyway. We're stuck in the middle of nowhere and I'm still not sure how we're getting out."

"I can't just sit here knowing Jake is alive somewhere and needs me!"

"Even if we left in the dark with no money and no car, where are we going to get him? Where do you think he is?"

"I don't know. He didn't tell me." The lack of information vexed her.

Will sighed, only in pity, not frustration.

She stiffened. "You think I'm crazy."

"No, I think you're distraught and exhausted."

He was right. She was tired and had no idea where they had taken Jake. It had to be enough to know he was alive, but the need for him burned deep in her marrow. "Alright, but we leave first thing tomorrow."

He kissed her forehead. "We'll see. You're still weak and need to eat. If we're walking out of here, which is the only way I see out at this point, you're going to need your strength."

He kept an arm around her waist and pulled her to the chair she sat in earlier.

"There aren't many choices for food here, but I can make some rice."

She watched him find a pot. "You cook?"

He winked and flashed his wicked smile. "I can do all sorts of things you probably never even thought of."

After Will started the rice, he sat in the chair and pulled her onto his lap.

She sat sideways, her head cradled on his shoulder. It felt odd not fighting with Will. She had an urge to touch him, but she suddenly felt shy. She hadn't been held by a man in a long time. He saw her at her worst, yet here he was, holding her. She tentatively reached her hand to his, which rested across her legs. He lifted it and laced her fingers through his.

She looked into his eyes. "You saved my life. Thank you."

He was silent for a moment. "I think this makes you my slave for life now." She heard the hint of a tease.

"Slave? Really? I thought I just owed you a favor or something."

His arm tightened around her back. "I prefer slave and all the connotations that go with it."

She snorted. "Yeah, don't get too carried away."

"Emma?" Will's free hand rubbed her arm.

"Umm?"

"Tell me about your tattoo."

Of all the things he could have asked, this one surprised her the most. "My tattoo?"

"The one on your shoulder."

"I haven't thought about it in awhile. I never see it since it's on my back." The familiar feeling of fear and helplessness rushed back at the memory.

"When did you get it?"

She hesitated. "Jake's father…I didn't really know him."

"How did you meet him?"

"At a party." Glad Will couldn't see her face, she bit her lip and grimaced. She had never told anyone before and she wasn't sure why she decided to tell him now. She knew she shouldn't be embarrassed, yet couldn't stop the shame. "I was a senior in college and I went to a party with a friend. There was a guy, and it was like this guy was waiting for me, like he knew I would be there. But I didn't decide to go until the last minute, so it was weird that he knew I'd be there." Feelings of shame slunk back, a heavy weight on her shoulders. She'd locked away the fear and guilt years ago. Why did he make her think about it now? "Why do you want to know?"

"Emma, you only have to tell me about the tattoo. I know you have a past." He shook his head. "I definitely do."

"I know, but it's part of it."

"Okay." He rubbed her arm again in encouragement.

****

The fall semester of her senior year in college wasn't turning out how Emma planned. And Emma had a master plan, one that mapped out the next ten years. But her long-term boyfriend suddenly decided he preferred blondes over brunettes, and the news shook her carefully orchestrated world. When not in classes, she spent the next two weeks in her apartment studying, crying, and adjusting to the tilting of her universe. Until one Friday night, as she focused on a complicated accounting equation, a friend called and invited her to a frat party. Emma had no desire to go, midterms were approaching, but her friend insisted that Emma get out and have some fun. Emma saw the logic in it.

She regretted her decision the moment she arrived. People crowded into the house and spilled out the front door in to the yard. Music blared through open windows as she approached, pounding her already aching head. Her friend insisted on staying, despite Emma's protests. As she walked toward the house, a sense of foreboding crawled up her spine and she considered walking the three miles home. She stood in the driveway, watching the crowd, hanging on her indecision.

That's when she saw him.

He leaned against the trunk of a giant oak tree, watching her. His posture suggested indifference, yet the way he tilted his head to the side reeked of arrogance. The air of a guy used to getting what he wanted. He appraised her as she turned to watch him, and his slow, spreading smile told her he liked what he saw. He pushed away from the tree and walked toward her.

"Hi," he said with a hint of cockiness. He was tall and blond and everything she never considered in a guy before. He linked his arm in hers. "I've been waiting for you."

She stared at him in surprise. "I'm sorry, but I think you have the wrong person."

He flashed a dazzling smile, looking like a Greek god with his blond curls, blue eyes and chiseled features. "No, I've been waiting for *you*, Emmanuella."

He led her into the house, sidestepping a rowdy group of guys shoving each other in the entryway. She tried to figure out how he knew her real name. She'd never told anyone at college. The deafening music made conversation impossible. He leaned over, his warm breath tickling her ear. "Let's go get a drink."

He pulled her to the kitchen and dropped her arm as he walked over to the cups. In a stupor, she watched as he made them both drinks. He glanced over his shoulder and winked, not a playful gesture, but laced with seduction. He handed her a plastic cup and lifted his.

"To a long-lasting relationship," he said and tapped his plastic cup into hers. He took a long drink as she sipped, watching him with caution. He grabbed her hand in his and pulled her toward the back door.

A fire burned in the pit in the center of the empty backyard. The sun had set, turning the fall air uncomfortably cool without a jacket. Two picnic table benches flanked the pit and he walked over to one, sitting down and pulling her with him. She never considered protesting. His beauty mesmerized her, which was odd, considering a man beautiful. He turned to her and laughed. Emma finally broke her gaze. "How did you know my name?"

He leaned over and whispered in her ear, soft and sensual. "I know lots of things about you." Chills tingled down her arm and he laughed again. He took her cup and put it down on the ground.

Another couple came out, boisterous and drunk.

He stiffened with irritation. "Leave us," he growled. His voice held an authority that surprised her almost as much as the fact they spun around and left. When the door closed, his shoulders relaxed.

"Who are you?" she asked, feeling a flicker of fear for the first time. The scent of dried leaves, musk, and smoke filled her nose.

He stared into the flames, a small smile lifting the corners of his mouth. "Fire is fascinating, isn't it?"

She had a sudden urge to pull away.

He sensed her apprehension and stroked the back of her hand with his thumb, his eyes still on the fire. "I won't hurt you, Emmanuella."

Her stomach knotted and her mouth went dry, not believing him. She gave a tentative tug, but his grip was too strong. The music was too loud for anyone to hear if she screamed.

"How do you know me?" she whispered.

He turned toward her. The flames were reflected in his eyes before they narrowed. "I've waited for you for a long time. I just didn't know where to find you."

"I don't understand…"

He lifted his free hand. His warm fingers trailed along her jaw line. "No, you wouldn't, but that's okay. You don't need to understand." He leaned down and gently touched his lips to hers.

He was gorgeous and under different circumstances, Emma might have enjoyed kissing him, but he frightened her.

He sensed her resistance. "Emmanuella, you can fight me if you want, but in the end, destiny is always fulfilled." His voice was warm and full of promise. He wrapped an arm around her back, pulling her to close, his lips on hers again, more insistent. She put her hands on his chest and pushed, but his hold tightened.

Her heart jumped to her throat. "Stop, please. I don't want to do this."

He studied her, his face glowing in the firelight. He was the most beautiful man she had ever seen, but his eyes glittered with evil.

"Emmanuella," he cooed. "We all have our parts to play. Yours is quite simple." He lowered his head to her neck and lightly bit her. She whimpered in pain and surprise. He chuckled. "Most women beg me for it. Are you telling me you won't?"

Her eyes welled with tears as she realized what he planned to do. His hand reached under her sweater, groping for her breast as his mouth trailed down her neck. "I wish we had more time, but unfortunately, we don't."

She jerked on his arm. He pushed her back on the bench and her head thudded on the wood. Pushing up her sweater, he tugged on her bra, his mouth replacing his hand. She prayed someone would show up to save her, yet feared someone finding her this way.

She shoved his shoulder and he fell to the ground next to the bench. Rolling off the seat, she tried to scramble away, but he grabbed her ankle and jerked. She fell on her chest, knocking the wind out of her. Still holding her leg, he dragged her back. The rock-strewn earth scraped her exposed stomach and her hands as she grasped for something to hold onto.

"No!" she gasped, trying to regain her breath

He flipped her over on her back, fury on his face. "I'm not so sure you *are* the one. If you were, you'd have the sense to want me."

"You're right," she cried, trying to crawl backward. "I'm not who you think I am."

He pinned her shoulders and paused, considering her words. "Maybe not, but there's only one way to know." He lost all pretense of concern and held her down, pulling down her jeans. They hung up on her shoes and he jerked them off and tossed them to the side, her jeans right behind.

"Please..." she whimpered.

His body crushed her as he pulled his pants down and straddled her. He laughed in her ear. "Now you beg me for it, *Your Highness*. Too late."

She wanted to close her eyes, but they refused to obey. The firelight cast an eerie glow and the smoke of the fire filled her nose making it difficult to breathe, or maybe because his body pinned hers to the ground, she wasn't sure which. She focused on the sharp points of the gravel that embedded in her back and the searing pain in her right shoulder blade. Ignoring the grunts in her ear, she looked into the starry sky and found Orion, her favorite constellation as a child. Finally his weight no longer smashed her and he stood up, pulling his pants on as he held out his arm to examine it. He dropped it in disgust.

"I was wrong." He sneered. "You're not her." Then he walked away, leaving her in the dirt and crumpled leaves.

She lay still for several moments, staring at the stars, pretending it hadn't happened. The cool air hit her bare legs and she shivered. The rocks still pierced into her back. She was too shocked to cry and unsure what to do. Ignoring the pain between her legs, she finally sat up. She found her panties and jeans and pulled them on with shaking hands. Unable to find her shoes, she crawled around on her hands and knees, searching in the dark. She found one, but not the other, and she finally broke, clutching the shoe to her chest. Releasing a sob, she chucked the shoe into the trees. *Stupid shoes*. She hated those shoes anyway.

Her feet froze as she made her way back into the house looking for her friend, who refused to leave early. Emma sat on the front porch for the next two hours, shivering from cold and fright. The fire pit would be warmer, but she refused to go back.

Once home hours later, she took a long shower, washing off the scent of his expensive cologne that intermingled with smoke. The hot water ran out but the filth still clung, like an oppressive cloud. She turned the water off and leaned into the shower wall, suppressing her tears. Tears wouldn't help her now. She wiped the fog-coated mirror with a towel and turned to see the damage the rocks had done to her back. Her heart stopped when she saw it. *A tattoo.* Two inches tall and an inch wide, permanently etched in her skin was the brand of fire. She barely made it to the toilet before she vomited in disgust and fear.

CHAPTER SIXTEEN

WILL sat in stunned silence, his arm tensed around her back. Finally, he kissed her temple. "I'm sorry." But inside, his anger simmered as he plotted how to find the son of a bitch and castrate him.

She relaxed and he hadn't realized how tense she'd been. Of all the unpardonable sins Will had committed, rape wasn't one of them. Even he had standards, and thank God, otherwise there was no way he could comfort her now.

"That was the night Jake was conceived?" He couldn't imagine how she could look at Jake every day and not see the man who raped her.

"Yes."

"And the mark appeared that night? It was flames?"

"Yes."

"Did you ever add to it? Try to cover it up?"

She leaned back and stared up at him, knitting her eyebrows together. "What do you mean 'add to it?'"

Will stood up, and pulled Emma by the hand to the bathroom. He turned her back to the small mirror and pulled her t-shirt opening down, exposing the marks on her shoulder. "Look at this."

Emma twisted her head to see the mirror.

"Oh my God…" She looked up at Will with wide eyes. "What does it mean?"

"I don't know. I was hoping you could tell me."

She leaned backward on the sink, examining the mark in the mirror. "Are those waves? Like ocean waves?" She turned to Will for confirmation.

He nodded. "That's what it looks like to me."

"But what's in the middle?" She leaned even closer, tittering on the sink edge.

"I think I can help with that one." Will held out his left arm, showing her his mark.

She grabbed his forearm and leaned over. "That looks like…" She trailed off as her eyes widened.

"Yes."

"But how did you get it? When?"

He paused. "Two nights ago, at the motel in the mountains. Jake gave it to me by the fire after you went to bed."

"*Jake?* How could Jake do this?"

"He had new powers. Could he read your mind and talk to you in your head?"

"Yes…"

"Me too, after he gave me this mark."

"But how could he do that?"

"With his hand, and it burned like hell."

Emma looked at her shoulder again and remembered the rest stop. "He must have done that to me, too. In the rest stop bathroom. We were hiding in the stall. Jake touched my shoulder and it burned. I didn't think anything about it since I was preoccupied at the time. But after he touched me… I could hear him in my head." Her voice trailed off as she leaned closer to the mirror. Emma slowly turned to face Will, her eyes widened and her face blanched. She slid off the edge of the sink. "Oh, my God."

"The fire tattoo showed up when you conceived Jake? So maybe fire represents Jake, which makes sense since he got his power from fire."

"What do you mean his power came from fire?" Her voice raised and she grabbed his arm, digging her nails into his flesh.

"He made flames from the fire shoot ten feet into the sky and he put the fire out with just the wave of his hand. He told me he got his power from fire."

"No. No!" She released his arm and shook her head slowly in horror. Her eyes squeezed shut, tears sliding out the corners. "No, not fire. God, please not fire."

Will placed his hand on her upper arm. "Oh God, Emma. I'm sorry."

Emma's eyes flew open, full of a fury that caught him off guard. "Stop telling me you're sorry! Sorry doesn't make any of this better." She pushed away from him and walked out of the room.

"I have to go get him. I have to save him." She moved a kitchen chair, searching under the table then moved to the cabinets, opening and slamming the doors closed.

Will stood next to the bathroom door watching her. "What are you looking for?"

"My clothes…"

"Emma, they're still wet. I washed them and they're outside drying. Besides we can't go anywhere tonight. It's almost dark. We're deep in a forest and don't have a car. Why don't you eat something and we'll talk about what to do."

Emma stopped to consider this, gazing out the window over the kitchen sink. She bit her lower lip and her eyes welled with tears. He saw the battle she waged, pitting logic versus the mother's protective instinct. "I have to save him, Will." The anger was gone, replaced with anguish.

"I know." Even though Will doubted Jake was alive, he refused to take her hope away. It seemed dishonest, but he would rather she have false hope than live with the devastating grief. "Let's eat and talk more about this. If we're walking out of here, you need your strength."

She didn't argue so he led her back to the chair and served the rice.

"I never considered it," Emma whispered. "Well, I guess I did. Magical tattoo appears. My son can see the future. But I refused to put them together. Refused to believe that monster had anything to do with my son. Jake is good and sweet and everything …" Her voice broke, "*he* was not."

"Emma, don't go there. It doesn't do any good."

"*Don't go there?*" she shouted. "How can I not go there? You just told me that my son has power from *fire*." She shook her head and sneered. "And how is it that you, who've only known him a few days, knows this when I don't?"

"He told me he had to be sure."

Her eyes narrowed. "Be sure of what?"

"He said he had to make sure I was *the one*." Will felt ridiculous saying it aloud.

"What are you talking about, Will? What do you mean *the one*?"

"That night by the fire." He hated to tell her after her revelation. "You went to bed and Jake and I stayed by the fire," he hesitated, unsure how to proceed. No matter what he said, it would hurt her and he was weary of hurting her.

"Go on." Her voice was harsh, not that he blamed her.

"Jake said he didn't have much time and he had to be sure I was..." He winced, not wanting to say it again. "He said he had to be sure for you. Then he asked if he could touch me and read me, or something like that. Has he ever done that before?"

She shook her head. "Not that I know of."

Will told her the rest of the story. "It was like he saw my thoughts and memories, and he went through everything in my head. I couldn't breathe and he said I was— the one." He lifted his forearm. "And then I had this mark."

Emma reached out her hand and brushed it with her fingertips. She traced the outline of the points, studying it.

"What does it mean?" she asked, her voice etched with pain.

He stared into her eyes and lost himself, like he did the night in the cornfield. "I think it means I'm yours," he said the words without thinking, but instantly knew they were true. He belonged to her and not the other way around. The truth of it was simultaneously frightening and exhilarating.

She looked startled, but the sureness of it washed through him. He rose on his knees and kissed her with a tenderness that surprised him. *Emma did that.* She brought out a soft side of him he had lost long ago.

"What the hell was that? Can't you ever be serious?" Her voice filled with rage.

He cringed at her rejection then recovered before she noticed. "Sorry, couldn't help myself," he winked, cockiness in his voice. Will slipped into it as easily as putting on a comfortable pair of jeans.

"Can we focus on Jake here, *please*?"

"Don't we always?"

"What the hell does that mean?"

He sighed. He wanted her to direct her anger on the situation and away from him. "I'm sorry, Emma. It doesn't mean anything. I don't even know why I said it. I'm tired and this is all a little overwhelming."

She watched him for a moment, still wary, but she seemed to buy his answer.

"So you're sure you didn't see anything else?" Will asked. "You never had a hint he got power from fire?"

"I never saw anything like that. He could only see things in the future and not everything. The first time something different showed up was when he spoke to me in my head."

"No," Will said, "things started sooner than that."

"What are you talking about?"

"When I showed up in the motel parking lot that first night, Jake came out of his trance. He wasn't scared anymore. He told me things changed because of me. He never got terrified again. I never saw him freaked out. I only took your word for it that he was. And his warning radar began to fail. He didn't know they were coming until they were there."

"Yes..."

"But you did."

They looked at each other, remembering she felt sick when the men showed up.

"I can't believe I didn't see all of this." She rested her elbow on the arm of the chair, slightly rubbing her forehead

"It's been a crazy few days."

"Is there anything else?"

Will didn't think he wanted to share the prophecy with her. It seemed too weird and he wasn't sure he could even say the words aloud. It all seemed so Lord of the Rings. But he also hated keeping anything from her.

"He said we would be enemies one day."

Her eyebrows scrunched in confusion. "Who?"

"Jake and I. One day we will be enemies."

"See, he *is* alive."

Will remained silent.

"You said he needed to know you were the one for me. Why?"

He gazed into her eyes. "He said I was to protect you."

"Against what?"

"He didn't say. I think it's safe to assume the men who...uh took Jake." He could have added the group who hired him, but no way in hell was he going there.

"So you protected me. Your job is done, then."

He knew his job was far from done, especially now that the unmentioned threat would soon join the hunt. "You think they're going to chase you for three years and give up now? They ran after us in the woods after they took Jake and something tells me they didn't want to have a tea party."

"What? So I'm chained to you like Princess Leia to Jabba the Hut?"

He cocked his head and gave her his lopsided grin. "I have to say, I've never been compared to Jabba the Hut before. Besides, most women don't complain."

"Be serious, Will."

"I *am* being serious."

"Ugh!" She pushed against his chest. "What about your job? If you're protecting me, how are you going to work? Are we going to run for the rest of our lives, like I have the last three years?"

"I don't know."

Her eyes bore into his. "You're giving up your life for me. Why would you do that?"

"I don't know."

"What *do* you know?"

"I know this is a fucking mess. I know that we both are in danger and right now we need each other to survive." He paused and decided to press on. "I know I'm not ready to let you go yet."

"So you're willing to give up your life for me?" She sounded incredulous.

"I'm willing to do what I need to do so we *both* survive."

She relaxed. "So what do we do?"

"Do you know how to shoot a gun? With accuracy?" He knew she had a gun and shot the man in the rest stop, but that was at close range.

"It's been awhile, but I've practiced in a shooting range before."

"Handgun?"

She nodded.

"What about a rifle?"

"No, but I'm willing to learn."

"Good, because tomorrow morning you're starting target practice. But first," he lifted the bowl forgotten in her lap. "You need to eat because I'm not carrying your sorry ass through the woods anymore."

Her expression softened. "Yeah, thanks for that."

"You can show me your appreciation. Later." He winked and stood up.

"Playing the 'I'm your slave' card now?" she asked with a snort.

"Emma, I assure you, I won't need it."

CHAPTER SEVENTEEN

EMMA woke the next morning, disappointed. She had hoped Jake would visit her dreams again. In the end, it didn't matter. She was still determined to find him.

She had slept more in the last day and a half than she had in weeks, so it surprised her that she hadn't woken sooner. Although she had missed some sleep the night before. Will definitely lived up to his hype. She wondered if sleeping with him was such a good idea, but it seemed a little late to change her mind and selfishly she didn't want it to.

Will was asleep and he lay on his side, rolled toward her. Even asleep he looked on edge, his brow furrowed. His hair was wild and unruly and smooshed on one side. She resisted the urge to reach up and smooth it. A couple of day's worth of stubble covered his face and she resisted the urge to touch it as well, which made her smile in spite of herself. It was hard to believe she wanted to touch him at all. His bare arm curled over the top of the blanket. She studied the muscles and the tan line that stopped mid bicep. His arm rested over the other, his mark only partially covered. Emma didn't know what to make of his mark. She couldn't wrap her head around the fact that Jake had made it, although she knew it was true. Just as she knew Jake had given her the new one on her back.

"Good morning."

He looked at her with one eye open. A slow grin spread across his face.

"Good morning."

He reached around her and pulled her close. "There, that's better."

"Don't we need to get up and start some target practice?"

"Not yet. We'll get to it soon enough."

She expected him to make some type of move, but he didn't. To her amazement he just held her. He actually seemed content. Will was full of surprises the last few days. Plus he smelled like a dirty dog. She knew she didn't smell much better.

"I need a shower," she mumbled into his chest.

His laughter rumbled in her ear. "Well, good luck there. We don't have a shower."

"What am I supposed to do? I can't go around stinking like this."

He laughed again. "We can heat some water and use a washrag. I volunteer to wash you."

"Will, be serious."

"Seriously, Emma, we have to hand-bathe."

"What about my hair?"

"We can heat enough water to wash it in the kitchen sink. There's water in the faucet, but it's only cold."

"Okay, that's first on the agenda. After that breakfast, then target practice."

"A list-maker, huh?"

"You forget I was an accountant. I'm all into details and order."

He pulled her even closer and kissed the top of her head. "Does that mean you'll do my taxes?"

"Something tells me your taxes would be a mess."

"Hmm…" His hand entwined in her hair, flooding her with a sense of belonging.

Belonging? With Will?

She had no delusions this was anything other than a temporary arrangement, but she had to admit, something about being in his arms felt *right*, in a visceral way. She nearly snorted the moment the thought popped into her head. But it hung there anyway, defying her to ignore its existence. It was dangerous to let her mind wander that direction. She already allowed this to happen, so she might as well enjoy it while it lasted, as long as she acknowledged what it really was: temporary. It occurred to her she still had no idea what his job was. In fact, she hardly knew anything about him at all.

"Will?"

"Yeah," His voice was lazy and sexy, sending a thrill racing through her blood.

"What do you do? Really?"

She felt him tense, barely noticeable, but there all the same.

"I told you, I'm a computer consultant."

"Who travels with guns?"

"Sure, why not? You're living proof that you never know when you need to protect yourself."

"Why won't you tell me the truth?"

He didn't respond, but she felt his right bicep twitch against her arm. After a moment, he finally spoke. "Emma, neither one of us is who we used to be, so it doesn't matter anymore. We can actually use this opportunity to become something else. I'm thinking about becoming a carnie." She heard the grin in his voice.

"I don't see how we can work together…" He cut her off by tilting her head up and giving her a kiss that left her dizzy and breathless.

He pulled back, grinning. "I think we should start heating some water so I can wash you."

"We need to talk about this."

"Emma, drop it." He kissed her again, leaving no doubt in her mind that he was in control at the moment. "I used to be a gigolo. Women used to pay me for what I'm giving you for free." His hands moved down her body and she soon forgot the question.

After they got up and washed, Will helped wash her hair in the sink. They dressed in their original clothes. Emma was thankful that Will had cleaned and hung them outside to dry the day before. Their shoes were still damp, as were their jeans, but only slightly. They decided to eat some of the canned goods for breakfast and use the empty cans for target practice.

Will showed her how to load one of the rifles and then had her try. Once he was satisfied with her progress, they moved outside with the cans.

The mid-morning sun was welcome after the rain and warmed the chill she felt from her damp hair. Emma paused and closed her eyes, enjoying the feel of the sunshine on her face and the chirping birds in the forest. While she waited for Will to set up, she thought of Jake. She prepared for the familiar fear to flood back, but a strange sense of peace filled her. She closed her eyes tighter and called out to him in her mind. Focused on reaching him in the distance, she nearly jumped when a dim light came into view and she saw his face. She couldn't believe it worked.

Mommy it's not safe for you to call me.

Jake, I have to know you are safe.

Mommy, I'm fine. I'm safe. You need to worry about you. He frowned. *You're in…*

"Ready?" Will called, shaking Emma out of her trance.

Her eyes flew open and she jumped. She quickly squeezed them shut, focusing on Jake, but he was gone. She sighed in disappointment.

Will dragged a fifty-five gallon metal drum between two trees and tipped it over. Four cans lined up along the top. He took the rifle and showed her how to stand and aim. After he warned her about recoil, he shot a can on the end, sending it flying off the metal drum. The birds in the trees scattered in all directions, screeching in protest. He turned to her with his smug grin. "See? Easy."

Emma rolled her eyes. He handed her the gun. She adjusted her stance and held the rifle up, looking through the sight at a can thirty feet away. Will stood behind her and reached around, lifting her arms.

"Hey, I was doing it right. I think you just wanted to put your arms around me."

Will chuckled in her ear. "And your point is?"

"My point is I have a gun and I might not be afraid to use it."

He dropped his arms, laughing. "The lady has spoken. Just be prepared for the recoil."

Emma viewed the can through the gun sight again, prepared herself and squeezed the trigger. She missed the can and the rifle jerked her back.

"Shit!" She rubbed her shoulder.

"That's okay, I would have been surprised if you got it the first time. You have to get used to the kickback."

She repeated the same maneuver several more times, missing each time.

"Son of a bitch!" Emma lowered the rifle and wheeled around to face Will. "Why can't I just use the pistol?"

"Because you can't shoot as far with it. You need to be able to use the rifle with some accuracy."

"This is going to take all friggin' day at this rate."

A slow smile lit up his face. "Lucky for you we have all friggin' day."

She glared. "No we don't. We need to leave."

"Not today we're not. You need another day to rest and you're already getting worn out with target practice."

"If I shoot the fucking tin can will you agree to leave today?"

Will folded his arms and shook his head with a look of exasperation. "Emma…"

"Can we or can't we?" She considered leaving without him, promise or no promise to Jake. Besides, if she took off ,Will would probably follow her.

"Only if you shoot the cans five times in a row."

"There's only three cans left."

He raised an eyebrow. "Now that's a dilemma, isn't it?"

She let loose a string of profanity that made him belly-laugh. She marched over to the drum and found the can on the ground and set it on the drum, turning it so that the side without a hole faced her. Will watched with a smirk as she walked back to her spot. Emma spun and glared at him in defiance. She aimed through the sight and braced for the recoil and squeezed the trigger. *Plink.* The can shot off the back of the drum onto the ground.

Emma grinned at Will. He crossed his arms and he nodded his head toward her. "Bravo. Now you only need four more *in a row.*"

"You don't think I can do four more in a row?"

He shoved his hands in his front pockets and shrugged, his lips pressed tight to keep from smiling. "Dunno, why don't you show me if you can?"

She turned back to face the drum and shot the next can.

"Lucky shot." Will said.

"Hmm, we'll see." She shot the remaining two cans.

"Well, well, all you needed was a little motivation. You still need one more."

"Why don't you be a dear and walk over and pick up one of those cans for me?" Emma pouted her lips and batted her eyelashes.

"I don't *even* think so," he laughed. "Seriously? Walk over there with you pointing a gun at me? No thanks."

"Afraid I'm going to shoot you?"

"The thought crossed my mind."

"You're safe— for now. I need you to get me out of here."

He walked over to her and pulled her in his arms, looking down into her eyes with a teasing glint in his eye. "Is that all I am to you, Emma? A trail guide?"

"A trail guide with perks." She reached up and kissed him. "Now about that can…"

He dropped his arms, grumbling as he walked to the metal drum, arms raised in self-defense. Emma kept the gun tip pointed to the ground, weight shifted to one side. Will picked up all four cans and set them back on the drum. He turned around and paused, a stunned expression on his face.

"What?" Emma asked.

"God, do you know how sexy you look right now?"

"Yeah, every man's fantasy— a woman with a rifle. Get out of the way."

Will chuckled and strode toward her. "I bet you can't shoot all four."

"What the hell? I only have to shoot one."

"True, but I bet you can't."

"And why would I want to? I'm not a guy, in case you hadn't noticed last night *and* this morning. I don't really get into pissing contests."

"We could wager on it."

"And what do you have that I would want?"

He held his hands out from his sides and flashed his cocky grin. "You're looking at it, sweetheart."

Emma snorted. "Please, like you're withholding yourself from me? All of a sudden you've become Virgin Will? Whatever. You've got nothin'."

"Don't be so sure about that. What do you want from me, other than my body and my ability to help you escape the woods?"

Emma stared at him, thinking. "Answers," she finally said. "I want some answers."

He looked sullen, but not surprised. "Agreed. You get three questions answered. Now, what do I get?"

"What do you want?"

A slow lazy smile lifted the corners of his mouth.

"Seriously, do you think of nothing else?"

"What can I say? I'm a guy."

"There's nothing else?"

He hesitated. "Yes, but you might not like it."

"What is it?"

He paused. His jaw tensed and his eyes grew serious. "At some point in the future, I'll ask you to do something and you have to do it, no questions asked. No balking, just do it."

She tilted her head, suspicious. "What is it?"

"I don't know yet. But I need to know that if we're in danger you'll do it, whatever it is."

She studied his face, all teasing gone. "You know that if I agree to this, I have to trust you."

"I know."

"That's hard for me. I don't know if I can."

"I know. It's a lot to ask, but I swear, Emma, I would never ask you to do anything that would hurt you. You'll just have to trust me."

He was completely serious. His seriousness worried her, made her wonder if he knew something she didn't. But he wouldn't tell her, even if she asked. It all depended on how lucky she felt.

Emma put her hand on her hip and lifted her chin. "You can't interfere in any way when I take my shots."

"You'd accuse me of cheating?" He didn't appear very offended, in fact looked like he lost his loop-hole.

"And I get my answers as soon as I ask the questions, no cheating and saying 'one a week' or something completely bull shit."

"All right, I'll answer the question when you ask it."

Emma stuck out her right hand. Will put his hand in hers and they shook, staring into each other's eyes. This should have been fun, they should be laughing, but Emma understood the gravity of the situation. They both offered something they weren't willing to give.

Emma took her stance and aimed, centering the tin can through her sight. She took a deep breath, released it, and shot. *Plink*. The can flew off the metal drum. She didn't turn around and gloat. There were three more cans to shoot to get her answers. She shot the second and third. Only one left.

Will stood silently behind her, although she could feel his nervousness. How was that possible? Could you feel nervousness in someone six feet away? She rolled back her shoulders and shook the feeling away then focused on the can. Her finger lightly looped the trigger, about to squeeze when her stomach cramped in an unexpected wave of nausea. She pulled the trigger instinctively as she doubled over in pain. Her shot missed the can and hit the metal drum.

"Emma?" Will was immediately by her side, hand on her back.

"I'm okay, I just felt sick all of a sudden." She twisted to glance at Will, who looked like he had the same fear.

"Can you walk to the cabin? We have to be prepared."

"No, go." She waved him away as she fought another surge of nausea and dropped the gun on ground next to her. She fell on her hands and knees in the grass. "You're wasting time," she moaned.

"No way I'm leaving you out here. You're coming with me."

"Sorry, but I'm a little busy right now." The nausea won out and she threw up on the damp grass, her hair falling around her face. "Damn it, I just washed that." She felt Will pull her hair back behind her back.

"Emma..."

The nausea seemed to have passed, if only temporarily, and she sat back on her heels, taking gasps of air. "I'm hurrying as fast as I can. Some freaking bizarre kind of alarm system this is. Why can't I just get a headache or something?"

Will grabbed the rifle then helped Emma to her feet. "I don't know. It worries me that it strikes out of nowhere and it's so debilitating. This could be dangerous."

"It's not a helluva lot of fun for me, either. Let's go."

Will took her hand as they walked toward the cabin. "We need a plan. I hadn't actually come up with one. I never thought they would find us here."

"That's reassuring."

"It is what it is. Let's get the guns and ammo and hide in the trees. We can use the element of surprise on them. If the other day is any indication, we don't have much time."

Will grabbed the other guns and some ammunition from the gun cabinet and laid them on the table as Emma's eyes still adjusted to the dark. He handed the pistol and several clips to Emma. "Here, this is your gun, load it."

"What about the rifle?" she asked as she inserted the clip into the base of the gun and the others in her jeans pocket.

"You're going to have that, too, but only use it as a necessity. I'm going to hide you in a tree and you will shoot only as a last resort. You don't have any practice shooting a moving target and I'm not having you draw attention to yourself." He handed her the rifle she had used and a clip. "Load this one too."

Will loaded the other rifles and stuffed extra clips into his jeans pockets. They walked out into the morning sunshine as another wave of nausea began to hit. "Oh no…" she moaned.

Will grabbed her arm and dragged her along behind him. She fought to stay upright. "Come on, hang in there until I get you up into a tree."

She doubled over as they reached the tree line.

"Slow deep breaths. We have to hurry."

It was so easy for him to say when he wasn't the one about to vomit again, but she also knew they were in jeopardy and she was slowing them down. "I'm sorry." She tried breathing through her nose, which seemed to help a little. Will pulled her fifty feet into the forest and stopped at the base of a large tree.

"Just try not to fall out of the tree if you barf. You've had enough drama the last few days."

"Yeah, thanks for the advice."

"I'm going to boost you up. Climb up and try to hide in the leaves. When it's over, I'll come get you." Will started to lift her up.

"Will, wait."

He stopped and waited.

"What are you going to do?" she asked, fear overriding the nausea.

He looked into her eyes. "I'm going to protect you. Now get up in the tree already." He lifted her up and she reached for a branch overhead. Will put his hands under her butt and pushed her up.

"Always looking for an opportunity to feel me up, huh?" She tried to tease, but her heart thumped wildly, making it difficult to breathe.

"Always." His tone was flat and she knew they were in trouble.

She pulled herself up onto the branch and gazed down. Will handed her the rifle, a worried expression on his face. She reached for the gun and realized there was something else in his face. Concern. For her. He was genuinely concerned for her safety. She knew it shouldn't surprise her. He'd spent the last few days taking care of her and saving her life. The significance of it hit her as she realized he could very easily run away into the woods, leaving her to fend for herself. He owed her nothing. Yet, here he was looking up at her with tenderness, and for the life of her she couldn't understand why.

"Will?"

He gazed up at her.

"Be careful."

His roguish smile lifted the corners of his mouth, but his voice was weary. "No worries, love, this is what I'm trained for. Now keep climbing."

She climbed about twenty feet and scooted out on a branch full of leaves. Fairly certain she was hidden, she also realized she couldn't see anything, bringing the now familiar rush of fear and anxiety. She wished she didn't have this stupid internal alarm. It made her ill enough that she had trouble escaping and it gave her little notice to get away, so what was the point? The sound of tires crunching on the gravel road echoed through the trees and she realized her nausea had disappeared. She wasn't nauseated when they showed up to kidnap Jake either.

Thoughts of Jake nearly suffocated her with worry until she heard the first gunshots, then her thoughts turned to Will.

CHAPTER EIGHTEEN

THE first SUV pulled up as Will positioned himself in a tree at the edge of the clearing. He didn't know why Emma became so violently ill when the men were close, but he was thankful for the warning. It would have been disastrous if the SUV pulled up while they were outside with only the one rifle. He tried to take comfort in knowing that Emma was hidden back in the trees, away from stray bullets. The doors of the SUV opened and four men stormed the cabin, with another SUV close behind.

They opened fire on the cabin, making it apparent they weren't looking to take prisoners. The cabin was destroyed in a matter of moments. Will tensed, thinking about Emma hiding only fifty feet away. It seemed far enough away before, but now he wasn't so sure. He waited. Once he started shooting, he'd give his position away.

Three men got out of the second SUV and joined the others. Seven men total. The sound of breaking glass, splintering wood and rapid gunfire echoed eerily through the woods. There was a chance they would shoot the cabin to oblivion and leave. He and Emma would be safe, but he wasn't willing to let them get away that easy. He thought of the hell Emma had been through and anger ignited his need for retribution.

Will waited until he had as many as possible in his view. He aimed and squeezed the trigger. In rapid fire succession he took out three men before they realized they were being attacked and spread out. Will jumped down from the tree and darted back into the woods, circling around the clearing, leading them away from Emma. The vantage point sucked compared to his previous spot, but it was safer for Emma if he stayed on the ground. If they realized that he'd hid in the trees, they might look for her there, too.

The attention of the remaining men turned from the cabin and focused on the tree line. Will shot a few more rounds, not necessarily to hit one, but to get their attention. Darting back into the woods, he circled, did a quarter turn directly across from where he started, and shot again. He hoped they didn't torch the cabin since he didn't have time to get many supplies out. Their main concern seemed to be finding the source of the gunfire. A man came into view, peering from behind one of the SUVs. He was an easy target for Will. Three or four left. He knew three would be too easy. Out of the corner of his eye, he saw two men slip into the forest, heading in Emma's direction.

Shit.

He had two choices: let them search and pray that Emma stayed hidden, or work his way back to her. He knew what he should do, but unsure if he could actually do it.

****

The storm of gunfire made Emma queasy, but for a different reason than before. Will was out there in the middle of all those flying bullets. What if he got hurt? Or killed? *Will can take care of himself.* Logically, she knew this, but he was only human; it only took one bullet. The vice on her chest tightened. *Not helping!* She had to think of something else, something other than what he was doing this very moment. Emma thought of the first time she saw him, leaning in the car window. *God, he'd been such an ass.* She still didn't know why he even got in the car in the first place, but she knew where she would be if Jake hadn't insisted she let him. Dead, without a doubt. And now he was out there risking his life to save her while she sat in a tree. She should be helping him. The sound of the gunfire slowed down. A fresh wave of worry caught her breath.

The gunshots stopped completely and an uneasiness wiggled up her back. Something was wrong. Will? No, she didn't think so. *Me.* She held her breath, the sound of crunching leaves and pine needles grew closer. It could be Will, but somehow she knew it wasn't. She hoped she was hidden enough; if she weren't, she'd be an easy shot. The thick foliage blocked her view, but she spotted a black object moving her direction through a gap in the leaves. Emma swung the rifle slowly over her shoulder, trying not to make any noise. She gripped the tree branch with her left hand and the rifle trigger with her right. Her heart beat so loudly she was sure the man below could hear it. More gunshots rang out toward the cabin and she jerked, rustling the leaves on her branch. The dark figure stopped almost directly underneath her tree. She held her breath and waited, her finger shaking on the trigger. *Should she shoot him?* Will told her to stay here and do nothing, but he never said what to do if one of them showed up underneath her. The man paused, turning slowly in a circle, his rifle swung around searching for her. More gunfire sounded in the distance. She was prepared for it this time and remained still. He walked forward a few feet, now directly underneath her. She had a perfect shot if she wanted to take it. Her heart beat savagely, making her breaths come in short bursts. What if she missed?

He glanced up and saw her, and for a brief second their eyes locked. His full of triumph, hers full of fear. But before he could raise his gun, she pointed hers and shot several rounds. He fell on his back, blood pouring onto the ground. The taste of bile and fear gagged her and she made herself look away. But her cover was blown; she needed to get out of the tree and move. She scrambled down, in spite of her violent shaking, ignoring the twigs that scraped her arms. To the left, a dark figure in the distance advanced toward her. She turned, bolting into the forest.

****

When Will heard the shots in the forest, his heart stopped. *If something happened to her...* He pushed the thought away. Will focused on Emma for a moment, wishing he could communicate with her and somehow, he knew she was alive. Stunned, he realized he could feel her presence. The thought was both reassuring and overwhelming.

He ran back into the forest toward Emma, no longer caring if he lured them to her. They were already there. The urge to defend her to his death was strong and surprising. He hadn't felt anything like it since he'd been in the military, yet even that was different from what he felt now.

He circled around to the tree Emma had climbed and found the dead man at the base. His heart sunk as he looked up already knowing she wasn't there. He paused, straining to pick up something, any clue to tell him where she was. The crackle of leaves echoed in front him. He crept silently in that direction.

****

Emma ran into the woods without a plan. *Think, Emma! Think!* She had to come up with something. Sounds followed her, confirming that she was being followed. An outcrop of rocks lay ahead. Could she find a place to hide? She headed toward it, but when she reached the rocks, she realized there was nothing deep enough to cover her. A branch snapped behind her and she turned to see a man dressed in a black shirt and jeans pointing a gun at her.

"Please," she said, holding up her hands. "I don't have anything you want."

"Actually, you do." He raised his rifle, a satisfied grin on his face.

Emma heard two shots and wondered why she didn't feel any pain. Maybe it didn't hurt to get shot. The man's face registered surprise and he fell to the ground, revealing Will behind him with his gun raised. He lowered his gun when he saw her, strode toward her in long steps and wrapped her into his embrace.

"Are you okay?"

"Yes," she answered, but her voice shook.

"That was too close."

She didn't answer, still trying to slow her racing heart.

"Come on, we need to take cover somewhere." He started walking toward the rocks. "This isn't over yet. There's still more out there. I think I should try to get more information from one of them."

"What do they want, Will?"

"I don't know. That's what I'd like to find out."

"Can't we just try to get away? What if something happens to you?" Emma panicked at the thought.

Will walked another ten feet past where Emma had stopped and found a crevice jutting into the bluff . "Nothing's going to happen to me. Now get into there and wait."

Emma wasn't going anywhere until she got some answers. "Will, these people are dangerous. How can you be so sure that you'll be okay? Especially if you try to catch one?"

"Emma, we don't have time for this."

"Will, please." She knew she sounded desperate, but she didn't care. She was terrified to let him go.

"Emma." He paused and stared into the trees above. With a sigh he turned back to her. She expected him to look impatient; instead, he appeared resigned. "You wanted some answers from me. Well, here's one. When I was in the military, this was part of what I did. I hunted people down and extracted information from them. I know what I'm doing. Now please, hide for me. Okay? I can't do my job if I'm worried about you."

"What if they find me?"

He pushed her down. "They only way they can get to you is to walk around this boulder. If someone appears in the opening, shoot first and ask questions later. When I come back, I'll tell you it's me so you won't have to worry about shooting me. Okay?"

It wasn't okay, far from it, but she knew she had no choice. Emma nodded.

"I've gotten most of them so don't be so worried. I'll be okay."

"Will, please be careful. I don't want anything to happen to you."

A genuine smile spread over his face. "Of course, you don't. Who else is going to put up with you knocking Tim McGraw?"

Her hand holding the gun shook as she watched him disappear.

****

Emma's hiding place wasn't as safe as he would like, but it was safer than a tree at this point. If he had been a few seconds later finding her… he refused to think about what would have happened. That was entirely too close. He hated to admit how much it freaked him out. He wanted nothing more than to stay with her, but there were still gunmen out there threatening her life. His goal was to keep them as far from her as possible. Plus, he wanted information. He kicked himself for not thinking of it sooner, but there it was. He wasn't thinking.

Will backtracked to the cabin. Chances were the men—however many might be left—had moved in his direction at this point. He slunk through trees in near silence, listening for signs of movement. Luring them out of the woods and back toward the cabin seemed like the best option.

There was no sign of them as he reached the tree line. He picked up a rock about the size of his fist and threw it at the headlight of a SUV. The sound of shattering glass filled the silence of the clearing. Scooping up a few smaller rocks, he climbed up into a tree and waited. To his left, he heard the barely audible sound of crunching leaves. The sound grew closer until a black figure approached about twenty feet away. The man paused, looking in the direction of the SUV. Will threw a stone against a tree behind him. The thunk echoed in the woods. Not fooled, the gunman turned in Will's direction and slowly made his way over.

Will waited, crouched on the tree branch about ten feet off the ground and opposite the gunman. The man paused several feet away, alert and listening. Will threw another rock behind him, farther away and into the tree branches. The whoosh of leaves drew the man's attention and he crept at a snail's pace in that direction. When he was next to the tree, Will jumped with the rifle in his hand, landing on the gunman's back. The man fell to the ground with Will landing on top of him. Will pointed his rifle tip into the man's back when he attempted to get up.

"I wouldn't do that if I were you." Will jabbed the gun into his back to prove his point.

The man eased back down onto the ground, his hands on either side of his head.

"Tell me who you work for."

"Why would I tell you that?" the man sneered.

"Because I have a high-powered rifle pointed at your back that will make a hole big enough to drive a car through."

"You're going to kill me anyway. So why would I tell you?"

He gouged the rifle tip into the man's back. "Maybe I'll let you live if you cooperate."

"I've got nothing to say."

Will sighed. "I really hoped you wouldn't say that."

****

Emma waited for what seemed like an eternity, ears straining for any hint of what was going on. She hadn't heard any new gunshots. The longer she waited, the more terrified she became. *What was taking Will so long?* She wasn't sure how long she should wait and had no idea how much time actually passed since he'd left. Her jangled nerves had her on the verge of going to find him when she heard the soft sound of leaves crunching in the distance. She held the rifle pointed in front, her trembling finger on the trigger.

"Emma?" Will's voice called.

"Will?"

"You can come out."

She crawled out, thankful he was safe. But as he walked toward her, she wasn't so sure His face was strained and blood splatters covered his arms and shirt.

She froze. "Oh God…"

"It's okay, Emma. It's not mine." His eyes were dull and expressionless.

"Then how….? I didn't hear any gunshots."

His jaw tightened and he swallowed. "I don't think you really want to know."

"What does that mean?"

He took her hand. "Come on, I'll get cleaned up and we'll get out of here. At least we have a way out now." He tried to sound aloof, although he wasn't succeeding.

"Will, what happened? What did you find out?"

He took both her hands in his and stared into her eyes. "Someone wants you dead and they are willing to pay a large sum of money to make that happen."

"Who?"

"I don't know. He didn't know. I'm sure he was just a middleman, someone hired to do the dirty work." He almost slipped and added *like me*.

"Why do they want me dead?" The words were heavy on her tongue.

"I don't know that either, but they didn't want you dead until after they blew up the truck. At that point, they wanted you alive. It was after the explosion that they got the assignment to kill you."

"What does that mean?" She could hardly breathe.

"I don't know." He sounded worried. "I know you're scared Emma and you have every right to be, but I *will* protect you."

"Why? Why would you do that?"

Will looked stumped by her question. He ran his free hand through his hair and sighed. Emma saw the blood stains he had tried to wipe off. Blood from someone he killed to protect her. Her chest tightened and she had trouble catching her breath.

"Honestly, I don't know," he said.

"That's not an answer Will!" She sounded hysterical, but she didn't care. "I'm supposed to count on you to protect me and you don't know why you're doing it? What happens if you suddenly decide you don't want to do it anymore?" She jerked her hand out of his. "I never asked you to do this Will. Never. You were the one who got in my car. You were the one who said we had to stay together. Why? Why would you do that?"

"Emma…" He reached out to her.

She backed up. "I need answers, Will."

"Sorry, sweetheart, you didn't win the bet." He gave her a wry smile, a half-assed attempt at his usual sarcasm, but it fell flat.

"Fuck the bet, Will."

"Emma, what matters is I'm here now and I'm not going anywhere."

"But why aren't you going anywhere? Why did you just risk your life to save me? How many men did you kill today? How many since you met me? You're one man, Will. *Just one man.* Why would you do it? Why *should* you do it?"

He moved in front of her, sincerity in his eyes. "Emma, I don't have any real answers. I wish I did. Maybe it's this goddamned mark. Maybe it's that I find you to be the most irritating, sexy woman I've ever met. You keep me on my toes and you don't take any shit from me."

Tears blurred her eyes and she looked away. Will put his hand under her chin and gently turned it back to face him.

"I'm not done yet. You asked me why. There's not one why. There's a bunch of whys. You're a good mother who gave up her entire life for her son to keep him safe. I think how amazing it would be if you gave me half that amount of devotion. Even now, your life in danger, you refuse to believe he is dead and you're determined to find him. I feel this overwhelming urge to protect you and to keep you safe. I don't know why, I only know it's there. When you were in the tree and I heard gunshots and I thought you might... I couldn't even let myself think it. And when that man almost shot you by the rocks... Emma." He pulled her against his chest and rested his cheek the top of her head. "I don't know why I feel this way, I only know that I do."

The answers he gave were more than she expected and it amazed her that they were enough. The scent of his sweat mixed with the rusty odor of blood on his shirt drove home the deeds he committed because of her. "You've killed so many men because of me. I'm sorry."

"I've killed many more and for less worthy causes." His lips found her and she realized how lucky she was to have him.

He pulled back and smiled. "Now let's get out of here."

Emma gave him a tentative smile. She had no choice but to trust him for now.

Will kept his arm around her back and turned back to the cabin then froze. She didn't have time to react before she heard the gunfire.

CHAPTER NINETEEN

WILL noticed a movement to his right. A man stood about thirty feet away with a handgun pointed at them. Will pushed Emma down to the ground, covering her body with his, but not before he heard the shots. His rifle was already up and shooting as they fell. The gunman took cover and disappeared.

"Are you okay?" Will asked.

"Yeah, I think so." She lay face down, muffling her voice.

"Stay down, crawl behind a tree, and wait for me. I'm going to get that son of a bitch." Will was furious. He thought he'd gotten them all.

Will rolled off Emma, chasing after the man who took off toward the cabin. The gunman was in the clearing, almost to the SUV, when Will caught up to him. Later, he admitted to himself that he shot the man more times than was necessary. But it appeased his need to make sure he was good and dead. Satisfied, he walked back to Emma.

A suffocating fear gripped him when he reached the spot he left her. A trail of blood disappeared behind a tree.

"*Emma?*"

He ran to the tree and found her sitting with her back against it, her legs extended. Her shaking hands pressed against her bloody left leg. Her face was ashen. "We have a bit of a problem," her voice cracked and she gave him a weak smile.

Will dropped to his knees and gently moved her hands away to reveal a bloody hole in her jeans. "Oh, Emma."

"Yeah, I think I got shot." She leaned her head back against the tree, closing her eyes.

Will pulled out a pocketknife and cut open her jeans to look at the wound. There was an entry wound but no exit, which meant the bullet was still in her leg. He didn't think it had hit her femoral artery, but there was a lot of blood and no doubt she needed medical attention. He stripped off his t-shirt and tied it around her leg.

"There you go again, taking off your clothes," she said, watching him through a half-open eye.

"Got to show you what you're getting, package deal." His voice was grim. "Although as a bodyguard, I obviously suck."

"No complaints from me. Shot in the leg beats dead any day."

He couldn't believe she could joke with him right now, but he also realized the pain hadn't fully hit her yet. "Emma I have to move you to an SUV. It's probably going to hurt."

"Well, it probably can't get much worse." Will scooped her up as she cried out. "Oh, I lied. It can."

"I'm sorry."

Her arms clung around his neck and she laid her head on his shoulder. "Can't be helped." But tears slid out of the corner of her eyes. He walked at an even pace, trying not to jostle her any more than necessary. She tensed and tried to suppress a moan with every step.

"Emma, it's okay. You can cry out."

She shook her head, biting her bottom lip. He reached the clearing around the cabin and realized he couldn't take her inside since there was little left of it. The back of one of the vehicles seemed the logical choice. He lifted the handle on the back door, praying it was unlocked and not booby-trapped. He was lucky on both counts. The back seat was empty and he slid her in as gently as possible.

"I'm sorry," he said as she cried out.

"Stop saying that already." She leaned back on her elbows. "Damn it, my leg's sticking out the door."

"I can come around and…"

She groaned. "I can do it."

"I need to go in and get some stuff before we go. I'll be right back."

He sprinted to the cabin, but stopped by one of the bodies and dug a cell phone out of its pocket. In the cabin, his water-soaked cell phone was, amazingly enough, still on the kitchen table. He pulled out the SIM card and replaced it with the card in the gunman's phone, then stuffed it into his jeans pocket. He found a pillowcase and filled it full of ammunition, clothes and linens, and headed out to the SUV.

Emma lay back against the door, eyes closed, chest rising and falling with her labored breathing.

"Emma, I want to change your bandage."

Her eyes slowly fluttered open. "You mean your shirt?

"Hey, we're short on compression bandages here." The shirt was almost completely soaked with blood. He crawled into the front and leaned over the back of the seat to work on her leg. He untied it and tossed it outside on the ground.

"You gonna just litter like that?"

"The way I see it, the grounds already littered with bodies anyway, what's another shirt?"

She lifted an eyebrow. "You have a point."

He folded up a towel and put it under her leg and opened a water bottle. "This might hurt a little. I've got to clean this out since it's covered in dirt." After he poured the entire bottle, Will dabbed the top of her leg and examined the hole closer. The entry was clean and he suspected no damage to her femur, but infection was a huge concern.

"I'm going to cut the rest of your pant leg off since it's wet." He removed the wet towel and placed a dry one on her wound then tied a clean shirt around her leg. "This isn't a tourniquet, but it will put pressure on it so you don't have to." He placed a pillow under her leg and covered her with a blanket. "How does one woman get into so much trouble?"

Her left shoulder slightly lifted in a shrug. "Don't ask me. Before this week I never had any drama."

"You mean other than running away from men who tried to kidnap your son for three years?"

"Well, yeah, there is *that*..." Her eyes were closed. "Now what, Will?"

"I don't know yet. Let's just get out of here and then we'll figure it out."

He was thankful the keys were still in the ignition as he started the vehicle and started down the gravel road. He knew the bumps made it rough on Emma from the moans in the backseat. He only hoped the road didn't go on for an eternity.

****

Emma sat in the backseat wondering if she was going to die. *Don't be ridiculous Emma, you only got shot in the leg. You are not going to die.* But the pain had become so intense she wondered if she would anyway. The bumpy drive didn't help matters.

"How much longer is this goddamned road?" she croaked out.

"I don't know."

She couldn't die now. Jake needed her to find him even if Will didn't believe he was alive. She knew she would convince him somehow and she needed Will to help her. Besides, she promised Jake she'd stay with Will. But this whole getting shot thing would totally delay finding Jake. The pain was bad at first, but now it felt like a hot poker had been stuck in her leg and left inside. She wasn't sure how much more she could stand, but she refused to scream. *Think cool thoughts. Ice, snow, arctic winds.*

"Finally," Will sighed. "The end of the gravel road is up ahead."

"Then where?"

"Denver."

"That far?" She panted through the pain. She didn't want to complain, but she didn't know how long she was going to last.

"I don't even know where we are. I don't want to use the GPS in case it tells the people who own this thing where we are."

"So how will you know?"

"I'll just stop somewhere and ask if I don't see a sign."

"A man who asks directions," Emma said. "I've seen it all now."

They drove several miles, seeing only trees and the winding road. "We are definitely out in the middle of nowhere," Will said. "How did they find us here?"

She didn't answer. She was too busy concentrating on trying to control the pain.

"How are you doing back there?"

"I've been better." She tried to remember some of her Lamaze breathing techniques. Maybe that would help. She needed a focal point. She found a spot on the back of the passenger headrest. Slow deep breath in, cleansing breath out.

The SUV pulled into the parking lot of a small gas station.

"I'm going to go get directions." Will said as he turned off the engine. He twisted around to look at her. "How bad is the pain, Emma? Scale of one to ten."

"Eight, maybe nine," she said between breaths.

He ran inside and returned a few minutes later with a bottle in a paper bag.

Emma glanced at him from the corner of her eye. "Little early … for you to be hitting… the bottle." The pain was getting worse. She leaned her head back praying for it to go away.

"It's not for me. It's for you." He took the bottle out of the bag and uncapped it as he leaned over the seat.

She looked down at the container he held in front of her. "I'm… not much… of a drinker." Her breath came in short pants. Her face and fingers tingled and she realized she was hyperventilating.

He held it up to her mouth. "Today you are. Drink up." He tipped the bottle. She opened her mouth and gulped. Her mouth burned and her throat quickly followed. She coughed in response. He tilted it again, filling her mouth. She tried to swallow, but she coughed again and spewed liquid in front of her and down her shirt.

"Let's do that again. Try to swallow this time."

She gulped the liquid, tears coming to her eyes as she suppressed a cough. "I'm going to get drunk if you keep doing that."

"That's the point, Princess. One more ought to do it if you're really not much of a drinker."

She gulped one last swig, tears streaming down her face. Her eyes closed as she felt the burn of the alcohol settle in her stomach and slowly spread throughout her body. Her leg was still ablaze, but the fuzziness everywhere else distracted her.

"Hang on, Princess." He kissed her forehead then started the car.

Soon, the hum of the car engine lulled her to sleep.

****

They were approaching Denver and Will still didn't have a plan. He wanted nothing more than to take her to the hospital, but the closer he got to Denver, the more he realized it wasn't an option. If they could be found in a cabin down a five-mile gravel road on the side of a mountain that didn't even get cell phone coverage, they could easily be tracked down in a hospital. He could notify police, but they'd get involved anyway since it was a gunshot wound. Will doubted they'd take the extent of the threat seriously enough which left Emma vulnerable. He was going to make damn sure it didn't happen again, but it severely limited his choices. Her leg needed to be cleaned out and she needed antibiotics, preferably by IV, but that didn't look like an option either. The trick was how to get his hands on some type of antibiotic. Maybe he could concentrate on cleaning out the wound first and get the antibiotic later. If nothing else, he could wait until nightfall and rob a pharmacy.

He needed sterile gauze and, at the very least, some antibiotic ointment. He glanced in the rearview mirror at Emma. Her eyes were closed, her face still pale, her breathing shallow. Blood seeped through the blanket over her legs. She could die, he realized. She had lost a lot of blood and was in shock. An infection could kill her.

Will pulled off onto an exit, searching for a drugstore. Pulling into a Walgreens parking lot, he found a space as far from the door as possible. He hated to leave Emma alone, but he was thankful she remained asleep.

He got several packages of sterile gauze, antibiotic ointment, a pair of tweezers and a couple bottles of saline. If she got a fever, he wanted to be sure he could take her temperature. He found the thermometers in front of the pharmacy window as he overheard the pharmacy tech on the phone.

"Patient name? Tyler Robinson...100 cc of Amoxicillin... Okay, tell the mother it will be ready in fifteen minutes."

Will couldn't believe his good luck. All he had to do was beat the mother here to pick up the antibiotic. He would have preferred Cipro, but it would do until he could figure something else out. He lowered his head so they didn't recognize him later and walked to the front of the store. After he paid for his items, he went back out to the SUV to wait fifteen minutes.

Picking up the antibiotic was even easier than Will expected. The kid's insurance card was on file, they didn't ask for ID, and he paid cash. He ran through a fast-food drive-thru before finding a motel with outside entrance doors to the rooms. Since he didn't want to use one of his credit cards, he had to settle for a seedy place that took cash.

The parking lot was nearly deserted so finding a spot in front of their room wasn't an issue. He carried everything in to the room before he disturbed her. Hurting her was the last thing he wanted, but moving her was necessary. He scanned the area to make sure no one was around, then opened the back door, catching her back so she didn't fall out as the door opened. She groaned as she fell back into his arms.

"Sorry." He slid her out and into his arms. She cried out in pain. "I know. I'm sorry." He almost wished he stuck around and tried to take someone's narcotics, but he knew they'd check his ID for that. It never would have worked.

"Will?" Her speech was slurred as she came around.

The door was only a few short steps from the SUV. He went through the door and shut it behind him with his foot. "Yeah?"

"Where are we?"

He hated to tell her, but there was no way to hide it. "We're in Denver. In a motel."

"Not a hospital?"

"No." He didn't want to lay her on the filthy bedspread. The whole goddamned place was a potential infection cesspool. He bent over, still holding her as he pulled back the bedspread, but he jostled her in the process and she cried out again. "I'm so sorry, Emma." He was sorry for so many things. After he laid her down, he knelt next to the bed and stroked her hair. Her face was pale, her eyes outlined by dark purple crescent moons. Her breath came in rapid pants.

"I can't take you to a hospital," Will said. "I'm afraid they'll find us there."

"Okay." She closed her eyes. "You know best, Will."

Her words were like a punch in the gut. Did he know best? If he did, they wouldn't be in this situation. "I have to clean out your wound, Emma. It's going to hurt. I'm sorry."

"I told you already, quit saying that." She paused and bit her lip. "Do what you need to do."

He cut her jeans all the way off with his pocketknife. Her leg was swollen around the wound and the hole oozed blood. He turned on a lamp by the table, jerked off the shade and held it over her leg. When he bent over and looked closely, he saw a few pieces of her jeans inside. He knew they had to come out, but he also knew there were probably some even deeper that he couldn't reach.

"Okay, time for another round of drinks. But first some water." He found a water bottle and reached around her back, pulling her up to drink. He held it to her mouth and she drank with her chapped and swollen lips. She stopped, panting from the exertion.

"Now, time to belly up to the bar." He tried to sound jovial, but failed. He held the bottle to her mouth and poured.

She swallowed and coughed. "What, couldn't spring for the good stuff?"

He smirked. "You must not be a drinker. This *is* the good stuff. Nothing but the best for you."

She panted and he waited for her to catch her breath. "You know…they say... it's bad…to drink…alone."

"I think we'll make an exception in this case." After he was satisfied she had enough to help with what he was about to do, he laid her back down. He washed his hands and the tweezers with hot soapy water. He bent over scalding his hands in an effort to sterilize them, agonizing over the fact that he was going to hurt her. He lifted his head and saw his reflection amazed to see the face of a man who cared. How long had it been since he'd cared about anything?

Goddamn it. He wanted to throw something, no to kill someone, the person who did this to her. He realized he had already done that, but it wasn't enough. He wanted the person behind this fucking mess. He took several deep breaths in to calm down.

When he went back into the room, he found her asleep, her breath now slow and steady. He hoped she stayed unconscious, but as he poured the saline into her wound, she began to scream in pain. If someone had ripped a hole in his own leg it would have been easier than listening to her anguish.

He stopped. "Emma, sweetheart, I know it hurts, I know. But you can't scream or someone might call the police."

"I'm sorry," she choked out through a sob.

He was about to implode from guilt. "No, don't say you're sorry. It's not your fault." He sucked in a ragged breath as he rubbed the back of his arm across his forehead, trying to regain control. He began to wonder if he could actually do this. What were his options? Leave the fabric in there and ensure without a doubt that she got an infection or try to get it out and hope she didn't. It had to be done.

"Okay, we're going to try this again," he said, trying not to sound so grim. "I know you can't help screaming so you have a couple of options. First is you can cover your face with a pillow and you can scream into it. I'd rather try that first."

"Okay."

"Maybe we should wait to do this," he said, although he knew he was putting off the inevitable.

"No… just get it over with." She grabbed the pillow and dragged it over her face. Will flipped on the television, turning the volume up to help drown out her cries, then washed his hands again. This time he pushed on, ignoring her cries and trying to see through the blur of tears in his eyes, until he was finally satisfied that he did the best he could with two bottles of saline and a pair of tweezers.

He pulled the pillow off her face.

She looked up at him, her face red and wet, her eyes swollen and glazed. "Thank you."

Will's tenuous grip on control snapped. After what he just put her through, she *thanked* him. "I'll be back in a minute," he choked out. "I've got to get something out of the car." He swiped the room key off the dresser and shot out the door, shutting it tight behind him. He leaned against the brick wall and covered his face with his hands, still covered in her blood. He slid down, ignoring the pain of his skin scraping against the brick, and for the first time in years he cried. It began as a trickle but once unleashed, it turned into gut-wrenching sobs. Of all the people he had hurt, and there were more than he could ever count, she was the one he regretted the most.

It shocked him that he cared. After so many years caring about only himself, he finally found someone he cared about more. But that wasn't accurate either. He stopped caring about himself the day his father turned him away. Will had lived without a purpose for the last three years, wandering through his life, living for the moment, but not really living at all. Before his court-martial, his life had been one endless con, trying to live up to who his father wanted him to be. But that ended in disappointment on both their parts. His father blamed him for a multitude of sins, most justifiable, yet here was Emma, who had every right to blame him, and she didn't. He hurt her because of his own negligence and she thanked him for it. How fucked up was that?

He had been waiting for her. He didn't know it before, but it was true. His whole life he had searched for some type of meaning and purpose. It wasn't the life his father groomed him for since he was a boy. It was her. Between the mark that Jake burned into his flesh and the glimmer of belonging she offered, he found it. Emma gave him a reason to live. The irony, of course, being that he discovered this as she might die. And it would be his own fault.

He sat with his legs extended, back to the wall, and watched the sunset over the graffiti-covered strip mall across the street. Only five days ago, he met her in a parking lot at sunset, yet it seemed so much longer ago. It all came full circle.

A car pulled into the lot, the pulsating bass of rap music blasting out the open windows. The two men inside glanced at him as they pulled into a parking space several units down. Will realized he had been out here longer than he intended. He should be inside watching over her, especially after what he just put her through. He wiped his face, stood up and took a deep breath before entering the room.

"Will?" Emma whispered.

He knelt down and stroked her hair. "Shh... I'm sorry I disturbed you."

Her mouth lifted into a tiny smile, her eyes full of tenderness. "It's not your fault."

He closed his eyes as he sucked his breath in.

"Will."

He looked at her only because she wanted him to.

"I don't blame you. Please don't blame yourself."

"Emma..."

"No, wait. There's something else. If something happens to me..."

"No, Emma, stop..."

"Will," she said firmly, in spite of her weakness. She stopped to catch her breath before continuing. "If something happens to me, promise you'll find Jake."

"Emma," he didn't care that his voice broke. He still didn't believe Jake was alive, but now wasn't time for a debate. "Nothing's going to happen to you. I won't let it."

She smiled again. "I know." The trust in her eyes shattered his already cracked resolve. "But in case you're not around and something does happen, please promise me you'll find him."

"I promise," he finally choked out. At that moment, he would give her anything.

"Thank you." She closed her eyes.

For the rest of the night, he sat in a chair by the bed, keeping watch as her wound turned red and hot, and red streaks branched out from the opening. She became feverish. Two more doses of antibiotic and ibuprofen didn't help and he knew things were desperate. Even after mulling over his options during several sleepless hours, he weighed them one more time before accepting it was his only choice. Just before sunrise, he dug out the cell phone buried in his pocket and checked his contacts, thankful the number he needed was still on the list. His thumb hovered over the send button. Once he hit send, it couldn't be undone. After all the years of brash decisions, he had to be sure of this one. He sighed and pressed the button, hoping he hadn't just signed their death sentences.

CHAPTER TWENTY

THEY told him to meet them at Centennial Airport in an hour and they would be waiting with a helicopter.

He drove up to the service entrance and entered in the security code they gave him. The metal gate slid open and he drove through, his chest tightening. A hundred feet in front of him sat a U.S. Army Black Hawk helicopter on the tarmac. He had spent enough time in them to recognize one. The blades spun, ready for takeoff and two men in military uniforms stood next to the open doors. A civilian helicopter he expected; a fucking Black Hawk he did not. This whole situation had government ties. He wondered again how it involved Emma. If the government wanted her, he didn't see how he could get her out of it. He steeled himself and drove the SUV around so the back doors faced the side of the aircraft. He got out, rifle in hand. He wasn't pointing it at them, just letting them know he had it.

They seemed unfazed by the gun. A quick glance of their stripes told him they were Army.

"You boys waiting for a delivery?" Will shouted over the whir of the blades.

"So we're told," one said.

"Any of you Kramer?" Will asked, but he already knew the answer.

"No."

"Before I make this transfer, you need to know I deliver her to Kramer himself. He's the one who hired me and after what we've been through, I trust no one. She transfers directly from me to him."

"We have orders to deliver you both. We hear she needs medical attention."

"Yeah, you could say that."

"Where is she?"

Will walked to the back of the SUV and opened the doors. Emma lay on the floor in the back, unconscious and covered with a blanket. "You boys got a stretcher? She sure as hell ain't walking."

The men pulled a stretcher from the helicopter. The one who looked like a medic peered inside the back of the vehicle.

Will stood to the side. "She got shot in the left thigh, a Glock by the looks of the gun. About thirty-foot range."

The medic climbed in and pulled back the blanket and bandages to examine her wound. "This looks more than a few hours old. When did she get shot?"

"Yesterday."

"Looks like it's been cleaned, though."

"I did the best I could with what I had. I'm sure I didn't get it all."

The medic accepted his answer with a nod. "You did a decent job, but she's got an infection."

"She dragged it through mildewy dirt. I'm sure there's all kinds of nasty shit out there."

The medic motioned for the other guy to help him move her to the stretcher. Will tried not to tense when they touched her, but he held his finger on the trigger of his gun. It was pretense. He'd never get away with shooting an Army helicopter crew, but it made him feel better, nevertheless. She cried out as they picked her up. He pretended not to care and watched as they began to move into the helicopter, trailing behind them.

"You gonna take care of that?" the other guy asked Will, pointing to the SUV.

"I don't give a shit what happens to it. It's not mine." He entered the aircraft and sat next to Emma as the medic started to work. The medic glanced up and pointed to the front. "You can sit up there."

"Let's get something straight here. I go where she goes. I stay where she stays. If she goes up front, then I go with her, but she looks like she's staying back here. So this is where I sit." He laid the rifle across his lap. "You're going to tell me everything you do before you do it. Is that clear?" Will shifted the gun slightly to reinforce his point.

The medic spoke in a hushed voice into the microphone on his headset, casting a glance toward Will. He waited for a response, then grimaced.

"You would make my job a lot easier if you let me just do it," the medic said.

"I don't give a shit what you want. My job is to deliver her alive. Her condition is already compromised and I don't get paid to deliver her dead. So forgive me if I try to insure my investment."

He shook his head in disgust. "I'm going to start an IV. Is that okay with you?"

"I want to see everything before it touches her and that includes a goddamned Kleenex. Got it?"

The medic's face turned red while his jaw clenched. "I've been ordered to humor you. So, fine. I'm tying this around her arm so I can find a vein. Then I'm going to stick a needle in her arm to start an IV. Do you want to see the needle?"

"Did I fucking stutter? I said I want to see everything."

He grunted in irritation and showed Will the needle, still in the package, and searched for veins in her right arm and hand. "I think she's dehydrated. I'm having trouble finding a vein."

Will tried to push water on her, but he knew the alcohol hadn't helped. The medic found a vein and inserted the needle. He showed Will a saline IV bag before he started an IV. "I'd give pain medication, but her blood pressure is low and she doesn't seem to need it at the moment."

The rest of the ride was silent. Will worried about what would happen when they landed. At some point he had to relinquish control of her and it agonized him to even consider it. But he had to pretend she meant nothing to him otherwise they would both be at risk. He just had to figure out how to convince them to keep him around.

They landed sooner than he would have liked. Several men ran up and opened the door. The medic helped them move the stretcher out. Will followed behind with his gun, stepping onto a concrete airstrip. It was a small airport, a private one from the looks of it, just one runway and a metal hangar at the opposite end. Several men dressed in civilian clothes stood by two dark sedans and a van. The sun rose low over the horizon and Will suddenly felt exhausted from lack of sleep and worry. But he knew this ordeal was just beginning. The van waited a short distance away, its back doors open and waiting. They slid the stretcher inside. Will began to climb in behind her but one of the men stopped him. Will held his gun up and turned around to face them. "Which one of you is Kramer?"

"He's back at the compound."

Will tried to contain his temper. "I seriously don't get you people. Are you fucking deaf? I told you I stay with her until I personally hand her to Kramer. So either I get in this van or she leaves with me."

They relented and he climbed into the back. He tried to look impartial, but his heart pounded against his chest wall. He was close to losing contact with her. He told himself this was all part of the plan yet it didn't make him feel better. The only thing saving his ass right now was years of training in the art of remaining calm.

The van took off, flanked front and back by the cars. He was surprised they let him keep his gun, especially since he used it as a threat, but they presumed he was on their side and protected what they so vehemently wanted.

A two-lane asphalt road stretched before them with no signs of any other traffic. They soon arrived at a compound of buildings behind a large chain link fence and guard station. They stopped at the station and the wooden gate lifted open for them to pass through. The motorcade drove down a long road that circled the perimeter of the compound with a row of buildings at the end opposite the guard station.

The van stopped in the front of a smaller building, the first structure in the row. The back doors opened and two men reached in to pull her out, Will right behind with his gun. "Just so it's clear, and since everyone conveniently keeps forgetting, where she goes, I go. We stay together until I personally hand her over to Kramer."

"Mr. Davenport?"

Will turned to see a tall, dark haired man in a suit approaching.

"And you would be?" Will asked, eyebrows raised.

"Scott Kramer." He held out his hand and Will's chest tightened as took his hand and shook it.

"We appreciate your diligence, but we'll take over from here."

Will watched them carry her into the building. Just like that, she was gone. He felt like someone had sucked the air out of him, but his face remained stoic.

"If you'll come with us, we can get you debriefed. First, it looks like you could use a hot shower." Kramer held his arm out prompting Will to walk with him. "Hope you don't mind a little walk. I'm in need of some fresh air."

Will followed. "What is this place?"

"This is one of our retreats. Our members rarely stay here, but it's here if needed, particularly in emergent situations such as this."

"You have a medical facility?" Emma's care was foremost in his mind.

"Yes, and a surprisingly good one considering the size of our compound. I hear you provided excellent care for our guest and it's most appreciated. She is extremely valuable to us."

"Really? Could have fooled me. You sent one man to get her and someone else sent scores. Not very good odds for something so valuable."

Kramer lifted an eyebrow. "Ah, but you are here, aren't you?"

"Yeah, at what cost to Emma? If she's so valuable, why risk her safety?"

Kramer laughed. "All very good questions, and I assure you they will be answered, but not now. However, I will tell you it was a test, which you passed."

"A test?" Will's voice rose to match his escalating anger.

Kramer stopped in front of what looked like a small office building. "All of your questions will be answered, Mr. Davenport." He opened a glass door and held it open. "But first, you appear in need of a shower, fresh clothes, and a good meal."

Will stared at Kramer with a narrow gaze. If it weren't for Emma, he'd leave and never look back. Instead, he entered through the door. Kramer followed and then walked beside him. "We have small apartments on the premises. I'll take you to one to decompress or do whatever you see fit." They stopped in front of an elevator. Kramer pushed the up button and the doors immediately opened. The elevator was encased in mahogany. No expenses spared here.

"Who exactly owns this place?" Will asked as they entered.

"Impatient." Kramer laughed again. "I like that about you. You're told to wait, but don't follow the rules. Some see it as a detriment. I see that you know what you want and you don't let anything get in your way." Kramer turned to face him and his gaze bore into Will's eyes. "Would you say that is a fair assessment of your character, Mr. Davenport?"

Will cocked his head and lifted an eyebrow. "If a man knows what he wants, why would he let someone stop him?"

The elevator chimed and the doors opened. "Exactly." Kramer led the way out and down the dimly lit hall. The floor was carpeted in a rich, ornately patterned carpet. Mahogany panels lined the walls. Art lights hung over oil paintings lining the walls, the only source of light in the hall other than a window at the end. Will suspected the paintings weren't the starving-artist sofa-size paintings he saw advertized on TV.

Kramer stopped in front of a wood-paneled door. "Yes, it is an admirable trait. But a wise man knows what's truly out of his grasp and lets it go."

The hair on the back of Will's neck stood on end.

Kramer's smile disappeared. "Some see it as a negative trait. I prefer to see it as the characteristic of a man who thinks outside the box. But it's a risk nonetheless." He opened the door and Will entered into an apartment nicer than any place he had ever stayed. "You have full access to everything here. But I ask you stay in the apartment until someone comes for you. Security measures and all."

"Of course." Will didn't hide his sarcasm.

"I will send for you in two hours, unless you need longer."

"Two hours should be long enough. I can usually do my makeup in less than ten minutes, fifteen if it's a formal affair."

Kramer smiled. "I had heard about your wit. I find it refreshing. The kitchen is fully stocked, but there is also a kitchen that provides room service if you need it. Just press zero."

"A real five star hotel you have here."

"Our members are used to such amenities. There's clothing in the bedroom for your disposal and toiletries in the bathroom. I'll leave you for now and see you in a few hours." He left Will alone in the empty apartment.

Will's thoughts immediately shifted to Emma. He realized he hadn't prepared her enough. He hadn't warned her that she probably wouldn't see him for a while. How would she react when she found out why he really helped her? Would she hate him?

He turned his attention to the apartment. Streamlined contemporary furniture decorated the living room. A large flat screen television hung on the wall. The living area was open to a kitchen filled with dark wood cabinets, granite counter tops, and stainless steel appliances. Will suspected the appliances were for show. Any one rich enough to stay here was unlikely to use them. A bowl of fruit sat on the counter and he grabbed an apple and took a bite, surprised at his sudden hunger.

Will moved to the double window. The Black Hills loomed in the distance, confirming they were in South Dakota. Was it her true ending place or a handoff location? He never cared to ask before.

He walked down a hallway past a guest room and into the master bedroom. The bed reminded him of his exhaustion and he promised himself a nap after his shower. The bathroom was marble encased, of course. He turned on the shower to warm up the water, switching on the full body sprayers. So this was how the rich lived.

Will hardly recognized himself behind three days' beard growth. He looked like he'd been to hell and back, and he supposed he had. When he finished shaving and showering, he crawled in the bed naked under a down quilt, making sure he set the alarm. He drifted off to sleep, in spite of his worry about Emma. His worry and his guilt.

CHAPTER TWENTY-ONE

THE shrill of an alarm woke Will from a deep sleep. He put on a pair of khaki pants and a long-sleeve shirt he found in the fully stocked closet. His escort arrived a few minutes later, taking him to the building's top level and exiting the elevator into a long hallway similar to the one on his floor. Will hid his disgust at the opulence displayed. Rich people always annoyed him with their greed and need to outdo one another. His escort took him into a large conference room with wall-to-wall windows overlooking the Black Hills. The view was impressive, but Will was more interested in the three suits sitting at the massive table before him.

"Mr. Davenport. Please join us." Kramer stood up and gestured to a seat across from the three men. "But first, are you hungry? Help yourself to some brunch." A small buffet was set up along the wall.

"No, thanks, I'll just have some coffee." Will poured himself a cup and sat down. "I have to say, gentlemen, this isn't how I'm used to doing things. Something tells me this isn't ordinary business."

"Very perceptive, Mr. Davenport. But we knew you were bright when we hired you." Kramer sat in the middle. He was flanked on his right by a middle-aged man, dark haired with touches of gray and crow's feet around his eyes. He leaned an elbow on the table and eyed Will with wariness. On Kramer's left sat a younger man with blond hair and a tan that didn't look like it came from working outside in the sun. He reminded Will of a model and his apparent disinterest made him wonder why he was there at all.

Kramer fingered the edges of a file in front of him as he spoke. "Tell us about your encounter with the people who attacked you."

"Which time?"

Kramer's eyebrows raised and he rested his elbows on the table. "You encountered them more than once?"

"Counting the night I obtained your guest?" Will used Kramer's word for Emma. "I believe there were four encounters."

All three men appeared surprised. Will noticed the younger one suddenly showed an interest in the conversation.

Will pushed his chair back from the table and crossed his legs. "I find it interesting that you haven't asked about the boy."

"The boy isn't our concern." Kramer said, but the younger man's chin lifted and his eyes narrowed, suggesting he had a different opinion.

Will stared directly at Mr. GQ and raised an eyebrow. "He was killed by the men following us."

The young man's eyes widened.

Kramer shrugged. "He's no concern to us."

"But this doesn't fit." The man to his right interjected. "This isn't part of the plan."

Kramer shifted his attention to the middle-aged man. "John, we'll discuss this in a moment."

"Plan? What plan?" Will asked.

Kramer turned back to Will, leaning back in his chair. "All in good time, Mr. Davenport. Your questions will be answered. You say the boy was killed. How did this happen?"

"Before I start story time, how about you tell me why you neglected to mention that I'd be dealing with truckloads of gunmen?"

Sighing, Kramer folded his hands together. "Honestly, Mr. Davenport, we never expected you to encounter them at all. Apparently they are more persistent than we expected, although I agree with John. For them to kill the boy is inconsistent with their primary objective."

"You mean you think they would have kidnapped him?"

"No, more like retained him."

"Like you have retained your guest?"

He shrugged. "In a matter of speaking. How do you know he was killed?"

"His mother and I were out of the truck when we were ambushed. We took cover in the trees along the road and the truck exploded."

"So you didn't see him actually die?"

Will paused and sipped his coffee as he watched the younger man. He tried to look unaffected by the conversation, but his face had lost some of its color. Will set the cup down on the table. "No, but I didn't see him get out either."

"This makes no sense," John said, turning to Kramer. "They would never kill him. Davenport lies."

Will shrugged and pretended to be bored with the conversation. "Ask his mother if you like. We saw the truck explode and then we were chased into the forest where they tried to kill us."

"You mean kill *you*?" John asked.

"No, the next time we encountered them one of them made it very clear that Emma was wanted dead. He said there was a bounty on her head. Her very dead head."

"That makes more sense, I can see why they would want her dead. But I don't believe the boy's dead. They wanted him alive for years." John calmed down as he reasoned with himself. The younger man's color had returned to his face. Will was no closer to comprehending any of it. He understood why someone would want Jake, but why Emma?

"They almost succeeded in killing her," Kramer stated. Will knew it was a question.

"The odds were stacked against us. Eight to one, the one being me."

"But you escaped unscathed," the young man said with a derisive tone. He narrowed his gaze at Will, making no attempt to hide his scorn.

Will turned his full attention to the man, their eyes locking. Will's cold, hard stare finally made the man look away. "As I said before, a little advance notice of our party guests would have been nice. I could have planned more accordingly. As it was, I did what I could with what I had."

"What took you so long to get here?" the young man asked with a sneer. "Your deadline was yesterday."

"As I mentioned before, we were detained. After the truck exploded, we were chased into the woods and we got lost. She wasn't in much shape to travel, considering she just watched her son die in an explosion."

"And it took you two days to get out?"

"We were on foot, unarmed at that point, lost in the woods. Your guest was incoherent with grief. We weren't traveling very quickly."

"How did you fight off eight men if you were unarmed?"

Will leaned forward with his elbows on the table, glaring at the younger man. "Is there a point to this conversation? Because last time I checked, I was hired to deliver her alive, which I did." Will leaned back again and shrugged. "Sure, she's slightly damaged, but after what we went through, you're lucky you got only slightly damaged."

"But you didn't deliver her on time." The young man's eyes narrowed on Will. "A lot of good she does us now." He turned to Kramer, curling his upper lip. "I still say she's not the one."

"Alex," Kramer said, his voice stern. "Many disagree with you. Even our opposition believes she is."

Will watched Alex out of the corner of his eye. He was a complete asshole but something else about him grated on Will.

"You were told to have her delivered by the fourth day," Alex said. "Today is the fifth. Even if it wasn't too late it would be most difficult given her condition."

"What would be most difficult?" Will asked, his instincts screaming something was off.

"Alex," Kramer interrupted. "I've told you time and time again that you can't force destiny. You can only try to harness your side to it."

"And as always Scott, we shall agree to disagree. We can't lie around waiting for things to happen. Sometimes we have to make them happen. We wouldn't be in this situation if you had listened to me sooner."

"Alex…"

Alex crossed his arms and scowled like a petulant child. Will would have found him amusing if he weren't so potentially dangerous to Emma.

"So you say I've delivered her too late," Will said. "If she's too late, then why have me deliver her at all?"

"Because not all of us fall under Alex's philosophy," Kramer said. "We shall simply wait."

"Wait?" Alex spit out in disgust. "That's all you do Scott, is wait. Waiting is what has us in this predicament."

"Alex, no one else sees a predicament but you."

"Again, I ask is there a point to this conversation?" Will interrupted. "She's here a day late and I'm more than a dollar short."

"If I have anything to say about it, you won't be paid at all," Alex said.

"Alex," A disarming smile lifted the corners of Will's mouth and his eyes held Alex with a razor-sharp focus. "I did not just go to hell and back to *not* be paid. However, you are correct. I did not meet your deadline. So if you choose to not pay me, I understand, but I will be taking your guest with me when I leave."

"Now, now," Kramer lifted his hands and patted the air. "This is nonsense. Mr. Davenport, you will most definitely be paid. The assignment turned out to be more than we expected which brings me to our next topic." He paused and opened the folder in front of him. "I told you this assignment was also a test, which, of course, you passed." He glanced up from the folder, a grim look on his face. "Things are changing."

Will felt the air around him turn cold. The mark on his arm grew uncomfortably warm as apprehension spread like a choking vine.

Kramer didn't seem to notice. "We are entering a new, unprecedented era. We find ourselves in need of associates with a different sort of skill sets than we are used to having at our immediate disposal. Skill sets you possess." Kramer looked down at the file. "William Marcus Davenport. Age: Thirty-two. Born: Kansas City, Missouri. Profession: Mercenary."

"Mercenary has such negative connotations," Will said with a sarcastic tone. "I prefer freelance security."

"University of Missouri, Bachelors' degree in history, summa cum laude."

"This blast from the past have a point?"

"Bear with me. You should be proud of these accomplishments."

"Yeah, that stellar history degree has been extremely helpful with my career choice."

"U.S. Marine Corp, Recon Unit, served seven years, rank E-6, dishonorable discharge, reason classified."

"Yeah, I could tell you but then I'd have to kill you," Will smirked. He really didn't like where this was headed.

Kramer smiled. "Lucky for us we have contacts who can obtain such information." He pulled a pair of glasses from inside his suit jacket and placed them on his nose. "Looks like a mission went bad, disobeying direct orders from a superior, a school full of children was involved." His face lifted as he peered over the top of his glasses at Will. "Does any of this sound familiar, Mr. Davenport?"

Will gripped his coffee cup, wondering how it didn't break from the pressure. If Emma weren't depending on him, he'd punch this guy and walk out. Instead, his cocky grin lifted one corner of his mouth and he winked. "Like I said, I'd have to kill you. Fortunately for you, I've reached my quota for the week."

"Were you given a direct order to not infiltrate the school?"

Will leaned back in his chair in a casual pose that belied his demeanor. "Tell me again why we're having this discussion?"

Kramer removed his glasses, setting them on the table. "I assure you, Mr. Davenport, it will be well worth your time."

"I had a decorated military history before the incident as well as an interesting and widely varied professional career since. Isn't that why you hired me, Mr. Kramer? I see no benefit to discussing it."

Kramer sat back in his chair, resting his elbows on the armrests and tapping his index fingers together. "I told you earlier I believe you are a man who sees what he wants and doesn't let things get in his way. Before your *incident* you had a history of ruthlessness. Was this the case in the incident involving the school?"

Inwardly, Will squirmed at the memory. He had spent the last three years doing his best to forget it. "I was given intelligence that led me to believe a high-ranking terrorist official was located on the premises. I believed we had the element of surprise on our side. I believed we could get in, capture him and get out without civilian casualties. I was wrong." He spoke with a casualness that surprised him. A few sentences of explanation that sounded so logical, so justified. If only it quieted the screams haunting his memories.

"And you were court-martialed?"

He sighed. This was pointless. "You have all of this information. What are you getting at?"

"Did you give any thought to the fact that you were disobeying direct orders?"

Will's face hardened. "I believed the benefits outweighed the risks."

"Excellent." Kramer's face beamed.

Will raised his eyebrows. "Excellent? Excellent that dozens of kids were killed?"

"No, of course the loss of the children's lives was most unfortunate, but did you obtain your suspect?"

"Yes."

"You saw your objective and you went after it. That is exactly the type of man we are looking for. We need someone to think bigger than the rules. We need him to consider the objective and to go after them, no matter what the cost. The end justifies the means."

"Even if forty kids lost their lives?"

"Your objective was achieved. How many men, women and children would your suspect have killed? Twenty? Fifty? One hundred? Thousands?"

Will shook his head. "You can't be serious."

"I'm deadly serious." The glint in Kramer's eye told Will he was. "We believe your skills will be a benefit to our organization."

"You're telling me that you want to hire me because I'm responsible for burning up a bunch of kids? What kind of organization do you run?" Will felt nauseated. It was bad enough he committed such a heinous act, now this guy applauded it. His skin crawled knowing these same people wanted Emma, for a reason he still didn't comprehend.

"One you want to work for," Kramer said with pride. "Our director will be arriving this evening to meet our guest. He will want to meet you as well and he'll share the details of your employment opportunity. I think we're done here."

Kramer closed the file, but Alex put his hand down on the table. "Not yet. I want to know what took him so long to bring her here."

Kramer turned to Alex. "That was already resolved.

"Not to my satisfaction." Alex drummed the table top with his fingers.

Will raised an eyebrow and waited.

"It's what, a two-day drive from Texas to South Dakota? You arrive in five days. The math doesn't add up, but then again, you were a history major. Maybe math isn't your thing."

Will wouldn't mind ripping this guy's head off and it looked like a pretty simple task. But outwardly, he appeared unperturbed. "Well, *Alex*, we had to make a few detours. You know what those are, right? When you can't go the way you're supposed to because something blocks your path? Yeah, well that just so happened to be a bunch of SUVs full of men with M16s. I was told you wanted your delivery alive so I did my best to ensure that happened. That meant hiding, sometimes backtracking and several times it meant actual gun battles. All of this added up to a few extra days. My apologies."

Alex didn't look appeased, but remained silent.

Kramer cleared his throat. "Mr. Davenport, I'm sure you're tired after the last few days so we'll have you escorted back to your apartment. I will let you know when you can expect to meet with Mr. Warren."

Will walked out of the room, his thoughts racing. Emma was deemed necessary, yet Alex didn't think she was *the one*. What did that mean and did it have anything to do with the marks on her shoulder? What would happen if Alex found out about them?

Alex was dangerous.

Worrying was wasted energy, yet his mind refused to listen and it spread like a cancer, eating through the neat little container he tried to contain it in. He wanted to chuck it all and go to Emma, to know that she was safe. But he'd just have to wait.

CHAPTER TWENTY-TWO

EMMA woke to searing pain in her leg. Her eyes flew open in alarm and realized she was in a hospital bed. She turned her head to scan the room. A nurse sat on a stool in the corner of the room, writing on a chart. An IV pole hung at the top of the bed, with several bags attached.

"Where's Will?" she asked, her voice a whisper from her scratchy throat.

The young woman glanced up from the chart with a smile. "Oh, you're awake." Putting down the pen, she walked over and put her stethoscope buds in her ears. "Are you in pain?" She placed the cold metal end on Emma's chest.

"My leg burns," Emma moaned and reached down, but the nurse grabbed her hand.

"That's normal. I can give you more pain medicine. Don't touch it, you don't want to rip out your stitches."

"Where's Will?"

The nurse took the stethoscope out of her ears and wrote something on the chart. "Who?"

"Will. Where's Will?"

The woman looked up, confused. "I'm sorry, I don't know who that is."

Emma's head swam with pain and confusion from the drugs. "He's the man who brought me here. Where is he?" Her voice raised in panic.

The nurse patted Emma's arm. "I'm sorry. I have no idea who that is but you need to calm down. You're body has been through enough stress."

"I want Will." Even through the foggy chaos swirling in her mind, she knew he wouldn't voluntarily leave her. Why didn't the nurse know who he was?

"Emmanuella, I don't know who Will is, but I can try to find out for you."

Terror kindled in her heart and spread like a wildfire, the flames licking at her limited control. The nurse knew her real name. "Why did you call me Emmanuella?" The monitor beeped faster.

"Emmanuella..." the nurse's voice rose in alarm.

"Stop calling me that!" Emma sat up in the bed. Pain shot through her leg and up to the rest of her body; she gasped in surprise. Blackness eroded the edges of her mind. She took a deep breath to push it away, jerking on the IV lines. She had to get out of here. She had to find Will.

The nurse pushed a call button. "I need help in here." She grabbed Emma's arm, trying to pull down. "Emmanuella, lay down. You just had surgery!"

"Let go of me!" Emma twisted out of her hold and threw the blanket off her leg, revealing a thick bandage wrapped around her left thigh.

Two men in dark uniforms rushed into the room. One stood next to the nurse and the other came around to the other side. The nurse ran to a cart next to the wall. The two men grabbed Emma's arms and pushed her down on her back.

She tried to pull away, but they pinned her shoulders and hips to the bed. Emma kicked and pain stabbed her left leg, overwhelming her consciousness.

"Emmanuella, you need to calm down!" the nurse shouted. "You're going to hurt yourself!"

"Stop calling me that! *Will!*" Emma screamed.

The nurse grabbed Emma's hand while Emma jerked and twisted.

"Hold her down! I've got to give her this sedative before she hurts herself."

One of the men lay across her upper arm and chest, smashing her into the bed. The pressure crushed her chest and she fought for breath, adding to her rising hysteria. Ice filled her veins and a dark heavy cloud filtered through her head until there was nothing.

****

Will stood at the entrance of the school. His team advanced past him, down the darkened hallways. The only light came from the small windows of the classroom doors. Children studied in their classes, eager for their day to be dismissed in another hour giving Will plenty of time to get in and out. Surveillance told him that the terrorist was holed up in the upper floor. It was perfect; the sick bastard was using kids as a shield. It gave him a false sense of security. No one would risk the lives of children to capture him.

The son of a bitch was wrong.

Will waved two fingers, telling the men to continue on down the hall. He had the element of surprise on his side and he planned to use it. The brass in D.C. had told him to wait, but they were notorious for waiting, wasting precious hours with their theoretical debates. It was so easy for them to sit in their comfy chairs in an air-conditioned room looking at their PowerPoints and scenario boards. Will and his men didn't have that luxury. They melted in 130-degree heat and faced the reality that men like this asshole created. How many terrorists had Will seen get away? How many times had *this* man gotten away? Will was done waiting.

The halls were ghostly quiet, more so than he would expect in a school full of children, but it was after lunch and the hottest part of the day. Everyone was sluggish, part of the reason he chose this hour for the assault. His team moved to the doorway leading to the upper level, flanking the door while Will held back, taking up the rear. They waited for his cue. A sudden chill ran up Will's back. Something was wrong. He froze, trying to determine the source while his men watched him, expectant. But, unable to discern a problem, he gave them the sign. One of his men jerked on the door and an explosion sucked the air out of the hall. Will flew several feet down the corridor, landing on his ass. He recovered seconds later, jumping to his feet. Half his team was gone and the end of the hall had erupted in a ball of flames. The surviving men scrambled in confusion. Will ordered them to get the kids out of the school.

Black smoke melded with the screams of the children. Will grabbed the first doorknob he came to, discovering it was locked. He peered in the window and saw small bodies huddled together in the center of the room. He beat on the door, trying to get them to open it, then ran to the next one and found it locked, too. Holding up his M4, he shot the door knob, splintering the wood and he kicked it in, shouting in his limited Arabic. "*Ekroj halan!*"

The children ran down the hall, crying and coughing.

He had only emptied two classrooms before he was forced to evacuate, but he took comfort knowing that his men had emptied others. Fresh air filled his lungs as he stumbled from the entrance, setting off a fit of coughing. The screams still filled his ears and he ran around the side of the building. Small bodies fell out the first-floor windows and he gasped in relief until he saw children trapped behind a partially open window. Will took off running toward them, their terrified faces pressed to the glass. Then he felt it, the anticipation of something about to happen. A moment later, the second explosion burst through the window, shattering glass and the sides of the concrete wall, the flames absorbing the screams.

A ringing jerked Will from his dream. He'd fallen asleep on the sofa, watching television. He ran his hands through his hair, sucking deep breaths to calm his growing hysteria. It took him several seconds to realize the sound was the phone in the kitchen.

"Hello?"

"Mr. Davenport," Kramer's voice greeted him. "I'm sorry to disturb you, but I have an unusual request."

Will forced himself to calm down and listen. "Yes?"

"Our guest keeps asking for you. We wouldn't disturb you with this, but she's in danger of injuring herself. The medical staff has sedated her several times, but every time she regains consciousness, she begins calling for you. Would you be willing to go see her? Since she's asking for you, they think perhaps you can convince her to cooperate. The medical staff is quite concerned she'll injure herself further."

Will's breath caught in his throat and it took him a moment to answer.

Kramer misunderstood his hesitation. "I realize this is unusual. I assure you this really is a special case."

"No, it's fine." Will shook his head to clear it. "I can see her."

"Someone will be there in a few moments."

Will paced the living room until the guard arrived to escort him to the medical facility. The sun was high when they exited the building and the day had warmed, making his skin clammy under the long sleeves of his shirt. He rolled them up as he walked, trying to hide his anxiety.

When they reached the building, they took an elevator to the second floor. As soon as the doors opened, he heard her cries. She was calling for him. Will forced himself to shorten his strides as he approached her room. He didn't need to ask which one was hers. He knew.

Walking to her bedside, he tried to appear detached, but the sight of her blew any chance of that. She struggled against two men who held her down on either side of the bed. Tears streamed down her face, but her eyes filled with relief when she saw him. When Will reached her, he pushed the man on his side out of the way .

"Will," she cried in a raspy voice.

Will noticed her arms. "Why is she tied down?" he asked over his shoulder as he worked to undo the restraint.

"She was hurting herself. We did it to protect her."

He untied her left arm and she bolted up, clinging to his shirt. He burned with anger and shame. He had been sleeping in an extravagant apartment while she was tied to a bed and terrified.

Will pulled her hand from his shirt and held it in his. "I'm coming around to the other side to untie you," he whispered in her ear.

Her desperate eyes searched his face for reassurance as he walked around the bed and began to work on the other restraint.

When freed, she threw her arms around his neck and pulled him down. "Where were you?"

Indecision stopped him, but her need won out. He sat on the side of the bed and held her in his arms. He stroked her hair. "Shh, it's okay. I'm here now."

"The nurse didn't know who you were. Why?"

"I don't know. I'm here now."

"Please, don't leave me."

"I won't." *Until they force me.* It was a matter of time before Kramer found out that Will had an attachment to her, then what would happen? "Emma, lay down, okay? You're going to hurt your leg."

"No. I want to leave. Now."

He buried his face into her hair, inhaling her scent. His gut tightened. "You got shot and almost died. They're taking care of you. You can't leave yet."

Emma pulled back and looked into his face, her eyes full of fear. "They know my real name, Will. Did you tell them?"

"No."

"Then how do they know?"

"I don't know."

She shook her head. "I'm not staying. I have to find Jake."

"Emma, be reasonable." He lowered his voice. "You almost died. Even if you leave right now, you can't find Jake in this condition."

"I'm scared," she whispered.

It surprised him she admitted her fear. *She trusts me.* He cleared his throat, trying to dislodge the choking lump of betrayal. "I'll stay with you, okay?"

Her lip quivered. "Thank you."

Will helped her lean back on the bed then sat next to her, holding her hand. Her eyes closed and she fell asleep. He watched the steady rise and fall of her chest, brooding for the thousandth time over how he would get her out of this.

****

Emma woke, her hand held down and panic returned. Until she spotted Will.

"Will? Where are we?"

He sighed and squeezed her hand tighter. His jaw tensed. "A place where you're safe."

"I don't feel safe."

"I know. I'll try to make sure that doesn't happen again." His eyes darkened. "Emma, no matter what happens, no matter what you hear, you have to know something."

"What?" she hesitated in apprehension, not sure she wanted to know.

"When we met, I may not have had the best of intentions. But they changed. *I* changed." He stopped, releasing a heavy exhale as he closed his eyes for a moment. When he opened them, they were filled with worry and dread. "You made me think I could be a better person. And you… I just couldn't do it. But then… I did it anyway and I'm so sorry."

"Will, you're not making any sense."

"I know." His eyes sunk closed and his face tensed. "None of this makes sense."

This was not the confident, in-control Will she knew and it scared her. He was all she had at the moment and she couldn't afford to lose him, too. Her nails dug into his palm as she tightened her grip. "It's okay, Will. Remember what you said? It doesn't matter what we did in the past. We're different people now."

He shook his head. "I wish it were that easy." he whispered, his eyes glistening. "You don't know what I've done. How can you just accept me without even knowing?"

"Because I know you, the real you. I saw through you a long time ago, Will."

He stood and leaned over her, gazing into her eyes. Then he kissed her with an intensity that made her anxious. "Emma, I love you."

Her breath caught in surprise. That was the last thing she expected him to say. Before she could respond, someone cleared his throat behind her. "Well, this does change things a bit."

Will froze, gripping her hand tighter. Emma turned to see a man standing in the doorway.

Both men locked gazes until the stranger stepped to the side of the bed and graced Emma with a smile that didn't reach his eyes. "Emmanuella, we haven't had the pleasure of meeting yet. I am Scott Kramer." He held his hand out.

Emma didn't take it. Will claimed she was safe here, but she had felt safer in the woods. At least out there she'd had a gun. "How do you people know my real name?"

"We know many things about you."

Emma's body tensed, shooting waves of pain through her leg. The beeping of her heart monitor increased. *I've heard those words before.*

Will straightened, squaring his shoulders. "She prefers Emma," he said, his tone a challenge.

Kramer glanced from Emma to Will, his eyes cold. "I see. I shall notify the staff. Mr. Davenport, I would like a word with you in the hall, please." He tilted his head toward Emma. "He shall only be a moment," Kramer said before he left the room .

"Will, what's going on? Who is he?" She searched his face for answers only to find more questions. Worry lines wrinkled his forehead.

He kissed her on the cheek. "Don't worry. I'll be back in a minute."

The nurse walked toward the bed with a syringe. Will grabbed her arm. "Don't you dare give her anything while I'm gone or you *will* regret it."

****

Will entered the hallway, expecting to face his sentencing. Kramer waited at the end of the hall, one hand tapping the other behind his back. He stared at the Black Hills in the distance. Will suspected he was considering his next move rather than enjoying the view. Will approached him in a defiant stance. No way in hell he would he slink to this man.

"I'll be honest; I'm not sure how to handle this development." Kramer kept his gaze on the landscape. "It makes perfect sense if you think about it. Destiny always has a way of working things out."

Will had no idea what he meant and remained silent.

Kramer looked down at Will's left forearm, the mark fully exposed.

Will inwardly cringed as the realization hit him. It wasn't his staying with Emma that sealed their fate. It was his mark.

"Mr. Warren will need to speak with you this evening. You can stay with her until then if you like," Kramer paused and stared into Will's eyes. "Of course, you will want to."

This wasn't what Will expected to happen. He paused and as he tried to process it. "Thank you."

"I cannot guarantee what will happen after tonight, but you have this afternoon." Kramer shook his head in bewilderment. "This is not what we anticipated at all." He walked to the men standing outside the door, leaving Will to follow behind.

"Mr. Davenport will stay with Ms. Thompson. He is not allowed to leave. See that he has anything he needs," He raised an eyebrow. "Within reason, of course."

"Afraid I'll request an AK-47?"

"The thought crossed my mind."

It crossed Will's as well.

"Mr. Davenport, one more thing. I completely understand your need to protect her, even more than you realize, but if you could refrain from terrorizing the civilian staff, it would be most appreciated."

"As long as no one hurts her, they have nothing to worry about."

Will walked past the guards, into the room. The nurse sat in a chair next to the bed. She looked up at the sound of the door opening. A wave of panic swept over her face when she saw Will.

"Did you give her anything?"

"No."

"What were you going to give her?"

"Pain medication."

Will took Emma's hand and his face softened. "Do you need anything for pain?"

Her eyes narrowed with confusion. "No."

Will turned back to the nurse. "Then leave."

The nurse's mouth dropped. "But I need to monitor her."

"You can come in every hour and check her vitals. Otherwise, get the hell out."

The nurse grabbed the chart and ran out the door.

"Will, what's going on?" Emma's voice rose in panic and her grip on his hand tightened.

"Emma, there's something I need to tell you. The real reason I helped you."

CHAPTER TWENTY-THREE

WILL sat in the chair next to the bed. He held her hand as his eyes sank closed. "Emma, I'm not who you think I am."

"Will?" She told herself to stay calm, but his nervousness made the hairs on her arms stand on end. What could he possibly tell her?

His eyes opened, full of regret. He rested his elbows on the bed, still holding her hand in a firm grasp.

She reminded herself this was Will, not the Will she met a week ago, but the Will who risked his life for her several times. What could he have done that would be that bad? "It's okay Will. You know what? I don't care. We'll just forget our pasts and move forward, just the three of us when we get Jake."

His mouth lifted into a wry smile. "I wish it were that easy." He paused. "Emma, I wasn't a good person before."

She shook her head, her eyes stinging. "Will, I don't care who you were. I only care about who you are now."

"Emma you need to know."

"Why?"

He grimaced. "Because if I don't tell you, Kramer and his people will."

"Who's Kramer?"

Will took a deep breath. "He works for an organization that I don't know much about." He paused and looked into her eyes. "They hired me to do a job."

Emma tensed, jerking her leg, but she forced herself to ignore the pain. Her next question could change everything. "What was your job?"

"Emma, do you trust me?"

Her voice hardened. "You didn't answer my question, Will."

"Answer mine first. Do you trust me?"

He had proven himself to her time and time again but could she trust him? She studied his face. His lips pressed together in determination while his eyes pleaded with her to understand. She steeled her heart, preparing for it to be broken. "Yes," she lied.

"My job was to find you."

She kept her face expressionless, but the wild beeping of the monitor gave her way. She reached over and jerked out the cord. "Why?"

"I didn't know. I was only told to find you and bring you to someone in South Dakota."

"Kramer?"

"Yes."

She ripped her hand out of Will's. "Are they going to kill me?"

"God, Emma, no. They won't hurt you. They wanted you alive. Do you really think I would bring you here if I thought they would hurt you?"

A day ago she would have sworn no. Now she wasn't so sure. "Why would they want me? Did they want Jake, too?"

"No, they didn't want Jake. That's what I didn't get after I met you. Why didn't they want Jake? He seemed like the obvious choice. But they only wanted you."

They didn't want Jake. Oh my God. Oh my God. Her eyes widened and she couldn't hold back her terror. "Did you have something to do with Jake?"

"No! I would never hurt you and I would never hurt Jake. I swear."

"How am I supposed to believe that? You brought me here!" She squashed the tears that burned her eyes. Tears wouldn't help her. She needed answers. "You were supposed to bring me here all along?"

"Yes." He paused. "But I changed my mind. In Kansas. When we went to Colorado instead of South Dakota, I was stalling."

"But the morning Jake was kidnapped you said we were going to South Dakota."

He shook his head. "I had this crazy idea that if I got rid of you my life would go back to normal. You scared me. You made me wonder if my life could be different and I didn't know how to handle it. But I wouldn't have handed you over. I regretted it the minute I made the decision that morning."

"But you brought me here anyway, Will. How can I trust you?"

"I didn't want to bring you here, but if I hadn't, you would have died."

"Why do they want me?" she asked, a hard edge in her voice.

"I don't know, I haven't figured it out yet." He ran his fingers through his hair with a groan. "I knew they wanted you alive. They were very explicit about that. So when you were shot and got so sick, this was the only safe place to bring you. I knew they had money and were powerful enough to protect you. If I took you to a hospital, the men who took Jake would have found you and finished their job. They would have killed you." His eyes clouded. "This was my only option."

She thought of everything he had done for her, how he risked his life to save her. Had it all been an act? Had he been doing it because he cared about her or because he was getting paid? She thought of the concern on his face when she climbed the tree in the woods. The panic in his eyes when he discovered she'd been shot. The way he'd taken care of her with such tenderness after Jake.

"Do you believe me?" he asked in a whisper.

Even now, she saw the devotion on his face. He brought her here, didn't that mean his job was done? Then why was he here with her now? "Yes." It might be insanity, but she did.

"Do you hate me?"

She moved her head with a slight, nearly imperceptible shake. "No." She felt betrayed and she didn't totally trust him, but when she searched her heart, there was no hate.

He grabbed her hand and closed his eyes in relief.

"So now what?" she asked. "You really don't know why they want me?"

"No.

"Then how do we find out?"

"I don't know, but I hope to get answers tonight. I'm supposed to meet with the director of the organization."

"So we have to wait?"

"It's our only option at this point."

"No, it's not. We can leave right now."

Guilt washed over his face before he hid it with a frown. "Emma, we already discussed this. You're too sick to leave. You need to stay until you're better."

"I can't leave, can I? Not because of my leg, but because I'm not allowed to."

He shifted his gaze and the muscles of his jaw tightened. "Yes."

She turned away from him, hurt anew. Even if everything he said was true, he had brought her to this prison. But he was her only ally she had at this point and being alone and tied down terrified her. "Will you stay with me until then?"

"Emma, I'm not leaving you unless I'm forced to."

She searched his face. "And will they make you?"

He hesitated. "Yes, at some point, but not right now. Kramer promised I could stay until I meet with the director."

Which meant that she had to trust Will to get her answers. The answers he chose to tell her.

"Emma, I promise you, I'll die before I will ever let anyone hurt you."

"Stop it, Will. I don't want to hear it."

"It's true. Remember when you asked me what my mark meant? I told you that it meant I'm yours."

"You were being a jerk."

"No. I was telling the truth. Jake tied us together. I'm bound to you now, whether you like it or not." He leaned forward. "And it means more than that, Emma. I love you."

"Cut the bullshit, Will. You brought me here. Your job is done."

"It's not bullshit." He groaned, rubbing his jaw with his palm. "Will you at least acknowledge that Jake wants us to be together?"

She gave him a curt nod.

"There's more. I think I'm bound to you on a deeper level… supernaturally."

She rolled her eyes in disgust. "What the hell does that mean?"

"In the woods before you got shot, I worried that something had happened to you. I concentrated on you and I could *feel* you, I knew you were alive. I think this is more than just a mark. It links me to you."

"You could *feel* me?" Sarcasm dripped from her words.

"Yes, I knew you were safe, scared, but safe. I know it sounds crazy, but how could it be crazier than anything else we've gone through?"

She tilted her head and glared. "Tell me what I'm thinking right now."

"I don't need to read your mind to know what you're thinking. Besides, I didn't read your thoughts. I just *felt* you."

"Fine, I'll pretend what you say is true. Does it work both ways? Can I feel you?"

"I don't know, but for some reason I don't think so. You have several symbols on your back. I only have one. I belong to you, not the other way around."

She shook her head. "This is bullshit, Will. You belong to me? What the fuck does that mean?"

"Honestly? I think it means I follow your orders."

"Finally, something I can use. I order you to get me out of here."

"I can't do that, Emma."

"Then what good are you, Will?"

His eyes widened in surprise and hurt. It pissed her off he had the nerve to look upset.

"There's something else," he said. "Jake told me a prophecy when he gave me the mark."

"What prophecy? Jake never told me a prophecy."

"He chanted it in another language when he was in his trance, but I understood it in my mind. Now it's burned into my head. I couldn't forget it if I wanted to."

"The land will fall desolate and cold
As it waits for the promised ones.
God resides within the queen
While she hides among the people of the exile land
Hunted for that which she must lose
One who is named protector, The Chosen One,
Shall be a shield, counselor, companion

"The elevated one will arise from great sorrow
In the full moon after the summer solstice

His powers will be mighty and powerful
He will rise up to rule the land
The supplanter will challenge him
But only one will be overcome
By that which has no price"

Emma shook her head. "What does that mean?"

"Everyone keeps saying things are changing. Jake said it. Kramer said it. Some kind of war is coming. Jake said I'm the Chosen One in the prophecy. I think you're the queen."

Emma snorted. "*I'm* a queen? You got that part wrong."

"Jake said I'm supposed to protect you, just like the prophecy says. The prophecy *Jake* gave me. Like it or not, you're the queen. It makes sense that I would serve you."

"No, that doesn't make sense at all. That's just plain crazy."

"Emma I've had days to think about this. *The queen hides among the people.* You've been hiding for years, trying to get lost in crowds of people. Right?"

"I guess…"

"*Hunted for what she must lose.*"

Emma looked up at him in surprise. "Jake." *Oh, my God.* Could what he said actually be true?

"Exactly. Jake told me I am The Chosen One —*shield, counselor, companion.* That's me. And you. Don't you see? Jake must have known something was going to happen to him. He said he had to be sure for *you*. I think I was hired for you by your son. He loved you, Emma and wanted to make sure you were okay."

Her eyes narrowed. "*Loves*. Not loved, Will. Jake is still alive."

"You're probably right. Kramer and his guys think so, too. Maybe that's part of the war, saving Jake. But what does the second part mean? Who is the Great One and who is the Supplanter? And what that has to do with us, I don't know."

She closed her eyes, overwhelmed. The ache in her leg had become a slow burn and she had trouble concentrating.

"You're overdoing it, Emma. Does your leg hurt?"

"No," she said through gritted teeth.

"Yes, it does. You're as pale as a ghost. I'll call the nurse to give you something for the pain."

"No!" She grabbed his hand. "It'll knock me out and I won't be able to wake up if I need to."

"Emma, you need to rest to get better. If I'm going to get you out of here, I need you as whole as possible."

She held her breath. "Are you really going to help me get out of here?"

"There's no way in hell I'll leave you."

She studied his face. "Okay."

Will pushed the call button. The nurse came in and saw the disconnected monitor cord, shooting a glare in Will's direction as she reconnected it. After she took Emma's vitals and checked her leg, she injected a syringe into Emma's IV.

"You should fall asleep in a few minutes." The nurse patted Emma's hand and glowered at Will before she left the room.

The drugs already made her groggy. "You made a friend there."

"It's my irresistible charm. What can I say? Women love me."

Her body tingled and her head became foggier. Panic rushed in as thoughts of being tied down popped into her head. "Don't leave me." She gripped his hand.

He reached up and brushed a strand of hair off her face. "I won't. I'll sit here while you sleep, okay?"

****

Will watched her fall asleep. Although the prophecy seemed to fit everything to this point, he wasn't sure he really believed it. For one thing, his gut told him they would take Emma away from him. He didn't see how he could protect her and be her companion if he wasn't with her. He'd figure out a way to get her out. He'd been in worse situations.

She turned her head and a strand of hair fell across her cheek. He carefully brushed it back, catching it in his fingers. He loved her long, thick hair. Memories of the morning by the fire pit washed through his mind. It was the first time he touched her hair. The first time he kissed her. No, attacked her would be more appropriate. It embarrassed him now that he treated her that way, especially after she told him about Jake's father. She deserved better.

He realized there was so much about her he didn't know, that he might never know. A pit of grief opened in his chest, mourning everything he would miss with her. He carefully lifted her hand to his lips and kissed it. When would he hold her hand again?

Will looked up at the clock on the wall. Seven o'clock. There couldn't be much time left.

As if on cue, the door opened and a man stood at the opening. It was time. Will lay her hand down. Would this be the last time he ever saw her? He stared at her sleeping face and bent over her, kissing her lips lightly. "I love you, Emma. I promise to get you out of this." He got up and followed the man out of the room.

CHAPTER TWENTY-FOUR

WILL moved down a hall flanked by the four men sent to escort him. He was somewhat flattered that they thought he needed four guards, but then again, he probably did. If Emma wasn't lying in a hospital bed and if he didn't have the hope of some answers waiting, he'd take them out and escape.

They walked across the compound, to the building with Will's quarters. The elevator took them to the floor of the conference room, and they stopped at a door at the opposite end of the hall. One of the guards knocked. The door swung open and two men in suits ushered Will through the door, pausing first to pat him down. They took the gun holstered to his leg and led him down a hall into a richly appointed living room, then left. Will was surprised they hadn't checked him for weapons sooner. But before this afternoon, they had no reason to.

"Good evening, Mr. Davenport. Please, come in. Can I make you a drink?" A man called from the far side of the room. He stood next to a wet bar and grabbed two glasses from a shelf. "I usually have someone do this, but I wanted more privacy this evening." The man was tall and movie-star handsome. He looked familiar.

"I'm not much of a drinker, actually."

"Well, tonight 's a special occasion. I insist. I'm having scotch."

"Then scotch it is." Will glanced around at the furnishings, disgusted. The money spent to decorate one room could have fed a Third World country for a year.

"I see you're admiring the décor." The man pulled a decanter off the counter and poured scotch into the glasses. "I prefer mine neat. Is that okay with you."

"Sure. Nice place you have here."

"It serves its purpose." He picked up both glasses and handed one to Will.

"And that purpose is?"

The man laughed. "Not one to beat around the bush, are you? I like that. Do you know who I am, Mr. Davenport?"

"No, can't say that I do."

"Not much into politics, I guess?"

"Not if I can help it."

The man laughed again and extended his hand to Will. "Let me formally introduce myself. Phillip Warren."

Even the politically ignorant knew the name Phillip Warren. It surprised Will that he didn't recognize him. He shook Warren's hand. "Senator, excuse my ignorance." The fact that he was shaking the hand of the senior senator for the state of California and a presidential candidate in the next election scared the shit out of him. What the hell kind of mess was Emma caught up in?

Senator Warren waved his hand. "Nonsense. It's good for me to be grounded every once in awhile. It's not advisable to have people fawn over you all the time. Please,

Mr. Davenport, have a seat." He walked toward a pair of club chairs by the window and sat in one.

"Thank you, Senator," Will said, sitting across from Warren.

"Please, call me Phillip." The senator leaned toward Will and held his glass up to Will's. "To a long and lasting partnership."

Will touched his glass to Phillip's and took a small sip. "In that case, please call me Will."

"Will, I've heard great things about you."

"Then you are a step ahead of me, Phillip. I've ignored politics for some time."

"I find it refreshing to start off at ground zero. I won't hold it against you. Scott thinks you would be a great asset to our organization."

"Again, I'm at a loss. I know nothing about your organization."

"No, you probably wouldn't and we try to keep it that way. We are a secret organization."

"So why tell me?" Will asked.

"You are part of us now." The senator sipped his drink.

Will ignored his statement. "What does Emma have to do with any of this?"

"There you go again, cutting right to the chase. I think Scott is right about you." The senator studied the glass in his hand. "I find it interesting that you don't ask what any of this has to do with you, but instead ask about Ms. Thompson."

"It seems I was pulled into this via Ms. Thompson."

"Not quite true. We've been aware of you for some time. We decided to use you to obtain Ms. Thompson as a test to see if you were a good fit for our organization. We didn't anticipate the trouble you would have. I confess it was short-sighted on our part." He pinched his lips together. "Several things were." He paused, swirling the amber liquid in his glass. "The irony is that we've waited so long yet we neglected some minor details that turned out to be quite important."

"And what would those minor details be?"

The senator set his glass on the table and looked at Will's arm. "I see that the mark is real. There was some question as whether it would be real or metaphoric."

Will said nothing.

The senator pointed to the mark. "That was an unexpected minor detail. However, maybe not so minor. Will, do you know what it means?"

Will decided playing stupid would be the best way to get more information. "The mark? No."

"May I first ask when and how you received it?"

"Several days ago. It just appeared." The less Warren knew, the better.

"Excellent. While you were in close proximity to Ms. Thompson?" He tapped his finger to his chin. "Many have wondered how it would happen. Would he be born with it? Would he have it tattooed without realizing what he had done? The purists said it would just appear and so it did."

"So what does it mean?"

"It means that you, William Davenport, are the long-awaited Chosen One."

"What does that mean?"

The senator waved his hands around in a circular motion. "It's shrouded in a lot of mumbo-jumbo. No one knows for sure, but many have desired the title. It appears Ms. Thompson was the one to give it to you. Some questioned that as well."

"Again, what the hell does it mean?"

"It's all a guess, of course. This is all enveloped in mysterious prophecies. But many speculate that you are bound to her now. That you will feel a tie to her. Do you feel these things, Will?"

Will scrutinized him. Phillip Warren was a very powerful politician for a reason, and that reason was his innate ability to make people trust him and do what he wanted. He reminded himself he couldn't trust this man.

"Not necessarily."

The senator laughed. "Bravo. Even now, you try to protect her. I heard about your afternoon in her room. There's no need to lie."

"In that case, there's no need for me to confess any feelings I may or may not have for Emma. You have your assumptions."

"Now, now, Will. No need to be defensive. Only an observation on my part. You've been anticipated for so long that there will be many questions. You should expect it. You should also expect many enemies. It was presumed a member of our organization would be the Chosen One. Many assumed it was dependent on Ms. Thompson, and they thought once she arrived they could approach her and see if it was one of them."

"My apologies for stealing their coveted crown. But what does any of this mean and what does it have to do with Emma?"

"It has everything to do with Emma. She is the prophesied mother of the elevated one."

"The elevated one? You mean Jake?" That would explain why the other group was after him for so long. He struggled to remember the lines.

"Jake? Her first son? No, many speculate that her second son will be the elevated one. It is believed that the Chosen One will be his father, which is what makes him the elevated one."

Will kept his anger in check. "How exactly were all those men going to see if they were the Chosen One?" He clenched his fist.

"Not what you think, Will. She would have been protected."

"*Would* have been?"

"The window of time has passed. It wouldn't do any good now."

"What window of time?" But it all came together as he asked the question. The deadline. Alex being upset she hadn't arrived on time. *Even if it wasn't too late, it would be most difficult given her condition.* The Chosen One was presumed to be the father of the elevated one. She was to arrive during the full moon. *The elevated one will arise from great sorrow* could only mean Emma's agony over Jake's death. *In the full moon after the summer solstice* was the first full moon after the official beginning of summer. His head swam.

That meant that he...

"You're a smart man, Will. I see you're putting the pieces together. Let me ask, did your mark show before or after you impregnated her?"

The fury spilled out before he could keep it in check and he hauled the senator out of his chair by his shirt.

"I really wouldn't do that if I were you," the senator said, lowering his voice. "You have far too much to lose."

Will released him with a shove.

"Have a seat, Will. If you can't control yourself, I'll be forced to have my bodyguards join us. But I prefer the privacy."

Will sat, taking deep breaths.

Phillip Warren assessed him with narrowed eyes. "You're a dilemma for us. You have significance, yet you're not one of us. Some will most likely want you dead, but we don't know the consequences of that, either. If you die, does your power transfer to someone else or is it simply gone? Is it worth the risk to find out? But alive, you are dangerous to us. If only there was some way to make sure you were on our side, to ensure your loyalty."

"Who *are* you people?"

The senator pulled a dining room chair from a table and sat down in front of Will, elbows on his knees, and leaning over to stare into Will's eyes.

"We are a secret organization, Vinco Potentia. A society formed by a select group of students at Brown University."

Will shook his head, trying to focus on the senator's words. He was still trying to process the senator's proclamation that he fathered a child. "Like the Skull and Bones society at Yale."

"Yes, very similar but much more powerful and much more secretive. Our group formed in the 1800s and recruited members who were interested in political influence. Former and present U.S. senators, congressmen, governors, political advisors. Men who made a mark on history with their leadership."

"What does any of that have to do with Emma or me?"

"One of our members was a philosophy major. While still in school, he had a job archiving documents for the philosophy department. One day he came across some documents written by a little-known Italian philosopher, Lorenzo de Luca. De Luca fancied himself to be like Nostradamus; he made predictions. These were generally disregarded and the archival was in regards to his philosophy papers, but our member studied the predictions and found that while on the vague side, they often correlated to incidents in history. He brought the papers to the attention of our organization."

"Does this little story have a point?"

"Patience, Will. We're getting there. The group was divided on the importance. Some thought it was nonsense, but others saw the validity of it. The group splintered and we formed our own sect, using the papers as a basis to help further our own political causes. The papers had predicted World War II, Kennedy's assassination, 9/11, among other things."

"Wait. You're telling me that these things were predicted, yet you did nothing to stop them?"

"Some things furthered our causes, others were too vague to completely understand until after their occurrence. Besides, there are others we did prevent, that the world never knew of."

"How long have you had these papers?"

"About fifty years."

"How many of you are there?"

"About thirty members, all very powerful men in politics or business. All with much to gain with the power that was foretold."

"I still don't get what kind of power you think I have."

"We're not sure of your power, nor Ms. Thompson's, other than she's the mother of the elevated one and the supplanter."

"What?"

"We believe her first son, Jake, is the supplanter, which is why the other group wants him. We disagree over who the winner is. We believe it is her child with you. The other group believes it to be Jake."

"Winner of what?"

Senator Warren sat back and crossed his legs. "Power. Control. Influence over the world."

"You're crazy."

"Any crazier than a mark appearing on your arm?"

Will grimaced at the reminder. Anything that gave this lunatic validity was bad.

"So what? You wait years for these boys to grow up and have some kind of showdown? Then the winner takes over the world?"

"We think that the boys will not necessarily rule themselves, but have influence. It could be that their battle occurs before adulthood."

Will remembered the prophecy that Jake gave him. It didn't fit with the senator's version. Jake's version sounded like the elevated one would rule.

"Can I hear the prophecy?" Will asked.

"I don't see the point."

"If this directly affects me, shouldn't I be allowed to know what it says?"

"Very well." The senator walked over to the bookcase and pulled a small bound book off the shelf.

"Are those the real papers?" If they were, perhaps he could steal them and hold them as ransom for Emma.

"No, the real papers are in a safety deposit box in Washington, D.C." The senator smiled and raised his eyebrows. "I'm not going to make it *that* easy for you." He opened the book and pulled a pair of reading glasses from his pocket.

"The Chosen one will serve
The mother of the two
Elevated and Supplanter
Will battle for control
Their influence will be felt
Across the lands

"The elevated one will

Conceive in the full moon
After the summer solstice
Born of great sorrow
The mother shall accept
Her Chosen One
And he will bear her mark
Protecting her until the end."

It's not the same prophecy.

The senator closed the book and raised a smug eyebrow. "Happy now?"

"Are you fucking kidding me? You're screwing up people's lives over *that*? That's the worst poem I ever heard not to mention a bunch of vague bullshit."

"Yes, I can see how you would think so, but there is other supporting evidence. Dates, locations, all written in a code we had cracked. How do you think we knew where to send you to find Ms. Thompson? How do you think the other people knew where to show up to find you and capture Jake?"

"Jake is dead. He was in the truck when we saw it explode."

"Yes, I know you insist on that, but we believe differently. It doesn't fit with the prophecy."

"Listen to yourself. A grown man talking about some fantasy. That's a bunch of bullshit and you know it."

Warren looked at him for a moment before answering. "You know, Will, I might be inclined to believe you if you hadn't shown up with a mark on your arm that matches the one in this book." When he opened the pages and showed

Will a drawing of his mark, Will knew he lost any chance of reasoning with him.

CHAPTER TWENTY-FIVE

"SO now what?" Will asked.

"Now we must decide what to do with you."

"What about Emma?"

The senator smiled. "You really do care, don't you? What if I told you that our plans are to kill her after she gives birth to her son?"

Will gripped the arms of the chair instead of breaking the senator's neck.

"Aww, just as I thought. I think we can work out an arrangement."

"What kind of arrangement?" Will asked through clenched teeth.

"Your cooperation in exchange for her life. You will work for us and we will provide for her safety."

"Somehow 'provide for her safety' means something completely different to me than 'we won't kill her'."

The senator shrugged. "In either case, she lives. Besides, you know even if we let her leave, the other group would kill her. So technically, we are providing her safety."

Warren was right. They would kill her. "So what am I supposed to do for you?"

"For now, I prefer to keep a close watch on you. The best way to do that is to make you a member of my personal security team."

Will laughed in disbelief. "Are you fucking kidding me?"

"Actually, no. It's brilliant, if I do say so myself. I can personally keep track of you and ensure your loyalty. And if something should happen to me that you caused or could have prevented, Ms. Thompson is disposed of."

Will scoured his mind thinking of a way out of this. The only one he could come up with was to try to escape.

"Will, you are much too obvious. I can see you are searching for another option, but there is none. Suppose you get past all the armed men here, and I must admit it is a possibility. Just remember that you will both be hunted, and not just by our group but the other group as well. This past week will seem like a cakewalk compared to the life you will live. What about when Emma is very pregnant? Or after the baby is born? How hard will it be to run then?"

He was right and Will hated him for it. They couldn't run forever, especially with a baby. Will sank into the chair.

"That's a good boy, listening to reason. I assure you, we will take very good care of her."

"I want more than your assurance, Senator. I want your guarantee. And I assure *you*, that if anyone hurts her I will hunt them down and kill them. But you Mr. Senator, will be first."

"Then I think we've reached an agreement." He beamed with approval. "First I want to meet with Emma, and then you and I will leave for Washington."

Will resisted the urge to ask what he planned to say to her. "I would like to see her before I go."

"I'm sure you would, but I'm not sure that's such a good idea," Senator Warren said.

"The only reason I spent the afternoon with her is because she kept asking for me and hurting herself trying to get to me. If I just disappear, the same thing will happen. Let me tell her goodbye. Please." Will had never begged before, but he was willing to do it for Emma.

Warren tilted his head and smiled. "This is why you will make a valuable asset to my team. You point out subtle things I might miss. See? I'm not a monster, Will. I'm a reasonable man."

Will disagreed, but kept his opinion to himself.

"Let's go see her then. I'm eager to get back to Washington. Lots of things to look forward to. Things are changing."

If one more person tells me that, I'm going to fucking punch them in the face.

The security detail accompanied them back to the medical building. Will found himself observing the guards, weighing the risks. Six men. It would be tricky, but he could do it. Then what? Emma couldn't run. He could use her as a hostage; they wanted her alive at this point. But that would never work. They knew he'd never hurt her. He could use the senator as a hostage instead. The thought excited him. It could work, but he'd have to hold Warren, and move Emma all the while keeping several men with guns at bay. It would be a logistical nightmare. Plus, they might use Emma against him. And even if they got away, then what?

The group continued across the compound, the thumping of the footsteps filling the silence, every step an albatross tugging on Will's resolve. How could he leave her here?

They entered the building and Will knew he had to make his decision soon. He glanced around. No vehicles out front; that could be a problem. He would need a getaway car. One guard sat at a desk in the front. He appeared bored until their group showed up, then snapped to attention. He would be more aware with the senator upstairs, but he looked like an easy target to get past. Will couldn't see what type of gun he had. Most likely a handgun. Most security guards did. The lax security earlier told him they weren't used to providing actual protection, which was surprising given the clientele they must be used to protecting. But then again, they were in a secret compound in rural South Dakota.

They reached the elevator bank. Two elevators, three floors; that would work against him. Emma was on the second floor. By the time he got Emma and Warren on the elevator and got to the first floor, every armed man would be waiting for the doors to open. It still might work; it would just be harder.

The group boarded the elevator. Will would have preferred to take the stairs. There were too many bodies on this elevator. He observed the operations panel. Emergency switch, phone, three floors and a basement. An escape hatch in the ceiling. If Emma wasn't hurt they could get on the elevator and climb out the top and buy themselves more time. But she was, so that wasn't an option. *Shit.* This fucking sucked.

The doors opened and they exited as a pack, Will in the center, Warren in the lead. Will wondered what Warren would say to her. That's what killed him the most, the thought of not being here to protect her. He couldn't bear the thought of her suffering anymore. If only he could be sure she would really be safe, and dare he hope, somewhat happy.

They reached her room and two more guards stood outside her door. A total of nine men. Still doable. He only had to overpower one, grab Warren and figure out the rest from there. The group stopped.

"How's our patient doing this evening?" Warren asked with a chipper tone.

The nurse's eyes widened and her face paled. "Senator Warren," she stammered, standing straighter. "Uh, she's been sleeping, Senator. She was much better after he showed up." She pointed to Will.

"Yes, I heard he had a calming influence on her. Let's hope it continues." He looked directly at Will and narrowed his eyes. "Will, I'm going to ask you to remain outside while we have our chat."

Will didn't like the order but knew he had no choice so he said nothing, in an attempt to look passive. But Warren read right through him and chuckled as he turned to walk in the room.

****

Emma woke to see a tall and handsome man standing next to her bed. His face lit up with a warm smile.

"Hello, Emma," the man said. "Glad to see that you're on the way to recovery. We were very worried about you."

She blinked. Who was he? He seemed familiar.

"I'm sorry, I haven't introduced myself." He extended his hand. "U.S. Senator Phillip Warren, from the great state of California."

She had no idea why a senator would be in her room, let alone Senator Warren. She knew he was running for president. She reached out her hand, but she was either weaker than she realized or the pain medication threw off her coordination and her hand fell before reaching his. He smiled at her and patted her hand in a fatherly gesture.

"That's okay. You're still tired."

She looked around for Will. "I don't understand why you're here."

"I had to meet our special guest. You have been much anticipated."

"I don't understand."

He waved to the chair by her bed. "May I?"

"Of course," she said, but her stomach clenched in spasms.

He sat down and leaned toward her. "I bet you have no idea how special you really are."

She stared at him in confusion.

"No, I can see that you don't. You, Emmanuella Thompson, are priceless."

The moment he called her Emmanuella the familiar feeling of dread sent prickles crawling up her back. "I don't understand..."

"What if I told you the fate of the world was in your hands?"

Emma stared at him in disbelief. "I'd tell you that you were crazy."

He laughed. "I think that's the second time tonight I've been called crazy. No, I can assure you that I'm not."

"Where's Will?" Something didn't feel right, no matter how friendly he appeared.

Senator Warren sat up. "He's busy at the moment."

"Could you tell him I need him? I'm sure he'll come right away."

The senator narrowed his eyes and tilted his head, appraising her. He caught himself and smiled again. "I'm sure he'll come when he's able."

Now, she worried for Will's safety. He said he'd stay with her until they made him leave. Anything could have happened to him while she was knocked out. While there was a chance that he had lied about staying, she didn't think he had.

Will said he could feel her in the woods and knew she was alive. He thought it was one sided, but if he told the truth and it really happened, maybe she could do the same for him. She closed her eyes and concentrated on the mark Jake had branded on her back, thinking of Will. A feeling of him rushed through her, strength and loyalty and an overwhelming surge of regret. He was anxious, but safe.

"Are you alright?" the senator's voice rose.

Emma opened her eyes. "I'm sorry. I'm still groggy and keep dozing off."

He cleared his throat. "As I was saying, you are a very important person to us. We realize you have been through quite an ordeal and would like to offer you our protection."

"Who is *we*?"

"Myself and my associates. We are friends to you and would like to keep you safe. Unfortunately, while I would love to personally oversee your convalescence, I have other pressing matters to attend to. My son Alex has graciously offered to see after you."

"That is very kind of you and your son, but it really isn't necessary. I'm sure Will can handle my care until I am well enough to take care of myself. Thank you."

His eyes hardened. "I'm sure Mr. Davenport is capable of many things, including overseeing your medical care. However, he'll be preoccupied. He has agreed to work for my security detail. In fact, we leave tonight. But there's nothing to worry about," he said, trying to sound light and jovial. "Alex is eager to step in and take over."

The way he said the last part raised a prickle of warning. "I really need to speak to Will."

"I'm sure he'll be around shortly. We'll see if he has time before he leaves for Washington."

"I'm quite certain he wouldn't leave without saying something to me."

He shrugged with a wave of his hand. "Perhaps."

"Senator Warren, you told me that the fate of the world rests on my shoulders. What makes you say that?"

His face brightened. "You, my dear, are very special. There have been prophecies about you. Your son will be a light unto the world."

"Jake?"

"No, not Jake. Your other son."

"I don't have another son."

He smiled with a glint in his eye. "Not yet."

The night of Jake's conception flooded back into her memory. She gripped the bedrail and gasped.

Senator Warren rose from his chair. "Are you all right? I'm sure it's a bit shocking to find out that you're pregnant this way."

"Pregnant?" How…? She hadn't even slept with anyone… *Will.* But it would be too soon to know. That was only a couple of days ago.

"Yes. You will have a son."

How would he know that? How did these people know about Jake and her real name? "Aren't you supposed to be accompanied by a chorus of angels to make an announcement like that?"

He laughed, his eyes twinkling with delight. "Oh, my dear, you are not what I expected."

"What did you expect?" she sneered.

He titled his head as he appraised her. "Someone more malleable."

"Sorry to disappoint."

"No disappointment at all. But I do say, you will be a challenge for my son," he said with a chuckle.

"I'll be a challenge for no one. I am not a possession to be handed around from person to person."

"That's where you're wrong. You are a valuable possession," his voice lowered, taking an ominous tone.

"I want Will."

"I told you, Will is busy."

"Will!" She called out. It worked before. If she called loud enough they might bring him again. "Will!"

"Emma, I must insist that you stop."

"I'll stop when you bring Will to see me."

He rolled his eyes, then he sighed. "Give me a moment." He stepped out into the hall.

****

Will tensed the moment heard her call his name. The guards around him reached for their guns and he stopped. Waiting. A moment later the senator came out and walked to him his mouth pursed into a grimace.

"She insists on seeing you and is being most uncooperative."

Will snorted. "That sounds like Emma."

"Maybe so, but I'll allow you into see her on the condition that you convince her to cooperate."

"Why would I do that?"

Warren raised an eyebrow with a leer. "Because her life depends on it. Yes, we need her alive to deliver this baby, but there's nothing that tells us we need her after."

Will wished he could kill this man with his bare hands, but he'd save that for another day. "What do you want me to tell her? I presume you don't want me to tell her what you just told me. That might not be very effective with Emma."

Warren scoffed. "Of course not. We don't need to make this difficult. Tell her to trust us. Tell her to cooperate. Tell her to give Alex a chance."

"*Alex*? Alex from the meeting this morning?" But now Will saw the resemblance.

"Yes, Alex is my son and will see to her care."

Will really didn't like the way he said "her care." And he really didn't like the thought of Alex being anywhere near her. Unfortunately, he didn't know what he could do about it. "All right."

Senator Warren smiled. "Excellent. You'll go in with me and convince her, then tell her goodbye. I've already told her that you're leaving with me tonight."

They walked through the door, Will still trying to figure out an escape plan until he saw her on the bed. She looked so pale and fragile he had no idea how he'd ever get her out. He reminded himself that he'd brought Emma here because she would have died without medical care. There was no way he could take her.

She saw him and the fury on her face melted into relief. His heart crumbled, unsure he could really do it. He couldn't take her, couldn't leave her. That didn't leave very many options. He walked to her side and took her hands in his, not caring if any of them saw. They knew he had a bond to her, why should he try to hide it?

"Will, he says you're leaving with him to go to Washington. What is he talking about?" She glared, chipping a crack in his resolve. He wasn't sure he could do this.

He took a deep breath. "Yes."

"What the hell, Will? Only a couple of hours ago you told me you wouldn't leave me. Then a U.S. senator offers you a job and you're off and running?"

He cringed. "Emma." He leaned his forehead against hers and cupped the back of her head. "I don't want to leave you, but I have to."

"Then tell me why? I don't understand."

"Will has been offered a job that is too good to pass up. Isn't that right Will?" Warren interrupted.

"Yes." His voice hardened.

Emma glanced from Warren to Will. She narrowed her eyes. He knew she was putting it together.

"Will is also here to convince you that we will provide excellent care for you. Isn't that right, Will?"

His jaw locked. "Yes,"

"Will, you don't sound very convincing," the senator said. "Need I remind you what's at stake?"

He hesitated, the pressure in his chest becoming unbearable. "Emma, I have to go, but they've promised to take care of you."

Emma shook her head. "No, I refuse to stay here."

"Emma, you don't have a choice."

"Then don't go, Will."

The anger in her voice nearly shattered his resolve. He didn't expect her to make it easy for him. "Emma, remember our bet? The one in the woods? I won, and I'm calling in my bet right now. You have to do something I ask, no questions asked. This is it."

She shook her head again. "No, Will. Don't do this."

"It's time to go, Will." Warren grabbed the door handle.

Emma clutched Will's hand in a tight grip, anger burning in her eyes. "What happened to 'I'll stay with you?' If you really care about me you will *not* walk out that door."

"I'm sorry, Emma." His voice cracked as he leaned down and kissed her.

She grabbed the back of his head and whispered in his face. "Don't do this, Will. I don't care what they threatened, please don't do this."

"God, Emma. I'm so sorry." He kissed her again and stood up, hoping he made the right decision.

"It's time to go, Will."

He prayed she would forgive him. "I love you." He turned and walked toward the door.

"Will!" she called out after him. Her voiced echoed in his head as the door shut behind him.

CHAPTER TWENTY-SIX

EMMA watched in stunned silence as Will walked out of the room. *He left me*. He swore he wouldn't leave her, yet he did. As she sorted through her rage and grief, a niggle of doubt crept into the mix. Will was either an incredibly good actor or he genuinely cared about her. She couldn't help but believe that the mark Jake burned on his arm helped ensure it. When she took several deep breaths and examined Will's actions the past few days, she came to a conclusion. Will would leave her only for a good reason. *Her*.

What had they threatened to do? Was she in danger now? Surely Will would never leave her if he thought she was in real danger.

The door opened and a young man entered the room. His stylish haircut and tailored shirt screamed money and sophistication. She knew him and instantly recognized the resemblance to his father. How had she not put it together? Air stuck in her chest.

"Hello, Emmanuella. I'm not sure if you remember me. I regret that I never officially introduced myself. I'm Alex." He paused and smiled a charming smile. He had the air of a man used to getting what he wanted. "We met several years ago and I must offer my apologies. Apparently you *are* the one."

Her lungs screamed in protest and she released her breath in a gasp as she stared into the face of the man who raped her nearly six years ago.

****

What have you done? The words echoed in his head until he thought he'd go mad. It was the only way. Was it the only way? He slid into the backseat of the sedan with the senator. Two armed men sat in the front seat.

"To the airport, gentlemen." Warren said. "I'm eager to shake the dust of South Dakota off my feet." He turned to Will. "I can't wait to show you Washington. I think you'll like it there, once you get used to it. Plenty of opportunities for someone like you."

Will refused to answer and instead slumped as he stared out the window. His arm tingled. He glanced down at his mark. It looked the same, but began to slowly burn. He sat up. Something was wrong. "What happened to Emma after we left?"

Warren shook his head in confusion. "Nothing happened. Alex was going to visit her."

"Would he hurt her?"

Warren waved his hand. "No, don't be ridiculous. She's much too valuable to him. He's been promised her child."

"You mean my child." Will hadn't stopped to consider the talk about a baby actually concerned his own son.

Senator Warren scoffed. "You won't be raising the boy. I thought that was well-established."

The burning of his mark increased. He thought about her, concentrating, slowly sensing her anger and terror.

"What was he going to do?" Will asked, his words clipped.

"Nothing. He was only going to visit her. What is this all about?"

Will concentrated again, pretending to look out the window as he shut his eyes. He thought about her, but went deeper, calling out to her through his mind, into hers.

Will? Her voice called his head. He nearly jumped. *He's here, Will. How could he be here? How did he find me?*

Will knew exactly who she meant. *He's there with you now?*

Yes.

I'm coming.

Two guards would be easy.

****

"How did you find me?" Emma asked. The monitor gave away her terror. She ripped out the cord.

"It's much too complicated for you to understand," Alex said, wrinkling his nose with impatience.

She narrowed her eyes. "Try me."

He walked to the chair by her bed and sat down. "I'd rather talk about my son."

"What are you talking about?" Her voice rose in anger.

"Come now, Emmanuella. I know I have a son. Tell me about him."

Her heart skipped, making her glad she had disconnected the monitor. He knew about Jake. Her anger burned, hot and fierce. "Have you been the one chasing us for the last three years?"

He crossed his legs, looking bored. "No, but I know who was."

"*Who?*"

"Emmanuella," Alex cooed in a soothing voice. "You really should calm down. It really doesn't concern you."

"The hell it *doesn't*. He's *my* son."

He raised his eyebrows with a smirk. "He's my son, too."

She gaped at him in disbelief. "Are you *kidding* me? Where have you been the last five years? No, forget that, because I guarantee if you had shown up I would have killed you."

Alex cocked his head and eyed her with interest. "You've changed, Emmanuella."

"Changed? How the hell would you know? You didn't know me at all. You used me and left me laying in the dirt."

"Yes, a most regrettable misunderstanding."

"*Misunderstanding?*"

"Emmanuella..."

"Stop calling me that! My name is Emma."

"*Emma*," he said her name with a condescending tone and a patronizing smile. "You need to calm down. You're going to harm the baby."

Emma's mouth fell open.

"I promise to be a better father for this one."

She took several deep breaths trying to regain control. "*Where is my son?*"

His mouth lifted into sardonic smile, giving his eyes an evil glint. "What's it worth to you?"

"What the hell does that mean?"

"I'm sure we can work out some kind of arrangement."

****

The car drove down the long circular drive leading from the compound. Will saw the guard station about five hundred feet ahead. The road ran parallel to a stretch of trees and would soon curve to the guard station. He knew it would be better to do this inside the compound than out, and he was running out of time.

Will jumped forward and wrapped his hands around the head and chest of the man in front of him. He jerked, snapping his neck. He reached into the man's jacket and pulled the gun out of the holster. Will pointed it toward the driver before he had a chance to grab his own gun.

"We're driving back to the medical building. Keep both hands on the steering wheel at all times, please." Will said in a deceptively polite tone.

The senator slid away from Will, holding up his hands. "Now, Will. There's no need for violence."

Will shot a quick glance at him, breaking eye contact on the driver for only a moment. "Senator, there wouldn't be if you hadn't forced me to it."

They were approaching the guard station. The road curved around but a side road turned to the guard station. "Keep circling around. You make any kind of move that tells them something's up and I'll blow your brains out. Got it?"

The man kept driving. Will was relieved when they passed and headed back to the medical building.

"Will, this is crazy. Let's not do anything rash." Warren used his constituent calming voice. "Obviously, I underestimated your need to be with her. Let's go somewhere and sit down and discuss this. I'm sure we can work something out."

"Oh, we'll work something out all right. Is there a road that goes behind the medical building?"

"Yes, but…"

Will pointed the gun at the back of the driver's head. "Take the back road. Here's what's going to happen when we get there. We're going to park really close to the back of the building. Then we're all going to inside together. Anyone makes a wrong move and the Senator gets a bullet to the head. Got it?"

The driver slowly nodded as he drove off the main road onto a road that circled around behind the buildings.

"Are there security cameras in the back?"

"No," Warren said.

Will pointed the gun at Warren's temple. "Are there security cameras in the back? If we get there and I find a single one, Warren's getting it in the head and you, Mr. Security, will be answering for it. So let me ask again. Are there security cameras in the back?"

"Yes," the man answered.

"That's better. Where? What are they pointed at?"

"The back door. The parking lot."

"Okay, good." They approached the building ahead. "How do we get in the back door?"

"We'll need a key."

"Do you have a key? What's your name?"

"Yes. Travis."

"Okay, Travis. You work with me and I won't kill you. I promise and I'm a man of my word. But you give me a reason to shoot you and I won't hesitate to do it. Agreed?"

"Yes."

"Good. Now park close to the door." Travis drove through a small parking lot and pulled up to the back of the building, parking next to the curb at the back door. "Keep your hands on the steering wheel. Now take out the keys with your right hand and slowly hand them to me. Are the keys to the back door on this key ring?"

"Yes," Travis said. He pulled the keys out of the ignition and handed them to Will.

"Now slowly, very slowly, pull your gun out with one finger and hold it up for me." He reached his hand into his jacket and removed his gun. Will took the firearm dangling from the guard's finger. "Okay, let's go. Everyone out Travis' side. Let's all stay close together, shall we? Just remember I have two guns, one on each of you."

The men got out and walked to the back door with Warren and the guard in front, Will directly behind. Will had Travis unlock the door while he kept a gun at Warren's back. Warren and the guard went through the door with Will following.

"Where's the staircase?"

Travis showed him the stairwell door close to the back door.

"After you, gentlemen."

Travis went in first, followed by Warren and then Will.

"Walk up side by side if you, please."

"Will," Warren said. "This is getting out of hand. You really don't expect to get out of here, do you?"

"Senator, if you don't shut the fuck up, I'll take great pleasure in doing it for you."

Warren released an exasperated sound.

They reached the landing between the first and second floor and started up the second set of stairs. When they reached the door, Will told them to stop.

"Now here's what's going to happen. We're going to walk to Emma's room and we're going to put her in a wheelchair. Travis is going to push it and the good senator is going to walk with me. Anyone tips off the men outside door and the senator gets shot. Sound good?"

"Will..." Warren started.

Will jammed the gun into his back. "Please, I'm begging you, give me a reason to go ahead and shoot you because it's taking every bit of restraint not to."

Warren shut up, giving Will momentary satisfaction. "Okay, everyone close together, the gun's trained on Warren." Will stuck the other weapon down into his front waistband. "Senator, you're going to tell them that you changed your mind and Emma's going to Washington D.C. with you. Let's go."

Travis opened the door and they moved down the hall. The guards looked surprised to see them, especially entering from the staircase.

"Senator?" one of the guards questioned.

"I've decided to bring our guest with me to D.C." Warren sounded amazingly genial. "Is there a wheelchair in her room?"

"Yes," the nurse answered, flustered at the change in plans.

"We'll just be a minute," Will told them as they entered the room.

****

Emma looked up when the door opened and sighed in relief. "Will."

The senator and a man entered the room with Will following. Will reached around and locked the door, then turned his attention to Alex.

Will's eyes darkened. "Is that him?"

Emma nodded.

Will strode to him and slammed the butt of his gun into Alex's head before he had time to react. Alex crumpled to the floor next to the bed.

"What is the meaning of this?" Warren asked, his voice rising in alarm as he moved to his son.

He pointed the gun toward Warren. "I would stay over there if I were you."

Alex lay on the floor in a fetal position, moaning. "Get up, you fucking maggot." Will kicked him in the stomach.

"Will, stop!" Emma reached over and pulled his arm.

"I'm going to kill him, Emma." His voice was calm, but the glare in his eyes told her he was serious.

"No, Will. Stop. He knows who was after Jake."

Emma felt his bicep tense. "How does he know?"

"I don't know, but he says he does."

"What is this about?" Warren's voice rose, indignant.

"Ask your precious son." Will spat and kicked Alex again. Alex groaned. "What? Not so tough with a man?

Only big and bad with defenseless women?" Will kicked him again. "Get up."

"Will, stop!"

Will jerked Alex up by his shirt and tossed him into the chair. He pulled the other gun out of the waistband of his pants and pointed it at Alex's forehead while the other stayed trained on Warren. Alex paled, in spite of his tan, and blood flowed down the side of his face from the gash made by the gun.

"Okay Alex, I'm gonna ask this nice only once. You've been warned. Where's Jake?"

"I don't know."

Will's face reddened and his jaw tightened. His finger twitched on the trigger.

Alex's eyes widened with fear. "But I know who took him if he's alive."

"Who?"

"The other group. The one that broke off of this one. They wanted him."

Will took a deep breath and glanced at Warren. His face was expressionless.

"So don't keep me waiting in suspense." Will gritted through his clenched mouth. "Where are they?"

"Ari ...zzzona." Alex stammered.

Emma heard the senator's sharp intake of breath. Apparently, Alex's information was news to him.

"Arizona's a big state with lots of desert, Alex. Afraid you'll need to be a tad bit more specific than that."

"I don't know, north of Tucson, about hundred miles northwest. That's all I know."

"I don't believe you." Will pushed the gun into his forehead.

Alex's eyes widened and his lip trembled. "I swear to God, that's all I know."

"What is the group called?"

Alex looked from Will to his father, then back to Will. "They go by 'the Cavallo.'"

Emma let a sigh of relief. It was something.

Will stuffed the gun in his right hand into his waistband and smashed his fist into Alex's nose. "You're lucky that's all you're getting from me but if I ever see you again, I *will* kill you." Will looked up. "Where's the wheelchair?"

Travis wheeled it to the bed. Will had him lower the guardrail. "Travis, you're going to carefully help her into the chair." He helped her slide over the side of the bed. She tried to ignore the pain shooting through her leg.

Emma wore a hospital gown that opened the back, it started to slip as she got down. Embarrassment should have been the last thing on her mind, but she felt her face redden anyway. Will walked up behind her and pulled the back closed as she sat in the chair. She panted as she recovered from the pain.

"Okay, Travis back over with Senator Warren."

Will leaned over her head from behind. "You okay?" he whispered.

"Yeah, I just want out of here."

He reached up and pulled her IV bags down and put them on her lap. He grabbed a blanket off the bed and tossed it over her legs, keeping the gun on the two men against the wall.

Will opened the drawers of the supply cart in the corner and pulled out a plastic bag. He had Travis stuff the bag with supplies while he kept a gun pointed at Senator Warren. Will took the bag and hung it on the back of the wheelchair.

"Okay, let's get this show on the road. Travis pushes Emma, then Warren in front of me. Sorry, Alex, you have to stay behind."

Alex had passed out in the chair.

Will unlocked the door. They filed out of the room and headed for the elevator. The guards watched with curiosity.

Will leaned toward Warren's ear and whispered something.

Senator Warren looked at the guards and smiled. "Alex needed a few minutes to make some calls so if you could leave him undisturbed for a while, it would be most appreciated."

Emma was amazed how calm the senator appeared.

The elevator doors opened. Travis wheeled the chair in with Senator Warren and Will following behind.

"You really don't think you're going to get away with this, do you?" Warren asked after the doors closed.

"Why, yes, Senator. I believe I will."

"I will track you down and I will collect what is mine." The hatred in his voice was unmistakable.

"In that case Senator, expect to collect a bullet in your head because that's the only thing I have that is *yours*."

The doors opened and the group emerged from the elevator. The security guard looked up from his desk in surprise.

Warren jerked slightly. "Good evening. We came to bring Ms. Thompson with us. We parked out back so we'll be headed that way."

The security guard nodded, unconcerned.

The sun was setting as they left through the back door. Shadows darkened the parking lot behind the building.

Will kept a gun on Warren's back while Travis helped Emma into the back seat.

"Okay, Travis, you get behind the wheel, and Senator, you sit in front with him."

"But there's a dead man in there," Warren protested.

"Somehow I don't think he'll mind sharing his seat."

Travis got behind the wheel, while Warren slid in next to the dead guard, cringing with disgust. Will climbed in the back seat next to Emma and pointed the gun at Warren's head. He reached forward and inserted the keys into the ignition.

"Let's get moving."

Travis drove around the back of the buildings, reconnecting with the circular drive. Half way between the buildings and the front gate, Will made Travis and Warren haul the dead body out of the front seat and into the trees along the side of the drive. They got back in and headed for the guard booth.

Travis slowed the car as they approached the station.

"Tell him we're headed to Rapid City," Will said.

He told the guard their destination and the guard waved them through. They turned onto the two-lane road, the opposite direction of the airfield.

Warren sat still for the next five miles, surprisingly quiet, although Emma was sure he wanted to say something by the way his jaw jutted forward and his lips twitched.

"Okay Travis, pull over here." They were in the middle of nowhere, wheat fields flanking the road.

Emma was glad Will told him to stop. She couldn't stand being in the same car with Senator Warren much longer. Will might have two guns, but Warren oozed power and control. He was not a man to be underestimated.

"Time to part ways, boys. I need you to get out and stand in front of the car." They opened the doors, leaving them open as they climbed out. Will slid out the back door, still pointing the guns toward them as they walked to the front. They raised their hands and squinted from the bright headlights.

"I'm going to have you boys hand over your cell phones, if you please. One at a time. You first, Travis." Will said, standing in front of the car, partially obscuring Emma's view of Travis. After a moment, Will leaned forward, taking the phone from Travis' outstretched hand.

"Senator?"

Senator Warren looked disgusted, but pulled his phone out of his pocket and handed it to Will.

"Now I'm going to have you boys move over to that side of the road." Will pointed to the road on the driver's side. "Be sure to stand on the shoulder so you don't get run over now."

"We will meet again, Mr. Davenport," Warren said as he walked across the road.

"Believe me, Senator Warren, I'm counting on it."

Will shut the passenger door then got in the driver's side, tossing the cell phones on the front seat. He lowered the driver's window and kept his gun pointed at them until he was a safe distance down the road.

Emma let out a sigh of relief. Will watched her in the rearview mirror, his face serious. But she saw the hint of a smile.

"What?" she asked.

"God, you're a hell of a lot of trouble."

She scowled at him. "Nobody asked you to come back, Will."

"Who said trouble was a bad thing?" He winked.

Emma cocked her head and glared. "I'm still pissed at you. You were just going to leave me there."

"I didn't think I had a choice, but once I realized who Alex was, there was no way in hell I could." His eyes turned serious. "It's not going to be easy, Emma. We're going to be running. I'm still not sure I made the right decision getting you out of there."

"I'd rather be running with you than imprisoned with them."

"I'll do everything I can to keep you safe. I swear to you, Emma."

She wondered if she should question his trustworthiness, but he just risked his life to get her out, not to mention pissing of a very powerful politician. "I know.

Now, let's just get the hell away from here. We need to go find Jake."

"Already issuing orders?"

"Didn't you tell me that was my job?"

"Yeah, I just didn't expect it so soon. Why do I think I'm going to regret that?"

"Shut up and drive, Will."

He looked in the mirror and smiled.

ACKNOWLEDGMENTS

AS always, I thank my children for tolerating Mommy jumping off the deep end to write this book. *Chosen* was my second completed novel and it grabbed me by the scruff of the neck and didn't let me go until I wrote *The End*. (Yes, I'm a dork and always write *The End* on first drafts.) This is when my children realized maybe Mommy was serious about this writing thing.

I also want to thank my daughter-in-law, Cody. If it weren't for Cody telling me that my then four-year-old son Ryan could only count if he touched her fingers, *Chosen* would never have been born.

Equally important in *Chosen's* birth is my dear friend David Paul. If it weren't for his continued encouragement and support, I would have stopped at chapter one. He always believed I was capable of telling this story even when I was sure I wasn't.

I also have to thank Brandy Underwood, who's read the first draft of everything I've written and still comes back for more. She's a huge support, encourager and self-proclaimed president of my (non-existent) fan club.

Of course, I couldn't have done this without my critique partners: Trisha Leigh, Eisley Jacobs and Kathy

Collins. They make me look good and keep me sane. Well, as sane as I am capable of.

Next comes a long list of people who read this book in its many edited forms and loved it. When I thought this book would die on my hard drive, someone else would ask "When is *Chosen* getting published? I want to share it with my friends." I wish I could name you all but unfortunately there's too many. (Probably fifty to sixty of you. I honestly lost count.)

I also want to thank the Baxter Boozers Bitchin' Book Club: Heather Ann McDonnell, Alison Turner Wilhem, A. Alex Hubbarth, Kelly Patterson, Lisa Kasko, Amy Anderson and a few others not mentioned. They read the earliest version of *Chosen* for their June 2010 book club then had a Skype chat with me to discuss it. Their enthusiasm made me believe I had something worth publishing.

And finally, I want to thank my copy editor Jim Thomsen, who could see things I couldn't, both good and bad, and helped me make *Chosen* even better.

ABOUT THE AUTHOR

Denise Grover Swank lives in Lee's Summit, Missouri. She has six children, two dogs, and an overactive imagination. She can be found dancing in her kitchen with her children, reading or writing her next book. You will rarely find her cleaning.

You can find out more about Denise and her other books at www.denisegroverswank.com

Made in the USA
Lexington, KY
11 June 2015